AHEAD OF HER TIME

AN SAT VOCABULARY NOVEL

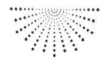

ERICA ABBETT

VOCABBETT

BIG WORDS MADE SIMPLE.

Ahead of Her Time

Copyright © 2019 by Erica Abbett

For permission requests, bulk purchases for academic institutions, and other questions, please email contact@vocabbett.com.

Cover art by Meredith Welborn.

ISBN (Paperback): 978-1-7340940-1-5
ISBN (Hardcover): 978-1-7340940-2-2
ISBN (ebook): 978-1-7340940-0-8

LETTER FROM THE EDITOR

Due to her unconventional upbringing, Noor's vocabulary is unusually large for a girl her age.

I attempted to persuade her to use simpler terms (really, who uses the word "impecunious" these days?), but she refused, making derisive comments about people "too slothful to open a dictionary."

We were able to negotiate a compromise. For the reader's convenience, the contextual definitions of lesser-known terms have been included at the bottom of each page.

There is also a glossary of more than 500 words at the back of the book.

Impecunious - Having little or no money
Derisive - Judgmental; expressing contempt or ridicule
Slothful - Lazy
Contextual - In-context

PART ONE

REPORT: U.S. STUDENT MISSING IN EGYPT

CAIRO - American university student Noor Cunningham has been reported missing in Egypt. She is described as petite, standing just over 5'1", with dark blonde hair and green eyes.

The daughter of archaeologists Frank and Mary Cunningham, Noor was raised in Egypt until her parents' death two years ago. Upon her parents' death, she was sent to live with her grandmother in Connecticut, where she spent her senior year of high school.

Cunningham returned to Egypt in the fall to pursue her undergraduate degree at The American University in Cairo.

The U.S. State Department has urged anyone with additional information to step forward.

* * *

I didn't read all the news reports until much later.

When I got back, I ended up telling the hordes of reporters I was kidnapped by terrorists, assuming that would be the hardest story to verify.

No one would believe me if I told them what really happened in those months, and frankly, I prefer it that way. It's far too dangerous for the public to know the truth.

There are only six people, besides me, who know it.

Hordes - A large group of people (often used in the context of an invasion)
Verify - Make sure something is true

CHAPTER ONE

"I HEAR SHE'S AN ORPHAN," Caitlyn pouted at the mirror in her locker, then turned to the gaggle of girls waiting for her.

"She's never even heard of Louis Vuitton. *Louis freaking Vuitton,*" Julia, Caitlyn's second-in-command, added. She was standing protectively between Caitlyn and the other girls, making sure no one stood closer to the fount of all popularity than she.

"What kind of a name is Noor?" Stephanie asked in a nasal voice. "It's like North, but North's parents are Kim and Kanye. It's not like *her* parents are famous or anything."

I — the Noor being discussed so openly — wasn't actually part of this conversation. From my position directly across Senior Hall, however, I was close enough to hear every word.

I slammed the door of my locker and spun to glare at them. Arms folded, I gritted my teeth and braced for a confrontation, but Caitlyn and her villainous hangers-on didn't even notice.

Gaggle - A flock of geese; a derogatory term for a group of people

Nasal - Coming from the nose

They were too busy dissecting my entire existence.

Yes, my name is Noor. Yes, I am an orphan.

A recent orphan.

I kicked a stray backpack and let out a frustrated "ugh!" as Caitlyn and her clique joined the wave of bodies being pulled toward the cafeteria. I had no choice but to slink into the crowd behind them.

It's not like I was going to chase these stupid girls, informing them that my parents *were* famous, even if they were too stupid to know it. My parents had been on *National Geographic* and *The History Channel* more times than I could count!

They'd discovered a sunken city no one else knew existed, buried by time and the Mediterranean Sea. It had been written up by the *BBC, CNN,* the *New York Times* — everyone!

Sadly, the city they discovered wasn't Atlantis, but it was every bit as extraordinary. Alexandria was the capital of Egypt for nearly 1,000 years. One of the richest cities in history, it was the seat of power under Cleopatra.

Before my parents, everyone assumed ancient Alexandria was trapped beneath modern Alexandria. That's how archaeology usually works; cities build on top of themselves. You can barely dig up a flowerbed in Rome without turning up an artifact.

Archaeologists were aching to dig it up, but the city's 5 million modern denizens were less keen on their roads and apartments being demolished so historians could play in the dirt.

Slink - Move quietly, unobtrusively

Denizens - Residents

Only my parents realized that, because Alexandria was on the coast, something might be different there. Hurricanes and other natural phenomena can raise the height of the sea. And if the sea had been creeping steadily inward, the city might move back with it...

In a nutshell? They were right.

Hiding in the Mediterranean, almost entirely engulfed by sediment and slime, they found the periphery of the ancient city.

Cleopatra's palace was already some distance removed from the mainland in her time, built on a little island called Antirhodos. Swallowed during a violent earthquake in the 4th century, it had been lost for nearly 2,000 years until my parents discovered it—"the Pompeii of the sea" one stunned reporter called it.

Deep beneath the waves, my parents found pharaonic sculptures as remarkable as anything at the British Museum, sphinxes so massive it took three cranes and two steamer ships to haul them from the depths.

My rage tied itself into a familiar knot in my stomach. The same knot showed up whenever I thought of my parents — that indefinable sense of dread, the reminder that life would never again be truly happy, the knowledge that my parents were really and truly gone.

My parents spent their lives studying the mysteries of the Mediterranean, never knowing that they were doomed to join its

---

Phenomena (*Plural of phenomenon*) - Something remarkable

Engulfed - Covered completely; swallowed whole

Sediment - Particles that settle at the bottom of a liquid

Periphery - Outer edges or boundaries

ranks. Three months ago I woke up, and they were gone. So was their scuba equipment. It didn't take a genius to connect the dots. Something had happened down there.

My grandma Mitzi flew over from Connecticut to coordinate the search. Unsatisfied with the steps being taken by the American and Egyptian governments, she organized search parties, chartered helicopters, and shoved anyone with a scuba license into the sea.

I spent every waking minute as Mitzi's translator, when I wasn't taking part in the search and rescue dives. By night, my sleepless mind played out possibilities of what could have happened, searching for any possible clue.

If sharks had gotten them, why had they attacked? My parents were too smart to dive with open cuts. What would've provoked them?

Had their gear malfunctioned? But that's why they always went together. What could've happened that would incapacitate both of them?

Something with the tide, the current maybe? But again, my parents were experienced divers. They knew not to fight a riptide, but to swim parallel to the shore until they could break free. They might have stumbled to shore a bit out of sorts, but they would've turned up eventually.

Ultimately, though, no one found any trace of my parents.

And now — as though fate hadn't cursed me enough — I was

Provoked - Caused something to happen

Incapacitate - Prevent from functioning normally

destined to spend my senior year of high school in the purgatory that is Connecticut.

* * *

"DARLING, THAT'S A WONDERFUL IDEA!" my grandma Mitzi cried. I'd just proposed throwing a massive party for my 17th birthday, just two weeks away.

According to the smattering of American television I'd seen back in Egypt, parties were *de rigueur* for American high school students. If they were the price of admission into the cliques of Connecticut, I was ready to pay. I couldn't bear the thought of fighting through every day of the next year.

I pulled out my phone, surreptitiously opening the only chain I cared about.

Harvey had been my partner in crime since before I could remember. The fellow child of archaeologists, he actually lived with us part of the year, and is the only person alive who can read my mind no matter what language I'm thinking in.

I still couldn't believe he was back in Egypt, and I was stuck here.

Our last conversation read:

ME: I HATE THIS PLACE, AND I WANT TO COME HOME.

Purgatory - A place of suffering where sinners wait before entering heaven, in Roman Catholic theology

Smattering - Small amount

De rigueur - Required by current trends (from French)

Surreptitiously - Secretly; trying to avoid attention

HARVEY: YOU CAN MAKE IT, NOOR. REMEMBER WHEN YOU FREED THE LION AFTER SEEING HOW DRUGGED & MISTREATED IT WAS? THOUGH THAT MIGHT NOT BE THE BEST EXAMPLE...I STILL HAVE THE SCARS TO PROVE IT. BUT THE POINT IS, YOU CAN SURVIVE A YEAR IN SUBURBIA. AND SOON ENOUGH, YOU'LL BE BACK IN EGYPT.

I found myself nodding at the text message. If parties were what American high school students enjoyed, I'd give them a party.

However, I wanted to make it 100 percent Egypt-themed so my classmates could see what I saw in the country — beauty, adventure, family.

"You're sure you don't mind?" I asked Mitzi for the third time.

"Don't be silly!" Mitzi took my hands in hers. Her nails were bright blue, courtesy of the manicurist she saw every Friday, and a diamond the size of Peru twinkled on her ring finger, courtesy of my late grandfather. "This house was made for parties," she continued, "and it's a *wonderful* way for you to make friends. You've been in school a month now, and..."

"Indeed," I gently extricated my hands, turning to scan Mitzi's backyard. It really was made for parties. A white porch circled the back of the house, overlooking an expanse of freshly manicured lawn. She lived next to a golf course, and your eyes tended to see the verdant hills as part of her land. As long as you didn't mind the stray golf ball underfoot, the view was well worth it.

Suburbia - The suburbs

Extricated - Freed; removed

Verdant - Green; rich with vegetation

My mind was spinning with possibilities. If my contemporaries were impressed by drinks and dimmed lights, what would they make of belly dancers and henna? For the next two weeks I thought of nothing else, and each night Mitzi and I finalized more details.

We began by sending out invitations to all 75 people in my grade. On the front was a Victorian woman on a camel in front of the pyramids, waving her parasol in delight. The back read: "Noor is turning 17! Join us Saturday, October 16 in celebrating her past and future. Dinner and galabeyas will be provided."

I'm not sure how, but Mitzi kept her promise and arranged for everything we planned. A procession of whirling dervishes, belly dancers, and henna artists filtered through the house in the days leading up to the party, strategizing where they would set up.

Most of them didn't speak Arabic, but when I found someone who did, it was like finding someone with whom I had a shared secret. We always greeted each other in "Salaam alaikums" rather than "hellos," and I relished whenever someone asked me for the *hamam* instead of the bathroom.

The morning of the party, I surveyed the yard. The manicured grass now housed a large Bedouin tent in the center. The walls were made of coarse, red cloth with patterned stripes, and wooden poles dug deep into the ground to hold it upright. A henna station would greet visitors who came in through the side fence, of-

---

Contemporaries - People who live at the same time
Henna - A dye often used to decorate the hair and body
Galabeya - A traditional Egyptian garment that looks like a big, long-sleeved dress

fering to transform their hands and feet into intricate works of art, and the fireplace had been turned into a spinning kebab grill.

The decor was more *Arabian Nights* than Hosni Mubarak — I'll admit that we were playing into oriental fantasies a bit — but Egypt is magical. You don't have to stretch the truth that much.

I had one final task to complete before the party could begin: hanging family photos throughout the tent.

Egypt to me represented, above all, family. If they weren't represented at the party, what was the point in having it?

Mitzi had already hung a long string across the back wall of the tent, clipping laundry hooks at regular intervals for me to hang the pictures.

"It adds a bit of a 'garden wedding' vibe," she admitted, "but since we'll be sitting on pillows on the floor, and the tables will be covered with food, there won't be much room for frames. It'll just have to do!"

I smiled and went back inside, passing through the kitchen on the way to my mom's old room. I could've taken the guest room, but hers was the only one I felt at home in.

A born linguist, my mom had moved to Italy when she was 17 to further her study of Latin and Italian. Apparently it was OK for *her* to spend her senior year abroad, but Connecticut was the only choice for me. I needed more "stability" during this "trying time."

I knew Mitzi only wanted what was best for me, but it was hard not to envy all the freedom she'd given my mom. After high

---

Intricate - Complicated; detailed
Intervals - Spaces between two things

school in Italy, she'd spent summers on archaeological digs in Greece, did her doctorate at Cambridge...

Cambridge was where she met my dad, by the way. My dad's British, and was studying archaeology at the time. He's really the archaeologist of the two of them; mom prefers — *preferred* — deciphering what they found to digging it all up. She was the linguist; he was the archaeologist. Together they were a perfect match.

Their professional compatibility was just a pleasant bonus, though. Their love for each other was obvious to anyone who knew them. At the time I found it gross. Now? I don't think I'd begrudge them anything now. Certainly not their love for each other.

Mitzi had never redecorated, and the room clung as stubbornly to my mother as I did. When I was lucky, it shared intimate moments from her past. I sometimes felt as though fate had stolen my parents, but had forgotten about this fragile bond. Knowing my mom had spent countless nights in this same room — and was just as desperate to escape this place as I was — gave me immense comfort.

I padded up the winding staircase and pushed open the turquoise doors that marked the entrance to her haven.

It looked more like a Moroccan *riad* than a teenage girl's bedroom. Gauzy cloth suspended from ceiling beams danced in front

---

Begrudge - Hand over unwillingly or resentfully

Haven - Safe place

Riad - A traditional Moroccan house or palace

of intricately-patterned wallpaper. A bulbous chandelier hung above the low bed. Books littered every possible surface, but the ones near her bed were obviously favorites — a collection of tomes in various languages, from Julius Caesar's journals to Howard Carter's field notes.[1]

I'd begun working my way through the books on the bedside table when I first got to Connecticut, and was planning on tackling the enormous bookshelf near the closet next. Made of dark wood and carved to a decorative arch at the top, it chronicled her obsession with the ancient world from childhood through her teenage years. I ran a hand along the titles, spotting *Peter Rabbit* in hieroglyphics, *Ritchie's Easy Stories* in Latin, and *The Little Prince* in hieratic. There were also books in Italian and Arabic.

Like Cleopatra, my mother spoke a staggering nine languages. I loved how Plutarch's words could apply to both women: "Her tongue, like an instrument of many strings, could readily turn to whatever language she pleased."

My mom had shared her passion with me, teaching me Latin, Greek, and ancient Egyptian as soon as I could speak English. I don't really remember learning Arabic; that one came naturally, through living in Egypt. When Harvey stayed with us, he received the same lessons I did.

Bulbous - Round or bulging

[1] *My editor has informed me that Carter's name is not a household one, and I must explain who he is. He only made the most thrilling archaeological discovery in history: King Tut's tomb. It was the only royal tomb that remained completely undisturbed (and unrobbed) since ancient times. There's just something about all that gold...*

Chronicled - Recorded, especially in a detailed way, organized by time

Reaching under the bed, I retrieved the suitcase where I kept my most valuable items. Inside was a worn manila envelope with the photos I needed. I began flipping through them, pausing at one capturing my parents stepping off a miniature aircraft.

My dad stood behind my mom, holding a suitcase in one hand and a fedora in the other, looking at some unknown object in the horizon. My mom looked like Grace Kelly in her humanitarian years — very little makeup, but impeccably sun-kissed, with wavy blonde hair cut to her shoulders. She was smiling at whomever took the photo. I turned it over and read the back: "Frank and Mary, Alexandria, 2009-2010."

I flipped to the next picture. My parents were standing on the sands of the Mediterranean, laughing and looking at one another as they removed their scuba gear.

Not long after taking that photo, they went on another dive and never returned.

Blinking rapidly, I placed the pictures on my bed and put the suitcase away. I'd hang everything up that afternoon, closer to the time of the actual party, since open-air tents and irreplaceable items don't go well together for long periods of time.

With that, I squared my shoulders and set off for what I hoped would be my final day as a misunderstood outcast.

* * *

"I THOUGHT THEY WORE, like, burkas over there?" Caitlyn said,

---

Impeccably - Perfectly; faultlessly

suspiciously eyeing the embroidered green galabeya Mitzi handed her.

"Well, you might see it every once in a while, but that's not very common in Egypt," I said. "Are you thinking about the hijab?"

"What?"

"Like, the headscarf?"

"Whatever." Caitlyn, having arrived fashionably late, snatched the garment and stormed over to her cohorts. They'd put their costumes on over their clothes and were standing in a tight-knit circle in the corner of the yard, as far from the vivid sights and smells as they could get.

I was amused to note that one of the belly dancers wasn't pleased by this development, and kept undulating closer to them as they slipped away.

Everyone else seemed to be enjoying themselves, however. The theater types were giggling and getting henna; the advanced math crowd dug into lamb kebabs and koshary. Whirling dervishes spun amid the groups, and my favorite Egyptian songs (a mixture of modern and classical) played in the background.

Mitzi and I regarded our handiwork and indulged in some self-appreciation.

"This is incredible," I remarked. "Truly, Mitzi, quite possibly the best party ever thrown."

"It is quite good, isn't it?" Colorful bracelets clanked on her

---

Cohorts - Companions

Vivid - Lively

Undulating - Moving in a wave-like motion

14

wrist as she took a sip of hibiscus tea. "One of the best I've attended, except that one with Jackie O."

Someone from my history class — what was his name? Adam? The guy who sat in the back and never spoke— approached me. Seeing him, Mitzi discreetly slipped away.

"Great party, Noor," Adam raised a glass in my direction. His face bobbed towards me, but he looked at the trees, his feet, anything but my face. "I know it's none of my business, but you should spend more time with Caitlyn. I, uh, I think she wants to be friends with you?"

My eyes narrowed, but his face betrayed nothing. "She told you that?" I asked, craning my head in an effort to make eye contact.

"Yeah. She's in the tent," he looked over his shoulder. "You should go."

"Thanks...I will." The conversation wasn't exactly scintillating, so I was glad to have a built-in reason to excuse myself.

As I walked from the porch to the tent, I once again wished we could've gotten a camel. But I suppose there were limitations to what even Mitzi could do. Maybe the zoo would have one in a few years, and if we asked nicely...

I opened the flap of the tent and saw Caitlyn and her set standing near my family photos, snickering.

My heart skipped a beat. Did I hang any funny photos? There was the one where Harvey and I were holding Egyptian asps —

Discreetly - In a not-obvious way; unobtrusively

Scintillating - Sparkling; clever

no, they were more likely to shriek than laugh over that.

Approaching them, I put on my best Mitzi imitation: "I hope you're all enjoying the party!"

They filtered back until only Caitlyn was standing before the photos, Sharpie in hand. When I saw what she had done, I experienced the closest thing I ever have to homicidal rage.

All of my family photos had been vandalized in some way — devil ears, a pointy tail, and Captain Hook mustaches were the recurring theme, but others had vulgar captions. In one, Harvey had a six-pack drawn over his clothes.

"He's not too hard on the eyes," Caitlyn said following my gaze. "Bet it was hard to leave him."

I wanted to strangle her. Blood coursed through my veins, my body begging me to respond to the attack. My throat felt tight, and the familiar knot in my stomach returned.

"Get out," I said, unable to control the shaking in my voice. "I swear to God if you don't leave right now, I will not be held accountable for what I do to you."

"It's not like you can't print more," Caitlyn's number two mumbled, nervously playing with her hair. "It's just a bit of fun."

"I *can't* print more," I bit the words off, rounding on her. "These are Polaroids. And in case you idiots didn't know, Polaroids leave you with only ONE COPY!!!!!!"

I ripped the Sharpie out of Caitlyn's clenched fist, then fought the urge to throw it at her. I'd shocked them at least, but whether

---

Recurring - Happening repeatedly

it was out of remorse that they'd vandalized the only pictures I had of my parents, or the fact that I was screaming at them, I didn't know.

I couldn't just walk away. Shocking them wasn't enough. I wanted to *scare* them. Punish them for what they'd done.

I began whispering harsh, unintelligible sounds.

"What is she doing?" Caitlyn took a step back.

I turned on her, whispering faster, raising my hands in front of me until they were pointing directly at her.

Then I switched to English, chanting: "Old gods, curse these wicked girls. Hound them with the ten plagues of Egypt. Let food turn to ash in their mouths; let boils and sores infect their skin. Haunt them with the curse of the pharaohs!"

It was horribly cliché, but it worked. Their faces turned pale. "You're crazy," Caitlyn said, throwing off her galabeya as if it were suddenly infested with fleas. She ran from the tent, and her cohorts emulated her.

I continued "cursing" them in a mixture of English and gibberish, hurling invisible lightning bolts with my hands until they were out of earshot.

A few seconds later, Mitzi opened the flap of the tent. "I take it something's happened?"

"*Look*," I pointed.

Mitzi came inside, inhaling sharply when she saw the photos.

"Girls are different now than in my day," Mitzi sank to one of

---

Remorse - Regret; shame

Unintelligible - Impossible to understand

Emulated - Copied

the pillows. "Sure, they could make your life hell. But they were more subtle about it — there was more scheming and tact. There's nothing clever about this."

"So if they'd been more clever, it would have been OK?"

Despite myself, I let out a half-laugh, half-sob, reminded of something my mom used to say. Whenever I did something stupid — like sneak past the "Do Not Enter" doors of the Louvre with Harvey — my mom would say: "If you're going to be stupid, at least be smart about it."

It wasn't the crime that rankled her so much as much as how stupidly I'd gone about it. She wasn't happy about the crime, mind you. But breaking the rules — and doing so in a stupid way — was an act of stupidity twice-over as far as she was concerned.

Mitzi smiled wearily, like she was recalling the same phrase. I sat down next to her, and she put a sun-spotted hand over mine. She always put on a brave face for me, but losing a daughter had been as hard for her as losing a mother had been for me. Last week I got a glass of water in the middle of the night, and I could hear her sobbing through the bedroom door.

"How can you stand it here?" I finally asked.

For the first time, I looked at Mitzi with a critical eye. She'd always just been Mitzi, my eccentric grandmother — a fixed point in time, one that nothing could ever change.

She had neatly highlighted blonde hair, thanks to art rather than nature, to match the other women of the community. But a

---

Subtle - Delicately complex or understated
Rankled - Bothered

certain *joie de vivre* rendered her completely unlike them.

While other women cruised around in Audis, BMWs, and Lexi,[2] Mitzi drove a decade-old Ford Explorer with an enormous red bow on top, like her car was a giant Christmas present. It wasn't because she couldn't afford anything nicer. It was because, as she said, "It's so much easier to find this way!"

She grew up in Greenwich, and with the exception of college at Sarah Lawrence, had lived there her whole life. I suppose that protected her somehow — she could be eccentric, but she was *their* eccentric. I was not.

"It hasn't always been easy," Mitzi admitted. "But it's my home. I think your life will be easier if it can be yours too. But this — you don't want to be at home with these girls, Noor. They're vile little trollops."

I gave a hesitant smile. "I was going to ask you about studying abroad again, but…you're the only family I have left. I want to leave them, not you."

Mitzi put her arm around me, giving my shoulder a little squeeze. "Forget these girls. If you stay out of their way, they'll stay out of yours."

I grunted. "So I go back to eating alone every day?"

"Maybe. So what? You eat alone here when I'm not around. Is it really so terrible? Anyway, it seems like there are some nice people in your class," Mitzi continued. "That Adam boy, the one who told you to come here. He told me after you left that they

---

Joie de Vivre - Liveliness; "joy of life" (from French)
2 *Any speaker of Latin will understand why I prefer "Lexi" to "Lexuses"*
Vile - Wicked; morally bad; terrible

were pulling some kind of prank. Seemed like he was trying to warn you, like he wanted you to get here in time to stop it."

"I wonder if he knew what they were going to do," I mused. "I appreciate that he didn't participate, and raised the alarm in his own shadowy way. But why are the only people with a spine here the horrid ones? If Harvey had been in his position, I can guarantee that none of this would have happened."

She laughed. "If they'd been men, they'd have gone running out of here with broken noses. Girls notwithstanding..."

"He would have tossed them into the pond by the 14th green," I said.

* * *

I WON'T BORE YOU with the details from the rest of the year. Suffice it to say that what I gleaned of the American education system didn't impress me. Half the time, the teachers were as bad as the students.

Sure, they started off all sympathetic, but they think you're playing a prank when you have no idea who Lewis and Clark are, and have heart attacks when you make polite suggestions on their Egypt presentations.

My history teacher was a decrepit old man named Mr. Sanders, who wore suspenders over checkered shirts and had

---

Mused - Wondered
Gleaned - Gathered; collected bit by bit
Decrepit - Old; worn out

bird-like, impatient eyes. I thought his class, "Roots of the Modern World: Ancient Egypt, Greece, and Rome," would be a safe haven, but I was a bit confused when we started with Ramses the Great's monuments at Abu Simbel.

"Why are we starting here?" I asked from my position in the front row. "This is New Kingdom art. Shouldn't we be starting in the Old Kingdom?"

"*Miss* Cunningham," Mr. Sanders wheeled on me, the projected images distorting his face. "Kindly hold your comments until *after* I've finished my lecture."

I bit my tongue as his embarrassment of a presentation progressed, Egyptian images jumbled in no discernible order. In what world does Cleopatra come *before* the pyramids? Hello! She was the last pharaoh of Egypt!

And if you're going to mention Cleopatra, why not illustrate how she rolled out of a rug, enchanting Julius Caesar with her unique entrance? Or how Caesar inadvertently burned down the Library of Alexandria — sacrificing the knowledge of the ancient world — while helping secure her throne? You could even discuss my parents' finds! They're the ones who found her palace, after all!

"And now," Mr. Sanders pushed his silver hair off his forehead, "you may ask your questions."

My hand shot up. "Were you just showing us highlights of Egyptian history? Because I've attempted to discern a comprehen-

---

Distorting - Disfiguring
Discernible - Understandable
Inadvertently - Accidentally

sible chronology from your presentation..."

Mr. Sanders began harrumphing noisily. "It is not your place, little lady, to question the methods and motivations of your elders —"

"Then, why did you say we could ask questions?"

"Questions about the *images*, not my teaching methods," he said. Then I heard him mutter: "Raised by wolves."

"Excuse me? What did you just say?"

"Enough!" he bellowed, suddenly clutching his heart.

Mr. Sanders collapsed and was rushed to the hospital. Before our substitute arrived, Caitlyn leaned forward and remarked: "Way to go, Noor. You just killed our teacher. Did you curse him too?"

I turned and gave her a long look. "Maybe I did. And by the way — that pimple on your forehead is just the beginning of what's in store for you."

Caitlyn's nostrils flared. Her minions gasped, raising shocked hands to their mouths.

The boys laughed, and Caitlyn's ex (how I learned these things, I cannot imagine) winked at me.

I raised my eyebrows and returned to my book.
142 days to go...

Comprehensible - Understandable

CHAPTER TWO: 143 DAYS LATER

THE CHAOS OF CAIRO always stuns me, like I've accidentally looked Medusa square in the eyes and been frozen senseless as a result. There are so many people, cars, odors, billboards, street vendors... The human brain is incapable of taking it all in without proper training.

Just because I grew up in Egypt, that doesn't mean I immediately felt at ease in every city within its borders. That's like saying someone who grew up in Des Moines should immediately feel at home in L.A. (*Take that, Mr. Sanders. I do know something about American geography*).[3]

Aside from occasional consultations at the Egyptian Museum or trips to the university to visit Harvey's dad, we spent very little time in Cairo.

We were almost always in Alexandria — a large city, admitted-

---

[3] *Mr. Sanders was fine, by the way. He just had severe indigestion. I wasn't surprised, given the food they serve in school cafeterias.*

ly, but it felt calmer because of its proximity to the Mediterranean. We were fortunate to live in an old Italian villa across the
street from the beach — absolutely beautiful on the outside, with
whitewashed stone and neoclassical paneling — but actually falling apart on the inside.

None of us minded the plaster peeling from the walls, though,
because we had enough room for Harvey to stay with us when the
professor was teaching.

Harvey's mom, an Egyptian, died in a car crash when he was
six. His dad — an Englishman everyone simply refers to as "the
professor" because of his single-minded devotion to his work at
the American University in Cairo — always did the best he could
after that.

My parents had known Salima and the professor since their
days back at Cambridge, and thought nothing of stepping in to
help after her death. I was exactly Harvey's age, after all. It would
be no trouble for him to sit in on the Latin, Italian, and Greek
lessons with my mom, or the Egyptology, science, and mathematics lessons with my dad.

It's not like Harvey could stay home by himself all day, and
full-time childcare wasn't easy to afford on a faculty salary. It just
made more sense for him to stay with us during the school year,
and for the professor to come visit on his many breaks.

Soon, our parents also began working together. My dad would
find the artifacts, my mom would decipher them, and the profes-

---

Proximity - Closeness (to)

Neoclassical - In the style of ancient art (literally "new" classical)

sor would publish and lecture on their findings. It was the perfect partnership.

Landing at the Cairo International Airport, I fancied my next chapter would be the inverse of our childhood: Harvey and I at The American University in Cairo under the professor's care, instead of in Alexandria under my parents'.

LOST IN THESE MUSINGS, I almost walked past the 6-foot tall mummy at baggage claim.

Children were yanking their parents' hands and pointing eagerly at the apparition. More than one adult gave an involuntary jump upon looking over.

I walked confidently up to the mummy, whose back was facing me, and tapped him on the shoulder. When he turned around, I saw that he was wearing one of those ridiculous glasses/big nose/mustache things comedians wear and holding a sign saying, "Welcome home, Noor."

I threw my arms around him, heedless of what my fellow travelers might think. Necromancy and embracing a member of the opposite sex are both frowned upon in Egypt, but at that moment, I didn't care.

"Harvey!" I buried my head in his bandaged shoulder.

"Welcome home, Noor," he smiled (I think). "Shall we get your bags?"

Inverse - Opposite

Apparition - A ghostlike image; an unexpected appearance

Heedless - Not caring

Necromancy - Communicating with the dead

I choked back a laugh. "What's with the get-up?"

"Who better to welcome home a daughter of Egypt than its most famous pharaoh?"

"Ah," I studied him quizzically. "So who are you, then? Ramses? Tutankhamun?"

"Seti, obviously," he responded, removing his glasses and giving them a polish with his bandaged fingers.

I smiled. "The notoriously well-preserved mummy, whom the Victorians found dashing and attractive?"

"The resemblance isn't clear?"

I gave him a jovial hit on the arm. "There's my bag," I pointed.

We angled our way through an international collection of travelers, trying to get closer to the carousel, murmuring apologies and excuse-me's in a number of languages.

Closing in on my tattered duffel, Harvey politely tapped the shoulder of an elderly Italian nun, asking in flawless Italian if he could squeeze by her for a moment. She nearly jumped out of her sensible shoes when she saw him, crossing herself and muttering prayers so quickly I could barely understand her.

I think Harvey forgot he was dressed as a mummy. Gentleman that he is, he thought the poor woman was having a fit and moved closer to ask if she was alright.

She scurried backwards as nimbly as a cricket, fairly climbing over bodies and suitcases, never taking her eyes off him.

"What's her problem?" Harvey asked, effortlessly swinging my 50-pound bag over his shoulder.

Jovial - Cheerful; friendly

26

I stifled my laughter. "Some people have no manners," I agreed. "Should we head for the taxi line?"

"Actually, the professor's got the car outside."

"Will he be dressed as a mummy, too?"

"Sadly, no." His tone turning uncharacteristically serious, Harvey continued, "But you should brace yourself for something... different."

"Care to be more specific?" I asked, angling sideways to allow a German tour group laden with fanny packs to pass.

Harvey started to speak, but we were immediately separated by another tour group — American, this time. Each of its members carried a giant shoulder bag emblazoned with the face of Nefertiti, presumably so the guide could locate them more easily if they got lost.

"Outside," Harvey gestured to the sliding glass doors. I nodded, and we made our way to the exit.

As the doors opened before me, I couldn't help but feel a little thrill as the air grew about 30 degrees hotter and 1,000 times more polluted.

A smile on my face, Harvey and I maneuvered to the street, settling ourselves among the crowd.

Harvey immediately started to remove his mummy suit, muttering that it was "too bloody hot." I poked him. "You were saying?"

"Hmm?"

Stifled - Restrained

Laden - Weighed down

Emblazoned - Conspicuously depicted

The suit seemed to be getting the better of him, wrapping its withered arm around his neck. I decided to intervene before Harvey became the latest victim of "the pharaoh's curse."

"That I should brace myself, before seeing the professor," I continued, releasing Harvey from the mummy's mortal grasp.

Harvey stepped out of the suit, gave himself a little shake, and threw the empty costume over the handle of my bag.

"Yes," Harvey rubbed the back of his neck. "I was saying...Dad took the death of your parents hard. *Very* hard."

"And?"

"And...He hasn't been able to move past it. For him, it hasn't been a year. It was yesterday."

My brow furrowed. I'd only just stopped crying myself to sleep every night, and wasn't looking to move backward in the stages of grief.

I was glad Harvey prepared me, though. When the professor pulled up in his old Renault, weaving through the frenzy of cabs and travelers that possesses every airport, he looked little like the erudite scholar I'd grown up with.

His linen suit was badly wrinkled. Some of that could be chalked up to the material, I guess, but even his tie showed signs of wear. His face hadn't been shaved in days, and his previously black hair was graying at the temples.

"Professor!" I clambered into the backseat, greeting him with a friendly hug. He returned it with a smile that displayed new wrin-

---

Erudite - Scholarly
Clambered - Climbed

28

kles around his eyes.

I yanked the car door shut, wincing as it slammed. Foreigners — specifically Americans — *always* slammed doors. It was one of the many ways you could pick them out in a crowd.

Now, I finally understood why. Doors were so much *lighter* in the rest of the world. Your arm goes on autopilot with a certain swing, but compared to Mitzi's Explorer, the Renault felt like it was made of tin.

Harvey got into the front seat, and the professor began to edge into traffic. Window rolled down, he used his arm to signal the taxis behind him, like a local.

I closed my eyes and took a deep breath, my lungs relishing the feeling of the dry, hot air. Opening my eyes, I noticed the professor watching me in the rearview mirror. He quickly looked away.

"Good to have you home, Noor," he said. "How was your flight?"

The conversation continued in that vein for 20 minutes — entirely appropriate, yet oddly forced. Both of us were trying not to speak of my parents, but their presence was so palpable, my dad may as well have been riding shotgun.

By the time we entered Zamalek, the island in the Nile where university housing was located, I was relieved to say goodbye. The professor's obvious inability to move on made me feel guilty that I had, if only a little.

Pulling to a stop in front of the entrance, the professor commented, "I'll let you two get unpacked and settled. Shall we plan

---

Palpable - Intense; practically touchable

on seeing each other again when classes start?"

"Works for me," Harvey said, already halfway out the car, grabbing our bags from the trunk.

The professor inhaled, like he was going to say something else, then stopped himself. My hand on the door, I gave him a quizzical look, urging him to go on.

But he just shook his head and waved me off. "Enjoy this time. You never know what will come next."

I swung my feet to the pavement with a sigh of relief, determined not to let the professor's melancholia infect me.

Harvey was waiting for me near the limestone stairs, taking in the scenery as much as I was. Though his father taught at the university, the Zamalek dorms were located far from where classes were held, so he'd had little reason to visit them.

The beautiful residence combined the high-rise practicality of an apartment building with graceful nods to Islamic architecture. Countless palm trees sheltered the building, and the ground-floor windows all ended in jaunty arches. The higher floors had protruding balconies with intricate carvings, and a bookstore sat directly to the right of the entrance.

I tried to see which books were on display as we made our way up the stairs. Spying one of my favorites — *Crocodile on the Sandbank* by Elizabeth Peters — I felt a rush of confidence.

I'd found a new home, a place where I could spend the next

Quizzical - Indicating mild or amused puzzlement

Melancholia - Gloom; sadness

Jaunty - Cheerful; self-confident

Protruding - Sticking out

four years, at least.

Little did I know how wrong I was.

* * *

HARVEY AND I parted ways after checking in, since the men's and women's dorms were located in separate wings of the building. A guard sat in a plastic chair in front of the women's-only staircase, lazily looking at his phone, but I had no doubt he would pounce if anyone made an attempt at co-ed mingling.

The stairs began as a wide, showy affair, then sharply turned so no peering male eyes could see all the way up. At the top was a communal bathroom, then straight ahead, rooms opened off to either side at regular intervals. After five or so, there was a common area with green couches, a microwave, then more rooms along the back wall.

I passed a fascinating array of nationalities while looking for my room, unabashedly eavesdropping through the open doors. Girls in colorful hijabs and bottom-hugging jeans (obviously from more liberal families) unpacked next to blonde Scandinavians and Americans of every background.

Suddenly I heard a crash. Something falling — not an explosion. But there were shouts! Angry shouts, in a mixture of languages. One was harsh, guttural, but not Arabic. Hebrew? The second was a language I'd know anywhere — Italian.

Unabashedly - Not embarrassed or ashamed

I hastened in the direction of the clamor. Spotting the number on the door, I paused. It was coming from the room I'd been assigned! Steeling myself, I pushed the door the rest of the way open, struck dumb by the sight before me.

A slender woman with tightly curled, blondish-brown hair had performed some type of Taekwondo maneuver to throw my other roommate on the floor.

"*Porca miseria!*" shouted the Italian, lying supine on the tile. "*Ma, sei pazza?!*"

"I don't speak *ee-talian*," the Israeli replied, in mockery of the other girl's accent or because that was her own, I wasn't sure. "I told you, I served two years in the Army."

"I believe you," the Italian grumbled, wiping dust off her shimmery, mint-green skirt. Her long legs were so encumbered by four-inch wedges as she tried to stand, she may as well have been wearing stilts.

As my eyes moved northward, so did my brows. Her skirt was (barely) acceptable by Egyptian standards, falling to mid-calf. But her white, sleeveless crop top, bearing both her stomach and slender, bronzed arms, would start a riot if she stepped outside the women's dorms. Her shiny black hair contrasted with the top in a way that was probably intentional, setting off its luster.

"Hi…" I ventured. "I'm Noor. I think we're roommates."

"*Si, si,*" the Italian responded. "Nice to meet you. You see what we'll be living with the next four months." She gestured expres-

---

Clamor - Loud, chaotic noise

Supine - Lying face-up

sively to the Israeli, who had returned to unpacking her standard-issue Army duffel.

I emitted an awkward noise that I think was half-laugh, half grunt, not wanting to offend either party. "What are your names?"

"Viviana," the Italian extended a bejeweled hand in my direction.

"And I'm Shira," the Israeli responded, tossing the words over her shoulder as she pulled a pile of folded pants out of her bag.

I cautiously took a few more steps inside. Two twin beds were pushed into the back corners of the room, and a third bed was perpendicular to the others, in the corner to my left. We'd each been given an armoire and a desk, both made of pale wood, which graced the walls next to our beds.

Three overflowing Louis Vuitton bags disfigured the center of the room.[4] Their contents seemed to have flown forth in every direction, like the ills from Pandora's box, covering all of our desks and armoires.

"Viviana," Shira said. "Time to move your things, eh? You think we brought nothing?"

"I hear you, I hear you," Viviana threw up her hands. "Such little space! They think we are animals, living here?"

"I only have the one suitcase," I pointed to my tattered leather bag. "If I have extra room, we can share my armoire."

"Thank you," Viviana responded. "I study fashion, you know,

Disfigured - Spoiled the attractiveness of

[4] Yes, I eventually figured out who "Louis freaking Vuitton" was

in Milan. I will have to ship what I buy from the *souk*, I suppose..."

"Fashion! That's interesting," I replied, thinking nothing could be less interesting. "Most people here study Egyptology or Middle Eastern politics."

"Mmm," Shira contributed in tacit agreement, folding her already-unpacked bag and sliding it under the bed.

"Yes, yes," Viviana said. "I was *fidanzato* — dating someone, you say — and we thought it would be a grand adventure to come here together. We are broken, no more together now. But I show him," she threw up her chin, sending her voluminous hair bouncing. "I come here on my own, to have the adventure myself."

"Good for you!" I said, watching her bask in the compliment. "And Shira, what brings you to Cairo?"

She sat on her bed, legs stretched towards us. She hesitated a moment before responding: "I study Middle Eastern Affairs at Tel Aviv University. All I want is peace, for the fighting to end. But that will only happen if we know each other. Some people here — they think we are devils, that we have horns. We must make friends if we are to find peace."

"Maybe no throwing people to the ground, if you want to make friends?" Viviana said, arranging makeup and hair products on her desk.

Shira cracked a sheepish smile. "I'm sorry, I didn't mean..."

"*Va bene, va bene,*" Viviana waved her aside. "I have brothers."

Tacit - Silent; understood without speaking

Bask - Bathe in; revel in

I smiled, recalling the people I had been surrounded by this time last year — empty shells, who didn't exist beyond their place in a contrived social hierarchy.

Viviana might be a fashionista, but she seemed to have a personality at least. And Lord knew things would never be boring with Shira around.

I THREW MY BELONGINGS in the armoire, then invited Viviana to territorialize the extra foot. After taking a quick shower and changing into fresh clothes, I remarked, "I'll be back in a few hours. Do you guys need anything while I'm out?"

"No, *grazie.*" Viviana stood in front of the full-length mirror, removing her makeup with a moist towelette. "I am going to shower myself and sleep for sixteen hours."

"It's only 6 o'clock!" Shira protested.

"*Eh,*" Viviana agreed. "Isn't it even later for you?"

I slipped out of the room while they were bickering, betting myself that they'd be best friends by the end of the week.

The bottom of the women's-only staircase opened onto the cafeteria, though it seemed to have become a *de facto* meeting spot. I suppose that's because it was one of the few places where girls and boys were allowed to mingle (though guards were still present to prevent anything untoward, of course).

I had to introduce myself to about 20 people before finding Harvey, who'd also been caught in the wave of introductions.

Contrived - Made-up; invented

De Facto - In effect, whether intentional or not

Everyone was beyond kind, eager to make friends where they had none. A continuing refrain was, "No way, me too!" as people clung to tenuous connections in a foreign land.

"I can't believe you're from Texas. Me too!" the blonde to my right said, eyes alight. The male with whom she was speaking seemed equally relieved to find a fellow southerner, and they began exchanging school histories.

I grabbed Harvey's arm and we made our escape. Catching my breath in the backseat of a cab bound for the Khan el-Khalili, I asked, "So, are your roommates as eccentric as mine?"

"I'm guessing not, if that's your first impression," he grimaced, rolling up his sleeves. "That bad?"

"Not bad," I protested. "Just...*lively*. I actually quite like them."

"Well, I've got an American and a Swede, so we'll have our hands full showing everyone the ropes."

"Can we take a break from the new and reminisce about the old for a moment? Bring me up to speed on the gossip. Is Khadija really engaged?"

"And utterly besotted. She'll speak of nothing else," Harvey replied. "Let's see, Layla is in medical school in France..."

We paid the cab driver, then continued chatting upon entering the labyrinthine alleys of the bazaar.

Crumbling arches and domed ceilings periodically appeared overhead, like the structure couldn't decide whether it wanted to

---

Refrain - A comment that is often repeated

Tenuous - Weak or slight

Reminisce - Talk about the past in an enjoyable way

Labyrinthine - Twisty and confusing, like a maze

be indoor or outdoor. Bulbous lamps and colorful scarves seemed to grow from the walls like climbing vines. Except for the occasional anachronistic item for sale, you could be stepping back in time hundreds of years upon entering.

"And Hakim has turned into such a cretin," Harvey added. "You know, the shiny-haired type who wears tight t-shirts, smokes cigarettes, and is constantly groping people?"

"Ugh," I snorted. "How do you even fall into that crowd?"

We continued exploring, with me asking nosy questions and Harvey supplying answers until we stumbled upon an antique jewelry shop. Unlike many of the open-air establishments, this one was firmly indoors, its golden wares winking to the street behind glass.

Normally I'm as interested in jewelry as American history (i.e., not at all), but they had a fascinating array of snake rings on display, neatly stacked on slender mannequin fingers.

"Do you mind if I take a look?" I asked. "I've wanted a snake ring for years. Makes me feel like Cleopatra."

"Erm — you know she killed herself with a snake, right? Had it bite her on the chest and all that?"

"I still want one."

He nodded with mock solemnity. "Then one you shall have."

I chose my favorite. Made of gold, it wrapped around my finger a full three times.

"*Salaam alaikum,*" I addressed the store owner. "How much for

---

Anachronistic - Belonging to a different time period

Cretin - An offensive term for a stupid person

this snake ring?"

The shopkeeper, an old man with two teeth and bright eyes, put on his glasses and took the ring. Turning the metal over in his fingers, he remarked, "300 *geneh*."

A pleasant interlude of bartering transpired, after which I began to reach for my wallet.

"My treat," Harvey passed a handful of pink and green bills to the shopkeeper.

"What? Nonsense."

"A welcome home gift, then?"

Harvey took my hand, sliding the ring onto my middle finger. It wound almost to my knuckle, ending with little red gems for eyes.

I loved it.

* * *

HARVEY AND I didn't return until late in the evening. I was about to walk up the stairs to the women's quarters when he remarked, "I forgot to tell you — we rented a dahabeeyah for tomorrow night."

I gave him a look of surprise. "Whatever for?"

"The university students do it all the time," he explained. "The boat essentially becomes a floating party by night. And where better to have our first college party than the center of the Nile?"

Geneh - A unit of Egyptian currency
Interlude - Period of time
Dahabeeyah - A type of sailboat popular among early 20th-century travelers

I bristled, the mention of the word "party" bringing to mind my horrendous experience in Connecticut.

"It'll be different this time," Harvey promised, before I'd voiced my concerns. "Feel free to bring your roommates, too, if you think it's safe to put them on a boat together."

I smiled. "Probably not, but I'll certainly invite them."

CHAPTER THREE

"MADONNA MIA, HE'S GOOD-LOOKING," Viviana muttered as we approached the dahabeeyah, a type of sailboat popular among early 20th-century explorers (and now, apparently, college students). I was amused to find her gazing in Harvey's direction.

"Harvey, you mean?"

"Oh, that is your Harvey? Yes, I did mean, but I meant no offense..."

"It's fine," I assured her. "He's like my brother. We're not together."

Viviana's perfectly plucked eyebrows rose. "But why! You have seen his physique? He looks like Italian with that tan, but his hair and those eyes! The blue-green, we have nothing like it in Italy. And look when he smiles! *Che bello!*"

"Um, well, I could introduce—"

"Viviana! Can't you control yourself for five minutes?" Shira interjected. "Don't you see how uncomfortable you're making her?"

"I didn't mean—"

As they bickered, I glanced in Harvey's direction. I suppose his unique ethnic background did make him quite pleasing to the eye. He'd inherited his mother's olive skin, but his hair was more susceptible to the sun's rays than some of his Egyptian compatriots, turning it a unique shade between black and brown.

Had he always looked this way? Growing up, the only distinctive feature I remembered was that he'd been the tallest in our group. We must have made a memorable pair: Harvey tall and dark, me tiny and blonde.

If I ever gave any thought to Harvey's height, it certainly wasn't in the style of Viviana. Rather, it was an inner musing, wondering why he always slouched.

I had my suspicions, though I'd never voice them out loud. While his coloring had largely come from his mother, his height had undoubtedly come from his father.

To my unending surprise, there were still people on both sides of the Mediterranean small-minded enough to frown on his parents' relationship. Several of his uncles wouldn't even speak to him, having disowned Salima when she married the professor. And while in England? He'd been called names I would never repeat.

Now that I thought about it, Harvey's penchant for disguises

Interjected - Said abruptly, usually interrupting a conversation

Penchant - Fondness (for)

made a lot more sense. People can't insult you if they don't know who you are.

There were times when his self-control would burst, of course, but as a rule, it was easier to make people laugh than to pummel them.

But still...there was something different about him now. He'd obviously retained a fondness for disguises, as the faux mummy at the airport made clear. But he didn't slouch anymore.

To my shame, I thought for the first time about what life had been like for Harvey in my absence. When I texted him, I pictured him in some sort of time capsule, as though everything had been upended for me, but nothing had changed for him back in Egypt.

But that made no sense. He lived with my family in Alexandria most of the year. Though he'd stayed in Egypt, he'd had to move to Cairo with his dad, making new friends, just as I had.

What had that been like? I was always Harvey's biggest defender, going ballistic on anyone who negatively mentioned his background, in either direction.

I forced myself to stop grinding my teeth. No one aboard had done such a thing, to the best of my knowledge.

And anyway, whatever reckoning he'd come to was obviously to his benefit. Standing up straight, it was like he'd cast off the burdens of his youth, deciding that people could either accept him or not, and he didn't much care one way or the other.

Retained - Hung on to

Faux - Fake

Upended - Turned upside down

* * *

MY ROOMMATES AND I were among the last to board, grasping the calloused hands of the captain and first-mate as we crossed the gangplank.

Stepping aboard, it was clear the night's entertainment had already begun. A playlist featuring hits from France, Egypt, and the States blared from the boat's tinny speakers, and drinks were being passed around freely.

The interior of the vessel was shaped like a shallow rectangle, with cushioned seating along the edges and standing room in the middle. If you were so inclined, you could lean over the edge and dip your hand in the water, though I wouldn't advise it, pollution and parasites being all-too prevalent.

A massive sail rose from the center, and for some reason, pink and green Christmas tree lights were wrapped around the exterior railings, casting neon shadows across the revelers' faces.

There were maybe 15 other people aboard, an international collection of students from the dorms. I brought Shira and Viviana in Harvey's direction, intending to introduce them, but Viviana beat me to it. She stumbled into his broad chest, forcing him to catch her lest she topple into the Nile.

She was on full display that night — big hair, big lips, and big boobs crammed into a tight white dress. Shira and I forced her to cover her shoulders with a pashmina during the journey over, but

---

Tinny - Having a thin, metallic sound
Prevalent - Widespread

she seemed to have lost it the moment we boarded.

"I'm so sorry!" she pouted up at him. "I don't know what happened. These ships are *soo* wobbly."

Amusement registered on Harvey's face. "Those shoes probably don't help."

I found myself scuttling backwards like a beetle, too embarrassed on Viviana's behalf to watch the hideously cliché exchange.

Shira followed suit. "That girl. In some ways, you have to admire her bravery. I'd never have pulled that off."

"Bravery is one word for it," I agreed. "I can think of others."

We began introducing ourselves to the rest of the group, soon meeting two lads studying abroad from a prestigious American military academy. Both were in excellent physical condition, and their cocky grins made it clear that they knew how their status and attractiveness affected most females.

Some time later, far from shore, I noticed one of them kept looking at me — Kevin, the one with dark hair and a plaid shirt.

"Why does he keep doing that?" I asked Shira, gesturing in Kevin's direction.

Shira looked over, then back at me in confusion. "Eh, because you are young and beautiful and he wants to talk to you?"

I snorted. "I think you're describing Viviana."

"I am," she admitted. "But also you. He's cute! Go talk to him. Flirt, as you say!"

"As I say? I say nothing of the sort. I'd have no idea what to

---

Prestigious - Having high status; respected
Grins - Smiles

say!"

"Of course you do! It is natural. Go!" she said, emphasizing the command with a little shove.

Blast. Kevin had observed the whole exchange. So had his friend. The friend slipped away, leaving Kevin standing there with a broad grin as I made my way over.

"Hello!" I said.

"Hi there," Kevin responded.

How to flirt...How to flirt...

"So, how are you liking Egypt?"

"It's incredible," Kevin responded. "The adventure, the history...and I'm meeting the most *beautiful* people."

The last bit was all meaningful eye contact and innuendo. I wrinkled my nose, thoroughly off-put by such an insipid line, and took a sip of my drink.

I don't know why I noticed. I wasn't *looking.* I just happened to look...and his fly was down. A bit of red boxer was poking through.

I cursed my fate. *Should I tell him? Should I jump overboard? Could I ever have normal social interactions with an American?*

"Your, ah—" I said. "That is, did you know..."

I stole a glance at Harvey. Viviana was still with him, laughing and touching his arm.

Catching my eye, Harvey raised his brows and gave me a "You OK?" look.

I nodded, but Harvey narrowed his eyes and transferred his

Innuendo - A suggestive reference

Insipid - Lacking flavor or interest

45

gaze to Kevin.

"Did I know...?" Kevin prompted.

"Did you know," I repeated, looking straight into his eyes, "that you pulled out a mummy's brain through its nose?"

Kevin's face underwent a series of rapid contortions, alternating between disgust, amusement, and concern over my mental state.

Mercifully, Shira interrupted before I could explain the process in greater detail. "How's it going?" she asked, looping her arm through mine.

"You know," Kevin took a sip of his drink, "I'm not quite sure."

Shira gave me a look of friendly exasperation, then said to Kevin, "By the way, your fly is down."

Kevin's hand instinctively reached for his pants. "Whoops!" He turned and fixed it, then said, "Now, Shira...remind me where you're from?"

Kevin's friend returned in time to hear the question. He was equally fit, his hair fair instead of dark, and he was awaiting Shira's answer with interest.

Eyeing her audience, Shira grimaced. I could almost *see* her guard going back up.

"Israel," she responded.

Kevin's interest piqued. "Is it true they teach you Krav Maga? Like, street fighting?"

Uncertain whether the question implied a subtle criticism, Shi-

---

Exasperation - Annoyance

Piqued - Awakened; made greater

ra responded: "An attack in Israel could mean anything. Often it's a fanatic with a knife on a bus, or in a shopping mall. If no one is armed, 'street moves,' as you call them, are the only way people can defend themselves."

"That's great," Kevin said. "I keep trying to get my sister to take a class. Some Krav Maga master opened up a studio in New York, but she's not interested."

Shira cracked a grin. I suppose that as an Israeli on her first public outing in Egypt, she was apt to be a bit cautious. The two countries may have signed a peace treaty, but their history was far from peaceful.

"It's great exercise, if your sister wants to get in shape. Kneeing would-be assailants in the balls is tiring work."

The guys laughed, raising their drinks to that. Shira and I raised ours as well, and as the conversation turned to more mundane matters, I said, "Shira, do you mind if I check on Harvey? Just want to make sure Viviana hasn't devoured him yet."

Shira assured me she was in good company, and I began weaving my way through the bodies, careful not to lose my footing amid the rocking waves. Harvey and Viviana were standing near the edge of the ship, where the crowd was less dense.

"Noor! There you are," Viviana said. "I was just speaking that the three of us should get dinner next weekend."

"Sure!" I said with forced enthusiasm.

"*Benissimo!*" Viviana hugged Harvey — though "pressed her

Apt - Appropriate under the circumstances

Assailant - Attacker

Mundane - Lacking interest or excitement

voluptuous body against" would be a more accurate description. The hug seemed very torso-centric.

Unfortunately Harvey had just taken a swig of his drink, and the unexpected embrace caused him to choke. He disentangled himself, coughing into his elbow.

Viviana seemed pleased by his reaction, smiling like the cat from *Alice in Wonderland* before making her exit. She wriggled her bottom and disappeared into the throng of people, heading back towards Shira.

"You OK?" I asked my recovering companion.

"Feel like I've just had a conversation with a bulldozer."

I snorted. "Now you get why Shira's first reaction was to lay violent hands on her."

"At least you're coming too. Not that she isn't an — erm, pulchritudinous — companion. But my God, she comes on a bit strong, doesn't she?"

"That's one way of putting it," I clapped him on the back. "Never fear, I'll protect you."

"Thank heaven for that."

As the night progressed, we drifted gently in the waves of the Nile as humanity had done for more than five thousand years. Though some on the boat were Egyptian and had taken many such excursions, the majority were foreign. At one point, near the center of the Nile, a collective silence settled over the rowdy

---

Voluptuous - Curvy and attractive
Disentangle - Free (from something)
Pulchritudinous - Beautiful

group. Conversation and lewd jokes temporarily halted as everyone admired the view.

Though the Nile is notoriously polluted, it isn't obviously so, like some other rivers. The Tiber in Rome seems to be covered with a layer of radioactive green slime, but the Nile's waves look as innocent as those that gave birth to Aphrodite. The waters were deep blue, almost black at that time of night, though the lights from our boat gave it intermittent pink and green hues. It spanned more than two miles across.

The city, a dusty gray during the day, seemed to have come alive after sunset. From our peaceful position on the river, we could see lights in every direction. Yellow flames danced across the water near the coastline. Minarets and skyscrapers rose above the fray, ancient and modern coexisting like nowhere else. I fancied I could even see the pyramids in the distance, but of course that was only my imagination. They were further south, in Giza.

We all murmured words like "beautiful" and "magical," but of course they were woefully inadequate. The ship's captain — a clean-shaven, middle-aged man wearing a gray galabeya — beamed, proud of the effect his country had on the *Inglizi* and *Amerikani*.

There was near-silence for several more minutes, the boat

Notoriously - Well known, usually in a bad way

Intermittent - Not consistent

Hues - Shades of color

Minaret - A tall, slender tower rising up from a mosque

Fray - A place of intense activity

Inadequate - Insufficient

slowly moving north with the current, before conversation resumed and the playlist that had mysteriously gone silent reemerged.

I'LL BE THE FIRST TO ADMIT that the events surrounding our disembarkation were a little fuzzy, but the general consensus among the group was clear: we wanted food.

"We" was Harvey, my roommates, and Kevin, whom I'd gladly surrendered to Shira.

The boat let us off near Tahrir Square, a bustling plaza full of shops, people, and redolent halal food carts. Even at that hour, nearly 1 o'clock in the morning, the square was as full as Manhattan at rush hour.

Though it's always crowded, Ramadan made it even more so. Unable to eat or drink during the day, most people rested during those hours, reemerging after sunset.

Kevin began wandering in the direction of a brightly illuminated food cart before Harvey stopped him, putting out an arm in what (I thought) was an unnecessarily rough gesture. Kevin bumped into it and staggered back.

"What the...?"

"Wouldn't do that, mate," Harvey said. "Street food here can churn the innards of those who aren't used to it."

Shira and Viviana, also drawn in by the smell, stopped advanc-

---

Disembarkation - Getting off a ship, aircraft, or other vehicle

Redolent - Smelling of

Halal - Having meat prepared in accordance with Islamic law

ing when they got close enough to see how the food was prepared.

"What am I looking at, exactly?" Shira gave a courteous wave to the vendor, who was enthusiastically inviting her to sample his wares.

He was wearing a once-white apron, now heavily soiled by the many ingredients he'd been cooking with. One of those ingredients appeared to be dirt.

At least seven flies were buzzing around his cart, occasionally dive-bombing the spit where shawarma was rotating. They'd crawl around for a few seconds, rubbing their feelers together like they were greatly enjoying the meal, before hopping over to sample the vegetables and dressing.

We were too close now to simply walk away. It would've been needlessly rude. Harvey handled it by addressing the man in Arabic. "One chicken shawarma, please."

Then, turning to us, Harvey said in a lower voice, "There's a place up the road that might be better for you."

I cleared my throat and addressed the vendor. "We'll have two actually. I'd like one, as well."

Harvey raised his eyebrows. I raised mine back, then fished around my bag for a few *geneh*.

Truthfully, the food was no more appealing to me than it was to my roommates. I wasn't above street food, but this was a particularly unsanitary specimen. It reminded me of a crepe stand in France where I'd seen the chef accidentally knock his tip jar into the batter. I assumed he'd dump it and start over, but he just gave

51

a furtive look around and kept stirring, watching the filthy coins sink to the bottom of the bowl.

Yet tonight, I felt the need to set myself apart from my squeamish co-habitants. How dare Harvey lump me in with them?

"It's fine!" I responded brightly. "Smells delicious!"

Harvey shrugged, and I tried not to watch the vendor wave away insects before slicing into the chicken. I deemed it safe to look up when Harvey placed the tinfoil-wrapped shawarma in my hands.

"*Shukran*," I thanked the chef for the food, sliding over the appropriate amount of cash. He wasn't wearing gloves, and immediately resumed work after putting my money in the register.

The moment we were out of earshot, Shira said, "You're not going to eat that, are you? You haven't taken a bite yet. You're not going to eat it."

"Of course I am!" I replied. "Why wouldn't I?"

"You'll get sick," Viviana said with a fastidious curl of her nose.

"*Foreigners* get sick. I grew up here."

I took a giant bite, only slightly surprised to find that the meat was seasoned to perfection, beautifully complemented by creamy tomatoes, lettuce, and onions. It required no undue effort on my part to continue eating as we picked up food for the others, then got Viviana a scarf from an open-air merchant.

When I was done, I crumpled the tinfoil wrapper in my hands, then tossed it into an overflowing wastebasket.

Furtive - Secretive, usually because of guilt

Fastidious - Attentive to detail/cleanliness

VIVIANA, SHIRA, AND I took a cab back to the dorms together; Harvey and Kevin took another. When we arrived, the omnipresent guard to the women's corridors was reading the Koran, so we walked past him in respectful silence, resuming conversation when we got upstairs.

Changing into our pajamas, Viviana asked Shira: "Could you teach me some of your karate moves? There are just so many men, men, men here and in Italy, grabbing you, shouting at you. You never know if one of them is *pazzo*."

"It's called Krav Maga, and yes!" Shira responded. "But what would be most useful...Ah. What to do if someone tries to strangle you."

Viviana opened her mouth, then closed it. "OK, what do I do?"

I sat cross-legged on my bed, taking notes as Shira wrapped her hands around Viviana's throat.

Transforming into instructor-mode, Shira asked Viviana how she would respond. Viviana flexed her hands, her painted nails turning into claws. "I'd scratch his eyes out," she said proudly.

"Wrong. Men are usually taller than women, so his arms will be longer than yours," Shira took a small step back. "Try to scratch my eyes out now. You can't."

"What do I do then?" Viviana sulked, like she just found out her favorite handbag was sold out.

"Let's reverse positions," Shira said. "Try to strangle me — not for real, you crazy! Just pretend."

Viviana adjusted her grip and Shira raised her right arm, stepping back with her left foot to twist her torso. She then pretended to ruthlessly crush her elbow on Viviana's forearm, collapsing her legs as she did so.

In effect, it forced all her weight on a vulnerable part of Viviana's arm.

"Then you can elbow his face, knee him in the groin, and *run away*," Shira remarked. "Always run away! The goal isn't to beat him up. It's to buy enough time to get help."

"Interesting... Now I try!" Viviana said, waving Shira towards her neck.

Viviana raised her arm and brought it down on Shira's, but forgot to turn her torso and collapse her weight. Her arm alone did little to break Shira's grip.

"Noor, come and attack me so Viviana can see," Shira said.

Eager to try, I scampered from the bed and lightly placed my hands on Shira's throat. She demonstrated several more times until Viviana began making noises of comprehension.

"I understand. Now I go again," Viviana decreed.

Viviana demonstrated the move to perfection, emulating Shira's sharp *whoosh* of breath with each step.

"Excellent!" Shira said, after having her repeat it several times. "Noor, now you."

Despite my notes, I didn't do it correctly the first time either. To be fair, though, my stomach was bubbling in a rather uncomfortable way, occupying the better part of my attention.

Viviana, now believing herself to be a self-defense expert, hopped back up from the bed to demonstrate once more. Then

Emulating - Copying

she turned me back over to Shira.

"Ok, arm up and twist—" I said, moving as I spoke, "then WHAM!"

"Two new pros!" Shira cried. "Keep practicing until it's your automatic response. You shouldn't even have to think about it."

I obliged, unable to stop laughing when I saw Viviana in my peripheral vision, jumping around her bed like Rocky Balboa, judo-chopping and kicking the air in her silk shorts and tank top.

Obliged - Did as someone asked or ordered
Peripheral - The outer edge (of something)

CHAPTER FOUR

I IMAGINED MYSELF Sir Richard Burton,[5] staggering through the Arabian Desert to an oasis of penicillin. Light-headed and weak, I stumbled past rows of manicured palm trees, no longer able to see anything but the university health center.

When I arrived, I found the state-of-the-art facility in a perplexing state of disarray. Janitors leaned against countertops, gossiping with nurses. Women in blouses and skirts powered past. Did they work here? If so, they didn't seem interested in helping an obviously sick person (me).

I walked with nothing but the strength of self-preservation to the woman at the front desk, and was curtly told to sit in the waiting area before being asked my name or anything else. I obliged with a sense of defeat.

Twenty minutes of sitting up unnaturally straight later, the

---

[5] *A Victorian explorer who searched for the source of the Nile*
Perplexing - Confusing; baffling

searing pain in my chest making anything else unthinkable, I realized I had clearly gotten lost in Egypt's bureaucracy.

Without acknowledging the cold receptionist who told me to sit down 20 minutes prior, I got up and wandered towards a doctor's office and was promptly waved in by a kindly, middle-aged woman. As though she'd been waiting, she tutted, "Come in, come in!"

Glancing at the clipboard of papers on her lap, she asked: "So, what exactly is wrong?"

I looked at the open door to my right. More accurately, I looked at the attractive Arab sitting just outside the open door to my right.

"Well, every time I breathe, there's a sharp pain right here," I indicated my ribs. She applied pressure to the area, leaving me breathless, and nodded.

"Is that all?" she asked. "How are your bowel movements?"

"Umm..." Looking purposefully at nothing in particular, my cheeks hot, I selected the word "spontaneous" and relayed it with little vocal inflection.

She nodded. "This is not uncommon, for Americans in Egypt..."

I began to protest, but started shivering again. A perpetual layer of cold sweat covered my face, and I'd been unable to participate in events more than 10 feet from a bathroom since eating at the food cart the weekend before.

"I'm prescribing you with *unpronounceable* and *gibberish*. You

---

Bowel movements - Number two's

57

will take the *unpronounceable* thirty minutes before eating, and the *gibberish* morning and night. If you are not feeling better in 72 hours, you may take *more unintelligible words.*"

Frustration tightened my throat. "What," I asked with a small cough, "do I have, exactly?"

None of the words she said made sense.

"Like...a lung infection?" I probed. "Food poisoning? The flu?"

"Yes, sort of," she replied. "If you don't want to take the medicine, we can give you shot, and you will feel better much sooner."

I made a face — I've never liked shots — but as she said it, she seemed increasingly convinced of the logic of the proposition. "Yes," she concluded, "you take the injection."

Aware that I was rapidly losing control, I endeavored to regain my composure.

"The medicine will be fine," I said clearly. "I'll take the medicine."

Brushing me off, the doctor began writing on her clipboard and said, "They will give you the shot now."

Seeing my look of mild panic, she stopped writing and looked at me. "Trust me, you will feel much better! It will be very easy!"

She stood up and handed me over to the cold receptionist who summarily dismissed me not 30 minutes prior, whose now-visible clothing indicated she was actually a nurse.

Without so much as a "hello," she brusquely motioned me into another office across the hall and followed me in. I sat on the

---

Unintelligible - Not capable of being understood
Probed - Questioned; tried to uncover information
Endeavored - Tried

padded, plastic chair and offered my arm like it was going to the chopping block.

"No, no" she said with the first semblance of a smile I had seen on her face, purposefully tugging on the back of her scrubs.

My eyes widened with understanding, once again unwilling. But she offered me no time to prevaricate, telling me to stand up, lean over, and lower my jeans. Grimacing, I lowered the right side and felt a needle go in the top-center, then the weird tightness you get after a shot. Thinking I was done, I suppressed a ragged cough and adjusted my pants.

"No, no..." she said, "another." My eyes widened with helpless outrage, but I did as I was told and felt another needle go in the exact same place.

Before I'd even buttoned my jeans, the awful woman whisked open the door and led me to another room down the hall. She pointed to a row of plastic beds, then departed with a soft slam of the door.

Lying down, the events replayed themselves in my mind in a jumble of mental photographs. I'd been so eager to get back to Egypt, but Egypt alone wasn't enough. My soul still longed for my parents.

I wanted them to say I'd be alright, for my mom to put cold washcloths on my forehead and brush the hair out of my face. I wanted my dad to bring me a warm cup of soup and tell me stories of the ancient Minoans. I wasn't a child anymore, but my

---

Semblance - Something that resembles something else
Prevaricate - Speak or act in an evasive manner, usually to try to get out of something

arms still ached with the emptiness of a hug gone missing.

I pulled out my phone, sending Mitzi a "How are you? I miss you" email. I didn't mention that I was at the doctor with an indefinable ailment. There was no need to worry her, but I wanted to feel close to someone who loved me.

If it hadn't been 5 a.m. in Connecticut, I would've called her. If my symptoms hadn't been so off-putting, I would've called Harvey. This just wasn't the sort of thing I wanted to share with him, and besides, he was in class.

I wiped a tear from my eye with a fist. It was just a touch of the Pharaoh's Curse, that's all.

I sank into an uneasy slumber, dreaming of the last time I'd seen my parents. They'd just made a "thrilling" discovery (though, to my dad, everything related to archaeology was thrilling). They promised they'd share it with me, but...

When I awoke, I was alarmed to see the crepuscular rays of sunset outside, framing the window in brilliant tones of red and orange. I took a deep breath and swung to my feet, deciding now was as good a time as any to leave. I'd die of old age before the nurse came to check on me.

I only hoped the shots had started kicking in. The bus home was over an hour — through Cairo traffic and across the Nile — and there was no bathroom.

WHEN I STUMBLED, pale-faced, back to our room, I found Vi-

Ailment - Illness

Crepuscular - Relating to twilight

viana standing in front of the mirror in a beaded black dress. The top covered her chest and shoulders, but everything above the bra line was sheer. The bottom ended mid-thigh.

"*Poverina!* You look even worse than you did this morning," she exclaimed. "You saw the doctor? What did they say?"

"Would you believe me if I said I don't know? It doesn't matter. I'll be feeling better in no time. But until then, I'm sorry. There's no way I'm getting dinner with you and Harvey tonight."

"Of course! I understand."

Her sympathetic, nodding smile seemed altruistic, but I suspected she was pleased not to have a chaperone. She resumed applying her makeup, and I crawled under the covers.

"I thought you were meeting at 7?" I asked. "It's already 7:15, and you just started your makeup."

"Let him wait," she said. "A man likes a girl he has to work for, no?"

"I suppose, but isn't that just rude?"

"In Italy, 7 means 7:30, maybe 8:00. He'll learn soon enough."

A flicker of annoyance shot through me, like when a piece of hair is on your shirt, tickling your arm, but you can't find it. Shaking my head, I burrowed beneath my thin blanket and drifted into a dizzy sleep.

VIVIANA DIDN'T RETURN until the wee hours of the morning. I awoke with a start, reaching for my pepper spray, since she slammed the door with such force it made my teeth rattle. But she

---

Altruistic - Selfless; kind

didn't appear to be angry. Rather, she was stumbling and laughing, and turned on the lights before remembering Shira and I were asleep.

"*Scusa!*" she shrieked in the shrill voice she believed to be a whisper. She flipped the lights back off and turned on her bedside lamp instead. I heard her fall a few more times as she tried to get changed.

"For heaven's sake, Viviana..." Shira muttered, putting a pillow over her head.

I couldn't help but agree. I wanted to ask how dinner went, but since it turned into a giddy, all-night affair, I imagined it went rather well. That old annoying feeling returned.

CHAPTER FIVE

SO THE NEXT FEW WEEKS progressed. Viviana grew increasingly giggly anytime someone mentioned Harvey, and I studiously refrained from asking about their blooming courtship. They were both adults, after all. They could do as they pleased.

To be honest, once school began, I saw Harvey far less than I anticipated. By some ridiculous twist of scheduling fate, despite the fact that he and I had the *exact* same academic background, we weren't in any classes together.

He was, however, in four classes with Viviana.

Accordingly, they took the bus together in the mornings, rode home together in the evenings, and sat by each other in class. She asked him to carry her books, no doubt.

Meanwhile, Shira and I were becoming closer. We'd only been in Egypt a month, but living together made it seem like far longer.

Studiously - Deliberately; on purpose
Refrained - Held back; stopped (oneself) from doing something

One miserably hot Wednesday, when flies were buzzing lazily around trash cans and the men sitting on the side of the road were too tired to cat-call, I asked Shira if she'd be heading back to Israel for Eid al-Fitr break.

We were carrying our groceries back to the dorms, discussing some of the more exciting trips people had booked. The holiday marked the end of Ramadan, and because it fell in the middle of the week this year, almost everyone was taking the whole week off.

The girls down the hall had already booked tickets to Istanbul, Kevin and his crowd were going to the beaches of Dahab, and some guys from my Egyptology class were going sandboarding in the Black and White desert.

"Home? Why come to Egypt just to go home? I want to see the tombs!" was her astonished reaction.

I smiled, happy to see her interest in archaeology take root. "We already saw the pyramids during orientation. How about a trip down to Luxor? There are no better tombs than those in the Valley of the Kings."

We'd reached the dorms by that point, and ran into Harvey and Viviana in the cafeteria on the way back up to our room. They were laughing and staring into each other's eyes, ignoring the food in front of them.

By some miracle, Harvey noticed our presence when we were a few feet away.

"Noor! Shira! I haven't seen you in days! Come sit with us," he pulled out a chair.

"Can't, groceries," Shira held up her bags. "But Viviana, Noor and I were just talking about Eid. Do you want to come to Luxor with us?"

She immediately agreed, but Harvey was more reserved.

"You're going to Luxor for Eid?" he looked at me and rubbed the back of his neck. "I figured we'd go to Alex, spend some time with the professor."

"That does sound nice," I said. "Next time, definitely."

I wasn't mad that he was spending all his time with Viviana, but I also wasn't going to wait around for the scraps that remained.

From there, the trip came together with surprising ease. Shira and I packed nothing more than a backpack and a purse for the four-day excursion; Viviana brought one of her giant wheelies. A toddler could have crawled into that thing and no one would've noticed.

No matter. There would be plenty of room on the train.

* * *

"VIVIANA, I KNOW YOU CAN DO THIS. On the count of three, relax," I said, feeling my hand go numb as my distraught roommate suppressed a wail.

She was squatting over a filthy, overflowing bucket on a third-class train from Cairo to Luxor, her arms spread like Jesus on the cross so Shira and I could keep her upright as she tried to pee. The floor was sticky, a brown substance was smeared on the wall, and

---

Suppressed - Held back; repressed

the one small window that existed was seemingly barred shut.

"I can't!" she whimpered, suppressing a gag while fighting to keep her balance. "What if it splashes? *Dio, che schifo,*" she said, this time gagging for real. "I cannot."

"Viviana," I twitched as one of the countless flies in the room buzzed near my face. "This is the third time we've done this. We're not turning back again. You're about to pee your pants — do it over the bucket instead."

Viviana made a face and, with a shrill cry, started to pee.

"You're doing it!" Shira said encouragingly, rubbing Viviana's back the way you might with a woman in labor. "Keep going!"

I eyed the bucket warily as Viviana exhausted her supply, acutely aware that at the next bump, it was going to spill over, and the urine and feces of countless Egyptians was going to drench our feet.

"That's it..." I adopted Shira's soothing tone as Viviana finished the task. "There you go..."

The second she was done, we yanked her to a standing position and she waddled forward, her pants still not pulled up. We all knew we had to get away from the bucket as quickly as possible. She could deal with her pants and belt at a safe distance.

"I'm getting off this train," Viviana declared, tears streaking her face. "I hate you both, and I am getting off this train."

"We want off this train as bad as you do," Shira reminded her. "At the next stop, we'll get off and figure something else out. I promise."

Acutely - Intensely

66

Viviana covered her hand with three alcohol wipes to open the door. There wasn't enough Purell in the world to get her to touch it, apparently. When the door was open, she dropped the wipes to the floor.

I was about to protest, but at that point, even I wouldn't have willingly touched them. The wipes immediately began to absorb certain liquids that occupy bathroom floors, and — though I know this isn't an excuse — the train was filthy already. You couldn't go more than a few steps without encountering detritus of some kind, whether it was discarded fast food bags, cigarette butts, or dusty, used tissues.

We started making our way back to our "seats," though technically our third-class carriage was standing-room only. We'd ended up there through a well-intentioned, if shortsighted, division of labor.

Thinking we'd have to reimburse each other less, I booked the hotel, Viviana booked the tours, and Shira took care of the transportation.

Unfortunately, Shira purchased our train tickets with the same mentality one uses when booking flights. She bought the cheapest option, assuming they were all equally unpleasant.

That may be the case with flights, but there are varying degrees of discomfort on an Egyptian train. I tried explaining this before our departure, but Viviana was delighted by the low price since it meant more pocket money for the *souk*, and Shira insisted

---

Detritus - Waste; debris

Reimburse - Pay back

that she could handle a little dust.

I gritted my teeth as we walked, trying to ignore the fifteen or so men who put their hands on my backside as we traversed the aisle, lazily reaching out to grope us from their seats.

I moved closer to Viviana, swatting away hands so she wouldn't have to remember that on top of the ordeal she'd just suffered. But there was nothing I could do for Shira, standing at the front of our group. I could see her shoulders tense as she braced for a fight, but she knew the odds were not in our favor.

"Miss, where you go? Where you go?" A scrawny young man wearing tight jeans and a neon orange t-shirt sidled up behind me. I thanked heaven that my backpack provided some barrier between us, even if I could hear him unzipping the front pocket. Let him take what he found. As best I could recall, that was where I kept emergency tampons. Hopefully he'd be so horrified he'd leave me alone.

I dismissed him with a curt Arabic phrase, to no avail. He continued pressing up against my back, repeating things like, "Why you no go with me? You have beautiful eyelash."

Soon, his arms reached under my backpack and began tapping my bottom, like he was playing upside-down drums.

I gasped, trying to use an elbow to stop him, but he just laughed and kept going.

Soon there were more men following us. *Three? Six?* Who knew. If we hadn't been walking down an aisle, we would've been

---

Traversed - Traveled through or across

(To no) avail - With little or no success

surrounded.

This was the one area where Connecticut beat Egypt, hands down. There, you could walk down the street unescorted and not attract a pack of stray males who were annoying at best, dangerous at worst.

As the tapping on my bottom became intolerable — and my requests for assistance from the other passengers were ignored, or simply attracted more predators — my brain clung to the safe and familiar: history.

I channeled Leonidas at the Battle of Thermopylae. I fantasized about kicking the men into a well, though it wouldn't make sense to shout, "THIS. IS. SPARTA!!!!!" Maybe "THIS. IS. WRONG!!!!"?

Either way, watching them flail as they fell to their deaths would be immensely satisfying.

Since there were no wells nearby, I considered the overarching lesson from the battle. In short, it was that a small group of people can take on a numerically superior force if they are funneled into a small space — like the aisle of a train.

At that moment, we were only a few steps from the women's-only carriage (the bathroom had been inexplicably locked for the past two hours, which was why we were forced to venture next door).

When Shira and Viviana were safely through to the other side, I abruptly stopped walking and shoved backwards with all my

---

Inexplicably - Impossible to explain

Venture - Undertake a risky journey

might, pressing my hands into the seats for extra momentum.

The man behind me stumbled back just enough for me to administer an elbow in the gut, then slam the heel of my boot onto his sandaled toes. I wanted to turn around and punch him, but decided not to press my luck. I ground my heel hard though, like he was a particularly large insect, and smiled when I felt a crunch.

The man howled, hopping and clutching his bleeding foot.

Meanwhile, I crossed into the safety of the women's-only carriage. The guard hadn't noticed anything amiss, and prevented the horde of outraged men from following.

* * *

THANKFULLY, EVEN VIVIANA admitted that the rest of the trip was a dream. We stayed at the Winter Palace, a tourist attraction in its own right since everyone from Howard Carter to Agatha Christie[6] has stayed there at some point. It was expensive, but the three of us shared a room, which made it more doable.

We got up early each morning, crossing the Nile in time to see the sun rise, painting the soaring cliffs impossible tones of orange and pink. We hiked all day, exploring Hatshepsut's mortuary temple at Deir el-Bahri,[7] Tutankhamun's tomb, and everything in between.

I relished my role as tour guide. Shira and Viviana were captivated as I told them about Lord Carnarvon's mysterious death

---

[6] *The best-selling fiction author of all time.*

[7] *Hatshepsut was one of the first female pharaohs, and her mortuary temple is stunning.*

after he discovered King Tut's tomb — how his dog back in England howled at the moon and dropped dead at the same moment he did, and how all the lights in Cairo went out at the same time.

"The 'curse of the pharaohs,' isn't real, of course," I concluded. "Lord Carnarvon may have funded the dig, but Howard Carter is the one who actually found King Tut, and he lived to the ripe old age of 64."

Shira clucked her tongue. "You were born ahead of your time, Noor. All this history — the way you tell it, you'd think you lived it."

I beamed with pride, even though I knew it was a rather unusual thing to be proud of.

By night, after a heavenly, cool shower upon our return from the dusty tombs, we'd enjoy the delicious fare of the hotel and sip drinks by the pool.

After four days, we were on a train back to Cairo (first class, by unanimous vote — I arranged for our old tickets to be donated). We were all several shades tanner, and our hair was noticeably lighter. I'd grown accustomed to my light brown hair in Connecticut, and was surprised to see myself going blonde again.

Our physical changes mirrored emotional ones. Once you've helped someone pee, you're kind of bound for life.

I no longer felt any resentment towards Viviana for all the time she was spending with Harvey. I still wasn't thrilled at Harvey, for some reason I couldn't quite conceptualize, but Viviana

---

Unanimous - Agreed on by everyone involved
Conceptualize - Form into an idea or concept

was open and sincere, sometimes to a fault, and didn't have a malicious bone in her body. There was a simplicity to her emotions that was refreshing after the girls I'd met in Connecticut. She didn't hide or hold on to anything. Her emotions boiled over quickly, but were soon forgotten.

Plus, I liked being able to speak Italian to someone.

I should have savored those days more while I had them, for I would soon be surrounded by the conflict of ages.

Malicious - Mean; bad; intending to do harm

CHAPTER SIX

BY MID-OCTOBER, I was ready to join Harvey and the professor in Alexandria. After two months of Cairo — and the inevitable madness of beginning a new school year, in any part of the world — I'd have done anything for a beach and some quiet.

Plus, I was worried about the professor. I saw him regularly, and had grabbed lunch with him more than once. He was teaching at the university I attended, after all.

But if something wasn't quite right with him, I doubted I'd find out during a quick bite between classes. I needed to get him away from the everyday distractions, from the convenience of a routine, to find out what was truly ailing him — or indeed, if anything still was.

Not only that, but I needed to get to the bottom of what ailed him *without* falling into the same sorrowful miasma myself. I

Inevitable - Unavoidable

Miasma - An unpleasant or oppressive atmosphere

wasn't looking forward to discussing my parents' disappearance again.

The setting would be ideal, at least. The professor had worked out some kind of deal with Mitzi that allowed him to stay at my parents' house in Alexandria when he wasn't teaching. I hadn't been back since being unceremoniously whisked to Connecticut more than a year ago, and to be honest, I was slightly apprehensive about returning.

I was mulling over the predicament while sitting on my bed, pseudo-studying for an upcoming art history exam. Shira was doing the same, and Viviana was reorganizing her clothes, muttering curses to herself in Italian.

*Shira and Viviana...*I shouldn't be leaving them in Cairo. They were capable of looking after themselves, but I'd come to learn that there was a sort of "code" in college: never leave a roommate behind.

The code applied on nights out, and (when studying abroad) to most trips.

*Not only that...*a sneaky voice in my head said, *but having Shira and Viviana along might help ward off excess emotion with the professor, grounding me in the present, so to speak...*

"Do you guys want to come to Alex with Harvey and me this weekend?" I asked. "The professor just discovered a new tablet with Ptolemaic remains. That's Cleopatra's family. You could see what maritime archaeology is like first-hand!"

Unceremoniously - Abruptly; with a lack of courtesy
Apprehensive - Nervous

Viviana's veneer of self-control burst. "Go to Alexandria? With you and Harvey? The man who said I was fat? Please! I spit on him."

I gasped, my pen clattering to the floor. "He said that?"

"He may as well have," Viviana sniffed. "He said I wasn't his type."

"Oh, um, well..."

"He is dead to me, *morto*," Viviana decreed. "You go to Alexandria to look at old rocks. I stay here."

"I better stay, too," Shira apologized. "Though *not* for the same reason. I have two exams next week."

"Alright, then!" I nodded, getting up to retrieve the errant writing utensil. "It's just a quick trip. I'll see you guys when I get back."

Would I still have gone, I wonder, if I'd known how that "quick trip" would change the course of human history?

* * *

HARVEY AND I TOOK the express train to Alexandria, which lasted around three hours and deposited us in the city at noon. Harvey was clearly trying to keep me distracted during the journey, insisting we play game after game of gin rummy. Nevertheless, I disembarked with mingled enthusiasm and dread.

"We'll drop off our things at the house, then head to the

Veneer - A thin layer of something

Errant - Not where it should be; looking for adventure

beach?" Harvey said.

"Sounds like a plan," I responded brightly.

He watched me for a moment, as if he wanted to say something, but decided against it.

We took a cab to the house, and time seemed to slow as we approached. Everything was just as I remembered. Intricate engravings on the facade enlivened the all-white exterior, and the hundred-year-old palm trees I'd been strictly forbidden to climb competed with the height of the roofline.

The roof was flat, since it doesn't often rain in Egypt, and we frequently made use of it to dine and watch the sunset. A low fence encircled the property, and the Mediterranean was just across the road.

Harvey let us in, since the professor had arrived the night before and was already out working. Stepping inside, I was nearly bowled over by how wonderful the place smelled. There isn't a perfume in the world more delicious than "sea breeze meets musty old house."

I made my way up the creaky, narrow staircase to my old room, and found that nothing — not even the books on my nightstand — had been moved. The only real difference between now and two years ago was that my clothes weren't strewn across the floor.

I changed and went back down to the kitchen, grabbing a bottle of water from the fridge as I waited for Harvey. The windows were open, admitting the rhythmic roar of the waves, and I felt

---

Facade - The face of a building

positively in heaven.

"Dressed for the beach I see," Harvey eyed my jeans and long-sleeved white shirt.

"You know the rules here as well as I do," I protested. "No swimsuits unless you're at a five-star hotel or *very* private residence. We're in the heart of the city!"

"I know. It was so much easier when we were kids, wasn't it? Though I do recall you starting to cover up as we got older. Confounded nuisance."

Alexandria was even more conservative than Cairo. While the hijab was common in the latter, it wasn't unusual to see women in all-enveloping shrouds in Alexandria, covered head-to-toe except a narrow slit for the eyes. Some even wore gloves to ensure the few square inches of skin on their hands wasn't exposed.

Needless to say, I couldn't exactly cross the street in a bikini.

Walking outside, I admired the sweeping coastline. Upon seeing its beauty in 331 B.C.E., Alexander the Great created the city and named it after himself. It went on to become the new capital of Egypt under his successors, the Ptolemies, the last of whom was also the last pharaoh of Egypt — Cleopatra.

I reluctantly abandoned my historical reverie in order to survive crossing the street. Harvey stood to the side of oncoming traffic, and when there was a pause in vehicles, we sprinted across the three lanes.

The ground immediately changed from black concrete to

Hijab - Headscarf; a garment to cover the hair
Enveloping - Covering; surrounding completely

rocky sand, the rocks thinning out as we got closer to the sea. There weren't many swimmers on this part of the beach. The only person waiting for us on the shore was the professor.

"Ah, Noor! Lovely to see you again." Even now, the professor always sounded so formal, like he was from the 1800s. I wondered what it would take to make him say "crap."

Clad entirely in linen, from his slacks to his white, button-down shirt, he rose from the boulder he'd been sitting on as we approached. I was pleased to see he looked more composed than the last time I'd seen him. His clothes were clean, his face shaved.

"Happy to be home," I responded, not hugging him this time for fear of offending any onlookers. "Now, what's this ground-breaking tablet Harvey's been telling me about?"

"It's rather a long discussion, actually. Why don't you two take in some of the sights, and we'll reconvene at dinner?"

The professor sat back down, continuing to dust off an ancient ring with single-minded fascination.

I didn't know whether to be amused or offended that we'd been so quickly dismissed. Harvey chose the latter. Seeing his clenched jaw, I intervened before he could say something rude.

"I haven't been to the Library of Alexandria in ages," I remarked. "Harvey, fancy taking a trip?"

Obviously the *real* Library of Alexandria burned down in ancient times, taking with it all the secrets of the ancient world. Ever wanted to know the truth about Noah's flood, the lost city of Atlantis, or where the story of the minotaur came from? The an-

---

Reconvene - Get back together

78

swers were probably in that library.

Losing the library, in modern terms, would be like losing Google (and all the other assorted search engines). Theoretically the information still existed *somewhere* — it just became nearly impossible to find.

Most of the documents in the Library of Alexandria were duplicates. By law, in ancient times, any ships passing through Alexandria were required to surrender what literature they had to the library.

Then — I love this part — the librarians would decide whether they wanted it. If they did, they made a copy, gave the owner back the *copy*, and kept the original for themselves!

But tragically, there were also documents whose copies have disappeared — like the aforementioned mysteries. To this day, that information has never been recovered.

You can blame Julius Caesar for the library's destruction. According to legend, he set his own ships on fire in 48 B.C.E. to prevent them from being used by Egyptian forces.

Caesar was helping Cleopatra secure her throne at the time. Though she had the support of the people, the Egyptian military backed her little brother, knowing he would be easier to control.

Caesar and Cleopatra won, of course, but not before the fire spread to the docks, the surrounding buildings, and...the rest is history.

"Always happy to visit the library's spectacular reincarnation, though I'd give my left arm to see the original," Harvey said, still

---

Reincarnation - A new version of something from the past; rebirth in a new body looking at his father in exasperation.

Valiantly, he took a deep breath and returned his full attention to me. "Shame they didn't make it a bit more historic-looking. I can't help but wonder what Cleopatra would make of the rebuild."

The architects had utilized the modern "style" when building a new "Library of Alexandria" in 2002. Constructed almost entirely of glass and concrete, the building was shaped like a giant circle, with a cut-out on the right side.

Some said it looked like a giant Pac-Man, ready to eat the rest of the city.

To be fair, no one knows what the original library looked like. Even ancient paintings were commissioned years after the library's destruction, and none of them looked anything alike.

I was pretty sure none of them looked like a giant, concrete Pac-Man though.

WE RETURNED HOME around 6 o'clock, just as the sun was beginning its drowsy descent to the west.

"I've already started cooking," the professor announced as we walked in the door. A white tea towel was draped over his shoulder as he chopped miscellaneous vegetables. "Salad and falafel for dinner, with baklava for dessert."

"You should consider yourself honored, Noor," Harvey clapped his dad on the back. "Most days he warms up peas from a tin."

"As all good archaeologists do," I replied. "Didn't Petrie give his entire crew food poisoning once?"

Commissioned - Ordered to be produced

I washed my hands, set the table, then asked the professor what else we could help with.

"Not a thing," he responded. "Why don't you go finish washing up? Dinner will be ready by the time you're done."

Soon enough, the delicious aroma of garlic and onion beckoned us back downstairs. Descending, I found the professor bringing large serving bowls to the wooden table just off the kitchen.

Harvey and I dug in, piling our plates high after a day of travel. The professor joined us, shaking out a napkin and placing it on his lap, but he didn't eat. Instead, he stared at his food like it was a rather troubling mathematics problem.

"I haven't forgotten your question, Noor, about the Ptolemaic tablet I've been working on," he eventually remarked, turning to me. "It's just that... It's a difficult conversation."

"Oh," I said, taken aback by the intensity of his tone. "Well, maybe Harvey and I can help. We probably have a better understanding of hieroglyphics than most experts at the university. And if it's in Greek or Latin..."

Harvey chuckled, raising his glass. "Ah, the benefits of being raised by linguists and archaeologists. You do realize how pompous you sound?"

I threw a roll at him, but the professor smoothly caught it and carried on. "The translation isn't the issue. But this does have to do with Frank and Mary."

Beckoned - Encouraged (someone) to come nearer
Pompous - Self-important; conceited

My parents. My body stiffened, unprepared for the conversation to begin so soon. "I see. Were you working on something similar with them?"

The professor put down the roll, then put his hand on mine. "Noor, what I'm about to say may strike you as odd. Cruel, even. But I beg you let me tell you the whole story before jumping to conclusions."

My arms erupted in gooseflesh. "*Okay.* Just what does this blasted tablet say?"

"It says," he remarked slowly, "'We are alive.' In English."

CHAPTER SEVEN

"SAY THAT AGAIN," I demanded. "It said what?"

"'We are alive.' And then beneath it, 'F + M.'"

"You're saying... What are you saying?"

"Noor, you may think I've been distant this past year, but everything I've done has been for you and your family. Please allow me to explain."

"By all means," I said, a little more sharply than intended.

I withdrew my hand, but the professor kept speaking. "Have you ever found it strange that no trace of your parents has ever been found?"

"Unless you could search the entire Mediterranean, how could there be?"

"That was my initial belief as well. The scuba equipment was gone, so were your parents. Combine that with a devastating, entirely unpredicted storm and the conclusion is hard to avoid. But it didn't make sense. Your parents would never go diving at night, alone, without telling anyone. What possible reason could they have for going? The objects we save are of the utmost delicacy. The ability to see what you're doing is crucial."

He looked at me as though expecting a response, but I remained silent.

"As you know, I halted my work for months after their death. I threw myself into exploring every alternative. Could they have gotten involved with a political organization unfriendly to the government, and abducted by the secret police? Kidnapped by extremists? I felt the evidence was too circumstantial to be accepted as fact. The scuba gear was in an unlocked shed. It could've been stolen, and we based our entire theory on it! But no other avenue proved worth investigating. Your parents were wholly dedicated to their work and their family.

"I eventually started looking into their work, beginning with the last dive site they were exploring," the professor continued. "Your parents made meticulous notes of everything within a specified grid. Yet when I made the dive myself, there was a tablet — quite obvious to the naked eye — that wasn't in any of their records. I don't believe I can describe the shock I experienced when I saw it. English writing on an ancient tablet! It defies logic! It resembled the surrounding artifacts in every way, untouched for thousands of years. Yet it was in English, and signed 'F + M.' Frank and Mary?

"I immediately brought the tablet to the surface and carbon

Circumstantial - Suggesting something without actually proving it
Meticulous - Careful; precise; showing great attention to detail

dated it," he said. "It's more than two thousand years old. This leaves only two possibilities: either your parents carved the message on an ancient rock while fighting for their lives in the storm, or..." he trailed off suggestively.

"Or...?" I asked.

"Or they were there when this was written, more than 2,000 years ago."

The professor actually looked a little sheepish, his cheeks reddening. "It's the only possible alternative. 'Once you eliminate the impossible, whatever remains, no matter how improbable—'"

"*Time travel?*" Harvey scoffed. He stood, chair scraping against the floor. "Father, I think we should go for a walk. This isn't..."

"There are actually two tablets at play here," the professor continued. "The one I discovered — with English writing — and the one your mother was working on before their disappearance. It took months, but I was finally able to decipher it. I could only show bits and pieces to my linguist acquaintances until I could put it all together for, if what I suspected were true, it was imperative no one gain access to the entire text. The consequences would be dire if this information fell into the wrong hands."

The professor pulled a piece of paper from his pocket, sliding it across the table to me. "Don't read it out loud, just in case."

The paper — handwritten in pencil — had a series of hieroglyphs at the top, then the English translation below. The English

---

Sheepish - Embarrassed

Imperative - Crucial

Dire - Deadly; something that presages disaster

read:

MY MOUTH HAS BEEN GIVEN TO ME THAT I MAY
SPEAK WITH IT
WHOMSOEVER IS ABLE MUST PROTECT, WITH THEIR
MIND AND THEIR BODY
THE SACRED HOUSE OF KNOWLEDGE
OH YOU GATES, YOU WHO KEEP THE GATES CLOSED
BECAUSE OF OSIRIS
OH YOU WHO GUARD THEM, I KNOW YOU AND I
KNOW YOUR NAMES
LET THE GATES BE OPENED

"You're saying," I said slowly, "that you believe my parents were sucked back in time?"

"My dear girl. That is exactly what I'm saying."

I LOOKED AT HIM for a long time. He sat, motionless, his hands clasped on the table, still looking for all the world like a respectable university professor. He might have just invited me to tea, except for his slightly accelerated breathing pattern.

"Professor," I finally asked. "Have there been any other...unusual...occurrences in your life lately? Did you at one point believe, for instance, that a spaceship landed on the Thames? Or that a werewolf was trapped in Buckingham Palace?"

"If you are questioning my sanity," he replied severely, "I can assure you, I have not begun seeing life as an episode of *Doctor Who*."

"Mmmhmm. And you haven't shown these tablets to your acquaintances because of the — 'dire consequences,' I believe you

86

said?"

"Time travel could do more harm than a nuclear bomb, in the wrong hands. Yet in the right hands..."

I caught his change of tone immediately. "What do you mean, 'the right hands'?"

"Well, obviously someone must explore this possibility. Equally obviously, that person cannot be me. Your parents had no choice in the matter — I don't believe they realized the ramifications of translating the text. But I could never intentionally leave Harvey and my studies."

"By all means," Harvey said coolly. "Translate away. This is the biggest load of—"

"You're saying me?" I squeaked. "You want me to go back in time?"

"But you are the ideal candidate!" the professor effused. "You are familiar with all of Egyptian history, though I believe you would be sent to 48 B.C.E. Protecting the 'sacred house of knowledge' must be a reference to the Library of Alexandria, and you can only protect it if you're sent to the time when it burned.

"You're fluent in ancient Egyptian — what we know of it at least — and your knowledge of Latin is as good as any professor's, so you could speak the *lingua franca* of the day!"

I raised my eyebrows. "I'm flattered that you think me capable of such a feat."

"Nothing is more noble than the pursuit of knowledge, Noor.

Ramifications - Consequences

Lingua Franca - Common language

Feat - Great achievement

To save the Library of Alexandria..."

"Professor, believe me, I would if I could."

He waved a hand. "More importantly, if you cannot save the library, perhaps you can save your parents."

My back stiffened. "Show me the tablets, please. The one my parents supposedly left us, and the one my mom was working on."

The professor went to his office across the hall, returning with a thick, white cloth. He draped it across the unoccupied half of the table to ensure any lingering food wouldn't damage the artifacts, then went back for the tablets.

He brought them in one at a time, placing them on the table with all the delicacy of putting a newborn to sleep. Both were a weathered gray stone, roughly two feet long by 16 inches wide. Thousands of years of sea slime had been washed off, but traces still clung to cracks and niches.

The first tablet, the one the professor discovered, was just as he described it. The stone was identical in appearance to the one next to it, the writing easily thousands of years old. There was even the same complex marine growth inside the cracks. Yet the text was in English: "WE ARE ALIVE. F + M."

It was impossible to say if it was my parents' handwriting, for I had never seen them carve anything in stone. Everything was capitalized, probably because the linear nature of the letters would be easier to carve. There were some places where the writing was shallow, as though it'd been written in a rush, but it was impossible to discern anything else from the stone itself.

Discern - Determine; figure out

The second tablet — the one my mom was working on when my parents disappeared — was written in hieroglyphics. But there were a number of characters I wasn't familiar with. An archaic form of the language, maybe?

"Professor, if I gave any credence to your proposition, what exactly would I have to do?"

He nodded vigorously, returning to his seat and folding his hands. "I can't tell you exactly, but I believe your mother was sounding out the text as she was translating it, inadvertently invoking whatever protective spell was placed on the library. Your father must have had some kind of physical contact with her at the time; perhaps he had his arm around her, or she was leaning on his shoulder while reading. This caused them both to be taken back, while the rest of us, occupying the same house, were left here."

His nose quivered, his speech growing increasingly animated as he concluded: "Speak the incantation, and the majestic gates to the past will be opened!"

Harvey looked at his father like he'd grown two heads. I wasn't far behind him.

"Okay!" I said brightly, unsure of how to speak with someone in the early stages of senility, or perhaps suffering some kind of nervous breakdown. "I will certainly consider this proposal."

Archaic - Old; outdated

Credence - Belief

Invoking - Calling on; summoning

Senility - The state of losing one's mental faculties as a result of old age

* * *

"IF I'D KNOWN this is what he was working on all those nights, I'd have put a stop to this long ago," Harvey said, slamming his drink down.

We were on the roof of the house, sitting next to each other at the simple wooden table. We'd chosen the bench facing the Mediterranean, even though it was too dark to distinguish the details of the sea. The roar of the waves provided a soundtrack to our discussion, and the celestial beings provided just enough light to make out the contours of Harvey's form.

"You're not seriously blaming yourself, are you?" I leaned on my elbow and turned to face him. "How could you have known he was working on a *time travel* theorem? It's absurd!"

"Thank God he hasn't shared his theory. I just hope we can set him right before he destroys the reputation he's spent a lifetime building."

There were no traces of the jokester, amused by everything and everyone, in Harvey now. He and I sat silently, the abyss of the sea before us, considering the startling revelations of the night.

"This reminds me of when we were little," I said finally. "Sneaking off to talk under the stars."

I sensed, rather than saw, Harvey's smile return. Then I felt his hand close over mine.

Celestial - Relating to the sky or heavens

Abyss - A deep or seemingly bottomless pit

Revelations - Something (often surprising) that is revealed

Harvey and I had never held hands before.

Surprised by how warm and capable it felt, I let it linger. When I started to pull away, his hand tightened, sending a pleasant wave of energy through my chest.

Harvey was looking at me intently now. "I'm sorry we haven't had much time together since you've been back."

"Yes, well, you've been busy," I shrugged, "between school and Viviana…"

He grimaced. "About that…"

"Yeah," I withdrew my hand, actually retrieving it this time. "What happened there?"

No longer holding mine, it seemed like he no longer knew what to do with his hands. "Viviana is a nice girl," he said, "but she's not… That is, there is more to a person…"

A dark flush rose up under his tan skin. He rubbed his chin.

"I get it," I responded. "She's sweet, but there's not much beneath the surface."

"That isn't what I was going to say." Harvey squared his shoulders and turned to face me. "She's sweet, but she isn't you."

"*Oh!*" Now it was my turn to flush.

"Noor, there's no one in this world like you. You're brilliant, beautiful, and stubborn as a mule. You drive me crazy with your harebrained schemes, but life without you is so inescapably *bland*. When you left, I thought I'd go mad without you. When you came back, I didn't want anything to change between us. I

Intently - Intensely

Grimaced - Made a pained, twisted face

Harebrained - Rash; not thought through

thought if I saw someone else I might start to feel differently, but..."

His gaze was so earnest, his eyes so pure, I felt an overwhelming desire to shield him, to protect him from the world.

And still, I didn't know what to say.

"Harvey, I...God, what a night."

I looked out at the sea, then back at him. I could see him trying to gauge my thoughts. He started to pull away, but before he did, I yanked him back by the shirtfront and kissed him.

Instinct took over. Years of pent-up emotion encircled us. Arms wrapped around one another, breathing ceased to be of importance. All coherent thoughts vanished. The only word in my head was *more*. I wanted *more*.

Some time later, a creak from the stairs made us pull apart in mutual alarm. Thankfully, no one was coming.

"Well!" Harvey let out a shaky laugh, running a hand through his hair.

"Well," I agreed.

We sat there, smiling at each other like idiots, until Harvey brought the conversation back to a respectable place.

"I suppose we'll need to decide what to do with the professor," he said. "What are you going to say when he tries to corner you again?"

I nestled into the crook of his shoulder as he put an arm around me. Breathing in the sea air with a sigh of contentment, I

Gauge - Measure

Ceased - Stopped

Coherent - Logical, rational

asked: "What if he's right?"

Harvey looked down at me in bewilderment, arm tensing. I returned his stare, our faces closer than they'd ever been prior to an hour ago.

"Harvey, your father is one of the foremost historians in the world. So what if he's a little more excitable than usual? He might have just discovered something more remarkable than anything we could possibly imagine!"

"Now you're starting to sound like him."

"'He,'" I corrected. "'Starting to sound like he does,' would be the full sentence."

Harvey suppressed a smile. "Only you would quibble over grammar at a time like this."

I bit my lip, pulling away. "Don't you think the possibility needs to be investigated, at least?"

"Noor, that's like investigating whether Bigfoot exists."

"Someone had to do it."

Harvey snorted. "There's no such thing as time travel, and we're not doing the professor any favors by encouraging his delusions."

"Easy for you to say. It's not your parents we're talking about."

Harvey pulled back as though I'd slapped him.

"How could you say that? You know how much I loved Frank and Mary. And, actually, it *is* my parents we're talking about — one of them at least."

Bewilderment - Confusion

Foremost - Best; most prominent or respected

Quibble - Object to something small or trivial

"Harvey, I didn't mean—"

"No, Noor. Listen." Harvey took a deep breath, his voice softening. "I know it's hard to accept, but your parents are gone. We can't do anything for them. Maybe we can for the professor."

My mind spun, unpredictable as a game of roulette. *Which emotion would it land on? Hope? Love? Stubbornness?*

"Maybe you're right," I conceded. "Either way, I have a lot to think about."

I stood up, but Harvey immediately objected. "Noor, don't...Let's not end things like this."

"Like what?"

"Like this! All awkward and prickly."

"I'm not prickly!"

"Mmhmm. Then why don't you sit back down? We could pick up where we left off, forget all about this time travel business..."

I could feel myself gravitating towards him, like a swimmer being pulled out to sea.

I was actually leaning forward, lips slightly parted, when I realized...how vulnerable I'd become? How quickly our dynamic had changed? How little I'd thought this through?

"Can't," I stammered, taking a clumsy step backwards. "Have to go to bed. See you in the morning."

And so I left him on the roof, confused and alone.

I RETREATED DOWN THE STAIRS, walking softly past the pro-

Conceded - Admitted

Gravitating - Moving (toward) something as a result of being pulled by gravity or another powerful force

fessor's door so I wouldn't wake him. When I reached my room at the end of the hall, I flung myself on the bed, mind racing with the implications of everything that had happened in just a few hours.

Could my parents still be alive? I didn't let myself feel much hope. The scenario was simply too far-fetched. But if the professor was right, and time travel was real...

My brain simply couldn't process it all. For Pete's sake, the water I'd put on the nightstand before dinner was still cold. I'd been to the moon and back, and my water hadn't even reached room temperature!

I put on my pajamas and began pacing in semi-circles around the bed.

If there was a way — *any* way — to save my parents, *and* go back to one of the most fascinating periods of history...Of course I would do it. I'd walk through fire to see my parents again.

And I can't pretend historical fever wasn't beginning to warm my brow. To see Caesar and Cleopatra fall in love? To save the Library of Alexandria? This is what dreams are made of.

What harm could there be in testing the professor's wild theory? The alternative — sitting across the table from Harvey tomorrow at breakfast, acting like nothing had happened in front of the professor...

We'd have to tell the professor, wouldn't we? Would he read it on our faces if we didn't? How long could we keep it a secret? What would I say to Viviana? Would this even continue? Was Harvey's mind racing as much as mine?

I shook my head, clearing the ridiculous stream of questions from my mind, and pulled out my computer. It wasn't even 10:30 p.m. — still mid-afternoon in Connecticut. Our tech-savvy neighbor had routed Skype through Mitzi's cell phone, and I clicked the green button to call her.

Bum bum bah dah bum! Bum bum bah dah bum.

"Darling! I was just thinking about you," trilled Mitzi's familiar voice. "Hang on while I figure out the video..."

"No problem! How are you?"

"All is well!" she replied, her face popping up on my screen. "Bunny is still cheating at poker, but no one wants to kick her out because she brings the best soufflé. I leave for Argentina on Tuesday, so it's out of my hands now..."

I grew suddenly sheepish as the chorus of familiar chatter washed over me. Surely, in the wake of something so life-changing, transatlantic thought waves would inform her? If she was going on about neighborhood gossip, it meant nothing had really happened. The professor's theory wasn't real.

I'd almost convinced myself that was true, but it wasn't fair to Mitzi. She wasn't a mind-reader. If I wanted her advice, I had to ask for it.

When she asked how I was doing, I admitted the truth. "Mitzi, I need your help."

WE SPENT THE NEXT HOUR discussing the professor's theory. I told her everything, answering questions about his well-being,

---

Sheepish - Embarrassed
Transatlantic - Across the Atlantic

the tablets, and my "gut," as Mitzi called it.

"Mmmm," Mitzi ruminated. "Seems to me like the professor might be onto something."

"*What?*"

"I've spent a long time thinking about that scuba equipment, Noor. I came to the same conclusion as the professor a long time ago. It was probably stolen."

"But — why didn't you say anything? If you don't think they died at sea, why aren't we looking for them elsewhere?"

"Believe me, darling, I've had many a stern conversation with the authorities. They dismissed me as a distraught mother — 'unwilling to accept reality,' was how they phrased it."

Bristling at the memory, she concluded, "I eventually came to accept that, even if your parents didn't die at sea, there were no other explanations that made sense."

"Of course there were!" I protested. "They could've been kidnapped by terrorists, the secret police..."

"Bah. An American and Englishman? Terrorists would want ransom or publicity, and the secret police know better than to bite the hand that feeds them. The treasure your parents found generates millions in revenue, to say nothing of the foreign aid at stake."

"I suppose..."

"Darling, I know nothing of archaeology, but how could English writing — and writing that says, 'We are alive. F+M,' no less

---

Ruminated - Thought deeply

Bristling - Reacting angrily or defensively

— end up on an ancient tablet? Not graffitied onto it later, mind you, but truly original? I could hear it in your voice. You couldn't come up with an explanation either."

"You think I should test the professor's theory, then?" I said tentatively.

Mitzi paused. "I couldn't possibly make such a decision for you. But there is something else to consider. If your parents haven't made it back..."

"There's a chance I wouldn't either."

Neither of us spoke, the thought of losing each other superseding all others. Then she sniffled and I bit my lip, knowing I couldn't possibly comfort her from thousands of miles away.

"I know how much you miss them," she eventually said, voice wobbling. "So you must decide, would you trade this life for a future with them? Not that I'm *entirely* convinced of the professor's theory, of course, but that's what it boils down to, isn't it?"

I grimaced. "I wish I could hug you through the phone, Mitzi."

"You too, darling. And just know — you have my support, either way."

We said our "I love you's," and I hung up, even more stunned than before.

It wasn't just the professor's crazy theory anymore. Mitzi thought he might be right, and in my gut, so did I.

I WASN'T SURE HE WAS RIGHT, obviously. But as I told Harvey,

Tentatively - Hesitantly
Superseding - Taking over; replacing

what was the harm in investigating?

If it didn't work, we were no worse off than we already were. My parents would still be gone; the library would still be destroyed. Both were burdens we already bore.

And if it did...Unconsciously, I began making a mental checklist of items I would need.

Presumably whatever force brought me back wouldn't be so kind as to provide a change of clothing, so I'd need to wear something contemporaneously appropriate.

According to tomb reliefs, Egyptian noblewomen tended to favor diaphanous shift dresses. The closest I had were some sheets in the linen closet.

Shoes, shoes... My trusty ankle boots seemed a little clunky next to an improvised toga-dress. But I *did* have a pair of gladiators; they were in vogue that year and I'd preferred their strappy practicality to the Viviana-esque heels at the store.

I snuck out to the linen closet, noting that a soft light still shone from under Harvey's door. On instinct, I almost knocked on it. But he'd made it abundantly clear that he wanted nothing to do with the professor's theory, and...

Well, things were different between us now. The thought of knocking on his door in the middle of the night made me cringe.

"Desperate" was the word they used in Connecticut, I believe.

Quietly grabbing the softest sheet available, I returned to my room to test out the new ensemble. I wasn't quite ready to aban-

---

Presumably - Something that is likely, but not certain (think: "probably")

Contemporaneously - With/for the time period

Diaphanous - Light; delicate; sometimes a little see-through

don my modern undergarments, so I wrapped the sheet in a way that covered both shoulders, V-ing at the neck, then wound down to my knees like a loosely-attired mummy. I strapped on my gladiators and slid on my snake ring like I was going into battle.

I surveyed the results in the mirror. I looked like America's Halloween-ified idea of a Roman senator (i.e. ridiculous and scantily clad).

But — I forced myself to remember — pre-Islam Egypt was an entirely different place. They didn't have our modern-day hang-ups about visible skin. If anything, I would be dressed more modestly than many.

Smoothing the wrinkles in my sheet, I considered the items I would hide in its folds.

Medicine, certainly. The doctor had given me an extra round of antibiotics in case symptoms persisted, and I slid the packet under one of the places the dress wrapped, near the hip.

What else... Money. We actually had a fairly large supply of coins from the era, since they're so durable and zillions were minted.

If this did work, could I possibly bring a backpack? Surveying my reflection, the antibiotics were already creating a rather unusual-looking bulge. Adding money and other essentials would only compound the predicament.

Hang it. I may not have grown up in the lap of luxury, but I've never lived in a world without toothbrushes. If this ridiculous

---

Compound - Make something bad even worse
Predicament - Problem

theory actually did pan out, I wasn't about to start the journey unprepared.

I began throwing necessities in my bag. Made of tan canvas with leather straps, it would draw less attention than my turquoise purse. Plus it was bigger, which meant I could pack more.

I relocated the aforementioned antibiotics, then added a few toiletries, a flashlight, pepper spray, a map of ancient Alexandria, and two photos. One was of my parents; the other was of Harvey and me exploring Etruscan tombs in Cerveteri.

There's always a small collection of junk floating around the bottom of my bags — gum, pens, ticket stubs. I didn't bother cleaning it out. It's not like I was going to test the theory that night. I was just laying the groundwork, gathering supplies and exploring the possibilities.

Should I get an entirely new bag? I wondered. The material wasn't flashy, but the buttons and zippers might get me in trouble if anyone got too close.

I needed a new one anyway. Viviana spilled nail polish remover all over it before I left for Alexandria, and I hadn't had time to get a new one yet.

In that case, I should probably get new shoes, too, I thought. The gladiators zipped at the back, and the stitching was too regular to have been done by hand. Surely they'd have something more authentic at the Khan el-Khalili?

Blast, did that mean I also couldn't bring a flashlight or pepper

---

Aforementioned - Previously mentioned

spray? Or was anything *inside* the backpack OK, as long as my outward appearance didn't betray anything untoward?

Shelving the questions for another day, I creaked open the door. Padding down the hundred year-old stairs, I made my way to the professor's office, where our coins were kept.

The room was dark, the smell of leather-bound books and ancient metal nearly overpowering the scent of the ocean.

I flipped on a dim lamp and headed towards the back wall, where one of the bookcases held a small fortune in ancient currency.

Mentally doing the math, I carefully slid out the book marked "Ptolemy XII Auletes." Rather than paper, the book held page after page of little plastic dividers, each one with twenty square containers for coins.

Auletes was Cleopatra's father, and though not alive at the time I was supposedly going back to, would be a safer bet currency-wise than she was. The incantation was all about saving the Library of Alexandria, which meant Cleopatra would still be fighting for her throne. Many of her coins wouldn't have been minted yet.

I carefully opened the binding and removed the first four pages, the ones containing the most valuable coins. My pilferage probably amounted to a few hundred dollars by today's standards.

Gently sliding the pages into my backpack, I made my way

Untoward - Unexpected; inappropriate; inconvenient

Padding - Walking quietly

Pilferage - The act of stealing something small

across the faded Persian rug to the professor's desk.

If I really did want to test out the theory, I needed a copy of the incantation. I wanted to be able to study it on my own — without the professor's overzealous commentary or Harvey's belittling remarks — and I wanted to start now.

The professor would give me a copy if I asked, of course, but then I'd have to wait until tomorrow. How could I possibly sleep knowing the key to finding my parents might be waiting downstairs?

Turning the golden key of the professor's desk drawer, I found what I'd hoped: the original inscription written in hieroglyphics, the phonetic version, where the sounds of the ancient tongue had been written in English letters, and the English translation.

I cast a sidelong glance at the staircase, hoping Harvey wouldn't find me in a sheet-dress breaking into his father's study. Quite understandably, he'd assume I'd gone mad, too.

Best be quick, then. I flipped on the lamp and took a closer look at the text, pulling out a blank sheet of paper from the center drawer for my own copy.

At first glance, it bore certain similarities to *The Book of the Dead*, the collection of spells that ancient nobles and pharaohs were buried with.

However, I instinctively knew that it was much, much older. It was like reading Dante's *Inferno* in the original Italian, or something written by Shakespeare. "What light through yonder win-

---

Overzealous - Too eager or enthusiastic
Phonetic - How something sounds
Sidelong - Sideways; from the side

dow breaks?" might technically be English, but no one still talks like that.

Here, too, the text was ancient Egyptian, but it possessed a weight that had been lost in later centuries.

My inner linguist was fascinated by the new hieroglyphs and, throwing caution to the wind, I began sounding out the words.

MY MOUTH HAS BEEN GIVEN TO ME THAT I MAY SPEAK WITH IT

WHOMSOEVER IS ABLE MUST PROTECT, WITH THEIR MIND AND THEIR BODY

THE SACRED HOUSE OF KNOWLEDGE

OH YOU GATES, YOU WHO KEEP THE GATES CLOSED BECAUSE OF OSIRIS

OH YOU WHO GUARD THEM, I KNOW YOU AND I KNOW YOUR NAMES

LET THE GATES BE OPENED

The wind outside grew stronger with each syllable. It began as a harsh whistle, causing frenzied branches to tap wildly at the windows.

Soon the sea joined the chaos, sending violent swells to attack the rocks. So absorbed was I in the text, I didn't notice until the final line, when the world around me rose to a deafening howl.

When I pronounced the final word, the cacophony of sounds immediately ceased, like when a choir director closes his fist for the end of a performance.

It was so silent, nothing in the world could have been happen-

---

Cacophony - A harsh, unpleasant mixture of sounds

ing. Time was stopped, or perhaps I was simply no longer attached to it.

Then the house began to collapse as though it were made of sand. I ran, desperate to to reach the staircase to warn Harvey and the professor, but the ground was already disappearing from under me.

PART TWO

CHAPTER EIGHT

I FOUND MYSELF sprawled on a cool, marble floor when I awoke. Only a few small fires — each one blazing in a large, elevated pot — attempted to combat the darkness. I could scarcely make out a gilded dome some two stories above, supported by grand arches open to the night sky.

I gave an involuntary start, scrambling backwards like a crab when I saw a man standing in the center of each arch. There were eight of them, each staring down at me with forbidding frowns. I held my breath, awaiting what was to come.

But no one moved. I stared into the darkest corner of the room to adjust my eyes, then back up at the men.

Statues! They were statues. No wonder I'd mistaken them for men. They were painted!

Statues of this sort haven't been painted since ancient times, a small

---

Gilded - Covered with a thin layer of gold

voice in my head remarked.

My immediate fears allayed, I gingerly rose to my feet. The professor's text fluttered from my trembling fingers, landing on the marble with a soft *scratch*.

I stared at it, open-mouthed, then quickly stooped to retrieve it, zipping it in the innermost compartment of my backpack.

A hypothesis had already begun to form in my brain, of course, but reason demanded unassailable proof.

My breathing was coming in faster than normal, which was probably why one of the first things I noticed was the air.

It was intoxicating — fresh as fields where a nymph might hide, but infused with the salt of the sea.

The stars were different, too. I was accustomed to only seeing the famous constellations — Orion's belt, the Dippers, the North Star.

Here, even through the narrow openings in the alcoves above, there were so many stars that the sky winked and waved, a woman bathed in diamonds.

Grabbing my little flashlight, I discovered that the circular room I was in wasn't isolated. Like beams from the sun, grand corridors led outward in every direction.

Picking one at random, I ventured forth before stopping dead in my tracks at the sight before me: bookshelf after bookshelf, lining the walls as far as the eye could see.

The shelves were divided into neat squares with organized

Allayed - Diminished; put to rest

Gingerly - Carefully; cautiously

Unassailable - Unable to be attacked, questioned, or defeated rolls of papyri. Cautiously, I drew closer to the nearest shelf. A beautiful, dark wood, the inscriptions were carved into gold panels.

"Socrates," I breathed.

Reaching a delicate hand to touch the scrolls, I continued walking through what must be the Greek section. "Thermopylae, Battle of," another inscription read; the one below it, "Leonidas, King." I smiled at my old friend, recalling how he'd helped me on the train to Luxor.

The beam of my flashlight made wild patterns as I greedily scanned my surroundings for mysteries and secrets. My hypothesis was looking increasingly likely — if, of course, this wasn't all a dream.

I withdrew a little notebook from my bag and began taking notes. Pacing and scribbling, I gasped when my eyes caught sight of the inscription: "Atlantis, City of."

In keeping with the subject's elusive nature, the scrolls were out of my reach. Rolling wooden ladders were attached to the bookcases, but the nearest one was some distance away.

I powered over, dragging the ladder back to the Atlantis section. It made quite a lot of noise, or perhaps there was just nothing to camouflage it — no cars in the distance, honking and humming— just the infinite lapping of the sea.

I reluctantly put away my flashlight, since I'd need both hands to climb the ladder, and hiked the sheet up to my thighs to permit

---

Papyri - The plural of "papyrus," the ancient Egyptian form of paper
Elusive - Difficult to find, catch, or achieve

the necessary movement.

By the time I was apprehended, I suppose I did look rather ridiculous. There was so much sheet around my midsection that it puffed out like a marshmallow, and my narrow legs protruded like toothpicks.

I was reaching for the scroll, and could literally feel its crispness in my fingers when I was stopped by a sharp, "Oy!"

Two heavily muscled men, dressed in white kilts and golden breastplates, stood ominously below. They held flaming torches and were shouting in heavily accented Greek.

Though there were parts of their dialect I didn't understand, I didn't need an interpreter to take their meaning. They wanted me to descend from my perch. Gesturing wildly, they had actually begun rattling the ladder in an attempt to shake me out, like a bird from its nest.

I gathered my dignity, letting the sheet fall back to its original position before descending. It was difficult with my movement restricted, but I managed by relying heavily on my upper body, hanging onto the rungs like monkey bars and dropping my feet as far as they would go, then repeating the process.

When I reached the ground, I tried to act like I scaled the shelves of the Library of Alexandria every night. I wiped the dust off my palms and gave them a friendly Greek, "Good evening."

Guard Number One scoffed, sending a calloused hand in my direction. I didn't know what he was going for, but instinctively

---

Apprehended - Caught; arrested
Ominously - Suggests something bad is going to happen
Scaled - Climbed

twisted out of his grasp. Guard Number Two came to his aid, and an undignified scuffle ensued.

I had nearly freed myself, and was stumbling backwards when my backpack collided with Guard Number One's torch. It caught fire with an explosive *whoosh*.

Viviana's spilled nail polish remover had turned me into a walking matchstick.

* * *

I CURSED, SCRAMBLING to get the thing off me. I actually threw it before remembering that the contents to my survival were in that bag. Swearing under my breath, I ran to it, wrapping a hand in my dress to unbuckle the burning clasp.

I tried to paw out anything that hadn't yet been engulfed, but was only able to recover the most pointless items: a ballpoint pen, pepper spray, and my cell phone.

I gingerly jumped back, unconsciously wondering where my captors had gone, before the answer became all too clear.

They'd gone to fetch water. My backpack wasn't all that was aflame.

The Library of Alexandria was on fire.

* * *

"NO, NO, NO!" I murmured. One of the papyri had caught fire

Engulfed - Covered completely; swallowed whole

111

when I threw my backpack, and from there, the rest of the library was kindling.

I desperately scanned my surroundings for anything that could contain the blaze. Shouldn't there be buckets of water in every room? Or sand, at least? What were these people thinking, leaving such knowledge unprotected?

The blaze was climbing the Atlantis bookcase faster than I had, spreading up as well as out. Perspiration prickling my brow, I fell backwards, then turned and fled to the circular atrium from which I'd come.

When I reached it, the statues overhead looked down at me even more critically than before. It was like they knew it was I who consigned them to their fiery fate.

Avoiding eye contact, I continued straight through to the next hallway, but there was no exit in sight. Rounding another corner in the labyrinth of bookshelves, I ran smack into the oily chest of Guard Number One.

He looked as surprised as I, but recovered more quickly. Snatching the collar of my dress, he sent up a shout. "GOT HER!" Then he gave me a shake, like a sadist with the scruff of a little dog. "You're coming wif me."

Any counterattack would be futile, possibly fatal. He knew the way out. I didn't.

Consigned - Committed decisively or permanently
Labyrinth - Maze
Sadist - A person who takes pleasure in hurting others
Futile - Pointless
Fatal - Deadly

Guard Number One led me back in the direction from which I'd come, keeping a fist clenched around the shoulder of my dress. We were walking briskly, but I could smell the smoke, and sweat beaded both of our brows.

Trying to look meek, I ventured in my politest tone, "So, what's your name?"

Guard Number One gave me another shake, and I stumbled before recovering myself.

"OK, then," I said. "If you don't want to answer, I'll just call you Bruno."

He looked like a Bruno. Somewhere in his 30's, he had dark oily hair that sat above a forbidding scowl. The name was more Italian than Greek, but once it popped into my head, it stuck.

We wove through the corridors of the library, and I succumbed so deeply to historical fever that I lost all sense of direction and self-preservation. My eyes glimpsed extraordinary inscriptions on the shelves surrounding us.

"Romulus, 1st king of Rome," one read. Nearby were the kings who followed him, Numa Pompilius and Tullus Hostilius. The Roman monarchy! A period almost entirely shrouded in myth.

I choked back a sob as we passed through the section on the Trojan War. The sob may have been caused by smoke, but losing the true story behind Homer's *Iliad* stung far worse than the pain in my lungs.

Though I was utterly lost, my hazy vision and burning lungs

Meek - Quiet; gentle; submissive

Succumbed - Yielded to an overpowering force or desire

left no doubt that we were heading back in the direction of the fire. *The place must be laid out like the Met in New York*, I thought bitterly. One main entrance meant people couldn't sneak off with the valuables, but it also meant you constantly got lost. I just hoped we could reach the exit before the fire did.

Bruno was clearly thinking the same thing. He muttered something in Greek that was obviously profane, followed by a shove and a command: "Run."

I didn't waste time following his order. I could see the flames now; so could Bruno. But I could also see the door. The flames were racing towards it, devouring the wooden beams and shattering the glass vases decorating the gallery.

I gasped as a shard impaled itself in my arm, then tasted only a moment of victory as I crossed over the threshold into the safety of the outdoors. Bruno gave me a hearty shove, and I promptly tumbled down the grand staircase.

Bruno was standing above me when I staggered to my feet, breathless.

"Serves you right," he said.

"You're very kind," I replied bitterly, wincing as I removed the shrapnel from my arm. "Where are we going now?"

But even as I spoke, my attention had begun to stray elsewhere. In the bay, just beyond the library, a battle was raging. The docks were on fire, and the fire had nearly reached the library.

Profane - Obscene; blasphemous; not respectable

Threshold - The bottom of a doorway; a symbolic point that must be exceeded for something to happen

Shrapnel - Fragments of a bomb or other item thrown by an explosion

I wiped my forehead with the back of my hand, my palms now covered in dust and blood. *Think, Noor.* A battle in the harbor. A fire at the library. This was what I had been sent here to prevent.

Assuming this wasn't all a dream, I now knew for certain where — and when — I stood.

It was 48 B.C.E., and Julius Caesar was in the harbor, just a stone's throw away, helping Cleopatra secure the throne of Egypt.

CHAPTER NINE

PRISON. That was where we were going, in case you were wondering. Specifically, the dungeons at Antirhodos.

Normally, any mention of the island would fill me with delight. Surrounded by panoramic Mediterranean views, it was the home of Egypt's royal family. However, the thought of languishing in its dungeons somewhat dampened my historical fervor.

"But, who's even *at* the palace now?" I argued. "Cleopatra and her brother are mid-battle for the throne. Perhaps it would be better..."

"Don't matter who's there," Bruno gave me another little shake. "Whoever wins, they'll want justice done by the witch that burned the library."

"Witch" might not have been an *exact* English translation. Bruno's dialect was a peculiar mixture of Thessalonian Greek and

---

Panoramic - Wide-ranging; including all aspects of a subject
Fervor - Passion; emotion

ancient Egyptian. Since the ancient Egyptians didn't write with vowels, our modern pronunciation of the language is, at best, a guess.

I sometimes had to close my eyes, imagining his words vowel-less and mixed with Greek, to take his meaning. However, I was certain he'd called me some sort of disparaging female word, and it gave me an idea.

"Still, we can't possibly go there *now!*" I eyed the harbor expressively. "A battle is raging. How could we sail through that?"

Bruno grunted. In some ways, it was easier to understand these monosyllabic emissions than his speech. Usually they meant, "be quiet, or I'll shake you again," but this one was a grunt of acknowledgement.

"I'll take you to Caesar's men," he decided with smug satisfaction. "Him's the real power round here now. He'll no' let you escape."

Bruno had a point. I had no counterpoint, so I shrugged and got to work refining my alibi.

We walked for over an hour through the city, encountering no one on the journey. One only needed to look at the harbor, stained with smoke and fire, to know why. Though the hour was early, the city wasn't asleep; it was abandoned.

Shops lined the streets to either side of us, but their doors were firmly closed, every window boarded. The only movement

---

Disparaging - Derogatory; critical

Monosyllabic - Having one syllable

Emissions - The production and discharge of something, usually air or gas

Alibi - A reason given to avoid blame

was the rising sun's reflection on the smooth stones underfoot; the only sound the slapping of our sandals and the faraway cries of battle.

Yet, withdrawn as the city was, its cosmopolitan nature was impossible to disguise. Above storefronts, signs were written in a mixture of languages, from Egyptian to Greek to Hebrew, advertising everything from spices to hand-blown glass vases.

When we reached the city walls, Bruno barked something at the guard and we were waved through. The guard didn't seem overly concerned about who was *leaving* the city, though, particularly through this exit. Caesar's camp was assembled just outside. They didn't need his help in matters of self-defense, his attitude seemed to say.

Seeing it, I repressed a whistle. For all intents and purposes, Caesar had built his own little city. Bruno had to state his credentials to another guard before we were allowed to enter, and then we were given an armed escort. Inside, tents were assembled in shades of beige and red, the latter clearly belonging to the highest-ranking officers.

The camp had a vacant feel, similar to the city, but there was more activity here. Guards stood sentry outside certain tents; messengers ran to and fro, their sandals leaving little clouds of dust on the neatly delineated paths.

The setup was all the more impressive considering it repre-

Cosmopolitan - Containing people from many different cultures
Repressed - Suppressed; held back
Sentry - Guard
Delineated - Outlined; portrayed precisely

sented only a fraction of Caesar's army. History informed me that Caesar had only 4,000 men in Egypt — roughly a tenth of what he had in Gaul, for instance — and (despite my attempts to confound Bruno earlier) — he'd really set up camp on the island of Antirhodos. These were just auxiliary troops.

None of this should have surprised me, though. A Roman legion could march 25 miles a day — each man carrying a 50-pound pack — then set up camp afterwards. Rome might not have been built in a day, but this outpost probably was.

There's a reason ancient sculptures are all so muscular.

The guard unerringly led us to one of the red tents in the center of camp. Outside, two more guards stood in full armor, their helmets even covering part of their cheeks.

As the various salutations, introductions, and permissions were exchanged, I gave my head a little shake. There would be time enough for historical observations later, assuming I could sell my story.

Just then, a moment of sheer terror gripped me. *What if my parents also thought they were in a dream?*

I realized I was so calm, partially, because I hadn't *really* accepted the reality of my surroundings. And I was better prepared than my parents, having been warned by the professor of what might happen if I read the text.

Unwarned and unarmed, I had no doubt my parents would

Auxiliary - Helping; giving supplemental assistance
Unerringly - Accurately; without hesitation
Salutations - Greetings

blithely indulge in their historical curiosity, as I had been doing, assuming they would "wake up" from anything too dangerous.

But if this was real?

I took a deep breath. It was time to focus on my survival, *really* focus. I just prayed my parents had come to the same conclusion before it was too late.

After a short wait, the tent flap opened and Bruno shoved me inside. I stumbled no more than a few steps, having grown accustomed to his interpersonal shortcomings.

When I looked up, I saw the most beautiful man ever created, calmly seated behind a wooden desk.

The immediate admiration I felt for him confused me. I am not a superficial person, and I had far more important matters on my mind. I struggle to even describe him on paper. In a purely top-level description, the seated Adonis could (shockingly) have passed for Bruno.

Both men were tan with dark, glossy hair, but Bruno was beefy, with a scar on his face that contorted every expression into a snarl.

This magnificent creature was proportioned to Michelangelo perfection, with a visage that could easily grace a statue of Apollo. He was also a good ten years younger than Bruno, putting him somewhere in his early twenties.

Catching the last of the introductions, I learned that his name

---

Blithely - Showing casual and cheerful indifference

Adonis - An extremely handsome person

Contorted - Twist or bent out of normal shape

Visage - Face

was Marcus Furius Camillus, and he was a tribune of the 6th legion.

I did my best to look calm as Bruno explained how I'd burned down the Library of Alexandria, for my newfound plan — hastily-devised though it was — depended entirely on my credibility.

It wasn't hard to look calm next to Bruno. Red-faced, spittle shot from his mouth as he described how I'd been lurking the great halls, plotting my crime.

"Thank you for bringing this to my attention," Marcus interrupted. "But perhaps your prisoner would like a chance to explain herself?"

By this point, Bruno had begun a bold exploration of my genealogical origins. According to him, one of my ancestors had clearly mated with an evil goat.

"Thank you," I said, with a graceful nod towards Marcus. "As you can see, I've had a rather trying night."

Bruno spat. "Now, don't go being the victim..."

"Silence," Marcus waved his hand. "Prisoner, proceed."

I took a deep breath and began to weave my tale, praying the yarn would hold. "Thank you. My name is Noor Cunningham. I am a sacred priestess of the goddess Isis, and I was warned that tonight, the Library of Alexandria would burn. I was sent not to set the fire, but to *stop* it."

I stuck to the truth as much as possible. There was no point in hiding my name. I'd read enough spy thrillers to know that it's best to use your own, otherwise you end up blowing your cover

---

Genealogical - Relating to one's ancestry

on something stupid, like failing to respond when someone offers you a biscuit.

Marcus cocked an eyebrow. "A priestess of the goddess Isis, you say? How nice." He leaned back in his chair. "May I ask, to which temple do you belong? I assume your sisters received this message, as well."

He was good.

Well, so was I.

"Respectfully, sir, I traveled many miles to be here tonight. My people are not from these parts, but the goddess sees all. Her powers know no borders."

"I see," Marcus strummed his fingers on his desk. "Her Majesty Queen Cleopatra is also a devotee. She believes she is Isis incarnate, in fact. When the battle is won, I shall take you to her. Until then, consider yourself a prisoner of the Sixth Legion."

Bruno smirked as our escort came to bind my wrists, using a thin strap of leather.

"There really has been a misunderstanding..." But even as I spoke, I knew my pleas would be in vain.

"Don't worry, priestess. The battle is almost over. If you are who you say, Cleopatra will free you, quick as Pan."

* * *

I THOUGHT THEY WOULD take me to a cell, but as it turned out, the Romans hadn't been in Egypt long enough to establish that

---

Incarnate - In human form

level of infrastructure. Prisons weren't high on their list of priorities. If you committed a crime, you were either executed or sent to the arena.

"We are holding a few men, of course, until their stories have been sorted," Marcus explained, when I expressed confusion about being led to the chair in the corner of his tent. "I could take you to them, but—"

"No, no," I waved my bound hands. "Quite alright here, thanks."

Marcus returned to his desk, and I unabashedly observed my surroundings. There was definitely a Romulus and Remus motif. I'd seen the twins on banners when we walked in, and the wall of Marcus' tent held the profile of a wolf.

"Where are you from?" Marcus asked abruptly. "Your speech is strange. It is an accent I have not heard."

"Hmm?" I rapidly considered and dismissed countries. Can't do Britain, Gaul, Greece, Egypt...Either I'd be enslaved (the former two), or my coloring would give me away (the latter two). "I'm American."

Honesty is the best policy, isn't it? And I technically *was* a citizen, even if I'd only spent a year in the country.

"American?" Marcus said quizzically. "I've never heard of America. Is it in Belgium?"

"Certainly not! It is many miles away, across a sea ten times as large as the *Mare Nostrum*."

Infrastructure - The basic structures and facilities needed for the operation of a society
Latter - Closer to the end than the beginning

Marcus raised his eyebrows. "The goddess helped you cross it, I presume."

"Naturally."

The lightening of the canvas walls indicated the sun had completed its ascent, and was now establishing itself high in the eastern sky.

"I'm surprised you were already on duty when we arrived," I said. "Do you make a habit of staying up all night?"

"Only when my men are in battle. Do you make a habit of questioning your captors?"

"Only when my captor seems amenable."

Marcus grinned. The sight almost knocked me over.

"May I ask, why are you not in battle with them?"

Marcus leaned back in his chair. "Only broad-stripe tribunes lead men into battle. My position here is...training...you might say. I'm here to learn the ways of battle, to gain the support of the men, so that I might one day serve in the Senate, not fight in battle myself."

"I see." He clearly came from an important family if he was already being groomed for the Senate, but it would've been indelicate to say so.

We continued to speak for most of the morning, and though I knew I was in grave danger, I couldn't help but enjoy myself. When else would I have the opportunity to exchange clever remarks with one of Caesar's men?

Presume - Assume

Ascent - The act of going up

Amenable - Agreeable; responsive

It wasn't just that he was one of Caesar's men, though, or that he could've served as Bernini's muse.

Marcus was an excellent conversationalist, his dialogue the perfect mixture of banter and honesty. At one point I found myself wondering why he was being so open with me, but eventually realized there wouldn't be many women in a Roman camp. I'd be enough of a novelty to keep his interest for a few hours, at least.

Not only that, but gender norms were different in ancient times. A big, strong Roman soldier wouldn't see little old me as a threat. Cleopatra was the obvious exception to this sexist standard, but once she became pharaoh, she would move into her own, non-gendered category.

Eventually a soldier came in, gave Marcus a salute, and passed him a scroll. Marcus cracked open the wax seal with a satisfying *snap*, then smiled as he scanned the text.

"Caesar has won. Come, priestess. It's time for you to meet the queen of Egypt."

* * *

THE SHIP WE TOOK to Antirhodos showed severe signs of wear. A mid-sized vessel, the sail was mended in multiple places, and the wood had little indentations where, presumably, swords had gone astray.

Contemplating the fighting that occurred where I stood — as

Muse (n.) - Someone who serves as the inspiration for an artist

Banter - A playful and friendly exchange of teasing remarks

Contemplating - Thinking about

well as the storm that left Caesar's other ships at the bottom of the sea — I felt a little queasy.

Mercifully, the feeling of unease didn't last long. Behind us, the coastline of Alexandria sparkled, its pristine visage uncontaminated by smoke or fog. Ahead to the left, the Lighthouse of Alexandria towered above the landscape, its fire burning bright even at this hour, beckoning distant travelers to Egypt's shores.

I bit my lip to stifle an undignified squeal. One of the lost wonders of the ancient world, right *there*!

To the right, Cleopatra's palace rested comfortably on the island of Antirhodos. The island was completely underwater in my time, having been eaten by the sea during a medieval earthquake. I was familiar with its contours, though, having dived the crumbling site more times than I could count. But to see it, actually *see* it!

I rose a hand to shield my eyes from the sun, leaning over the railing to take a closer look. Unlike the sand-colored palette I'd grown accustomed to in modern Egypt, the palace glittered with reds and golds and blues. The corners were still sharp right angles, and columns decorated to look like blooming lotuses supported the roof. Palm trees dotted the scenery, and a long row of sphinxes marked the entrance.

Had my parents seen this too? One of their biggest profession-

---

Visage - Sight

Stifle - Restrain

Medieval - Relating to the Middle Ages, a time period that lasted from around the 5th to the 15th century

Contours - An outline representing the shape or form of something

al accomplishments was discovering Cleopatra's palace. Before they brought it to light, no one had known of its location for almost 1,000 years. If seeing the palace affected me this way, what had it done to them?

My giddy excitement turned to steely determination. Heaven help me; if they were here, I was going to find them.

We disembarked before the avenue of sphinxes. I gave Marcus a wide-eyed, "are you seeing this too?" look, and he just chuckled.

"Never been to a palace before, priestess?" he asked.

"None like this," I answered honestly.

What I would've given to wander around each sphinx, observing it as though I were in a museum! Especially that one...the third on the right. I could've sworn it looked familiar. Sworn I'd *seen* it before. Could that be one of the sphinxes my parents discovered?

Impossible, I thought.

But logic reminded me that anything they found *had* to have been here at some point. I winked at the statue, choosing to interpret its presence as a positive omen.

By the same logic, there was no reason my parents couldn't have left the message the professor discovered. They knew these ruins better than anyone. They would've known exactly where to plant an artifact to give it the best chance of survival.

I took a deep breath as we disembarked, then crossed the double gates heralding the entrance to the palace grounds. Egyptian

---

Giddy - Excited to the point of being dizzy or unsteady
Disembarked - Got off a ship, aircraft, or other vehicle
Omen - A sign of good or bad things to come

guards with curved swords at their waistbands stood to either side of the entrance, but they didn't challenge our arrival.

The sand beneath my feet immediately turned to stone, and another row of sphinxes led us to the palace itself. Ceilings soared 40 feet high and large windows opened to the sea, its breeze lightening the burden of the Egyptian sun.

I stopped dead in my tracks when we entered the Great Hall. Innumerable people milled around me, but my eyes went directly to *her*. She was seated at the back of the room, her throne on a platform high above the crowd. Her comparative height might have been part of the reason she stood out, but I don't think that was entirely it.

Cleopatra was resplendent in gold and linen. Her beaded wig ended in a chic, shoulder-length bob, and a snake made of gold rested directly atop her head, where her hair would have parted.

Her physical appearance was only part of her magnetism, though. There was just something *more* about her.

I can't really explain it. The closest comparison, I think, would be meeting the president. But even presidents — no offense — don't have the same kind of longevity as Cleopatra. There are plenty of presidents whose names I don't know a mere 200 years later. People would remember Cleopatra for millennia.

Innumerable - Too many to count

Milled - Moved around in a confused mass

Comparative - Involving a comparison

Resplendent - Shining brilliantly

Longevity - Having a long existence or life

Millennia - Thousands of years (the plural of millennium)

I scanned the room, but Caesar was nowhere to be seen. I narrowed my eyes in confusion before realizing just how significant his absence was. I'd have been willing to bet my snake ring that he wasn't just sleeping off a night of battle. He and Cleopatra were making it clear that *she* was the pharaoh of Egypt. If Caesar was standing behind her, she would look like a mere puppet of Rome.

Instead, Cleopatra was doing what monarchs do best — acting regally superior and arbitrating the occasional dispute. *Man,* these two were smart.

At that moment, a man was kneeling before Cleopatra, pleading for the life of his son, who had been sentenced to death after stealing his neighbor's goat.

"He never would have done it, Your Majesty. But the taxes have been so heavy, and his sister was so hungry..."

Cleopatra's eyes softened as she looked down at the man. Though she was responding to him, her words were calculated to reach everyone in the room.

"I know the burden you have borne," she said in carrying tones, "and I regret the suffering my brother caused so he could sit here, on my throne. Your son will be freed, and I will repay your neighbor with one of the palace goats. Does this satisfy you?"

The man's eyes welled with tears. Clutching his ragged hat in both hands, he said, "Yes, Your Majesty. Thank you, Your Majesty!"

Cleopatra nodded, her slender wrists never leaving the arms of

---

Monarchs - Kings, queens, or emperors

Regally - Fit for a king or queen; magnificent and dignified

her throne, then summoned the next petitioner. Matters contin-ued in this vein for some time, with Cleopatra always choosing the diplomatic response, the one guaranteed to sway the most people to her cause.

Belatedly, I noticed we were in line, and the line was moving forward. We were actually quite close to the front.

"How is this going to work?" I whispered to Marcus.

He'd removed the binding from my wrists on the journey over. In my naiveté, I assumed our easy friendship meant he would help free me from my present dilemma.

"Your old friend — the one who brought you to me — is here. He's going to tell Cleopatra what he saw, and she will decide what to do with you."

"Bruno?!" I gasped. "You're going to let Bruno make my case?"

"It's not up to me, priestess, and I think his name is Hector. But he was the witness, not I."

We were next in line now, and I saw Bruno a.k.a. Hector standing on the side wall. He didn't have to mingle with the riff raff. He was a guard of rank, here to make a case, not plead one.

I was in more trouble than I thought. I believed Marcus was going to state the facts of my case, and I'd spent the better part of the day getting to know him. I knew he would be fair and impar-tial.

Not that I should be found innocent, even in a fair trial, my guilty conscience said. But at that moment, my sense of self-preserva-

---

(In this/that) Vein - In a certain way

Belatedly - Later than should be the case

Naiveté - Lack of experience, wisdom, or judgement

tion overpowered the agony of guilt. And if Bruno was making my case, I was desperately, hopelessly in danger.

But there wasn't a moment to strategize before, suddenly, it was my turn. My stomach tightened as I stepped before the crowd.

"Your Majesty, you are no doubt familiar with the tragedy in last night's triumph," Bruno began, his rough dialect now replaced with palace Egyptian. "We were able to save a small section of the Sacred House of Knowledge, but there is much that can never be replaced. And I personally saw *this girl* start the fire!"

As Bruno pointed at me with a flourish, the collective gaze of the crowd hardened into naked hatred. Several old women hissed; others made signs with their fingers to ward off evil.

I felt like I was back in Connecticut, giving my Senior Speech. Caitlyn and her cronies had acted much the same when I took the stage.

My cheeks flushed, but I forced myself not to look down. "Your Majesty, if I may..."

Cleopatra looked at me with such venom that I felt an overwhelming desire to run and hide. She said nothing, however, and I seized my chance.

"I was not there to start the fire, but to prevent it!" I proclaimed loudly, projecting so the crowd could hear me as well as they'd heard Bruno. "I was sent by the all-knowing, all-caring goddess Isis, who watches over Egypt as she does her own family.

Flourish - A bold or extravagant gesture

131

She foretold the disaster and wished to avert it!"

With a flick of her dainty finger, Cleopatra summoned the slave to her right. She was about the queen's age, with similar coloring, but wore a simple white dress in place of the queen's regalia.

Cleopatra said something in tones too low to be overheard. The slave nodded, then spoke. "If the mother goddess wished to forestall such a tragedy, why did she not tell the queen, her most beloved daughter? Why are you the one to whom the message was sent?"

Of course. It would be beneath Cleopatra's dignity to cross-examine me. Lucky for me, Mitzi was a fan of *Law and Order*.

"The goddess knew Her Majesty had more pressing matters to attend to. She did not wish to task her with such an onerous burden on the night of her triumph. She chose me because — quite simply — I am special."

Bruno scoffed.

"I can prove it," I said. "I have with me two gifts from the goddess. And as we all know, the gods almost never grant such tangible gifts. Ergo, I have been chosen."

"Proceed," the slave said.

I pulled the ballpoint pen from my dress, which — for some

Avert - Prevent

Regalia - The emblems, insignia, or wardrobe of royalty

Forestall - Prevent

Onerous - An extremely burdensome amount of effort

Tangible - Touchable

Ergo - Therefore

inconceivable reason — I'd stashed where the cloth tied around my waist.

"Behold!" I transformed from courtroom lawyer to stage magician. "I have in my hands a stylus one need never wet or refill. One can write for hours, days, without pause. And it dries immediately, without the need for powder!"

The crowd was silent, unimpressed, lacking any of the "ooohs" or "aaahs" I'd hoped for.

I wanted to kick myself. Most of the crowd was probably illiterate. Why would they care about pens?

"But that's not all!" I withdrew the cell phone from my bra, ignoring the looks of confusion from the crowd. "This device is one of great magic. It plays music unlike anything you've ever heard."

I opened the music app and rapidly considered which playlist would be most appropriate. "Dahabeeyah Nights" might be a little too intense. "Calm Study," perhaps?

I hit play and turned up the volume, gratified to hear gasps of amazement.

"Magic!" someone whispered. "But how?" another cried.

"But wait; there's more!" I closed the app and opened the camera. "Your Majesty, this gift enables me to become the greatest artist the world has ever seen. With it, I can paint a miniature portrait in seconds, perfectly reproducing anything I see. Every jewel in Her Majesty's crown, every carving on the wall — what

---

Inconceivable - Unbelievable; not able to be understood

Illiterate - Unable to read or write

Gratified - Pleased; satisfied

took others a lifetime to create, I can recreate in an instant."

Murmurs of disbelief swirled in the air.

"Would you like a sample?"

Cleopatra gave her approval with a barely perceptible nod.

"Of whom would you like the portrait?"

"Her Majesty, naturally," the slave responded. "Art is not for peasants."

Her words belied the mood of the room. Every face was held in rapt attention, though no one seemed to take offense at her remarks.

I held up the phone to Cleopatra, then zoomed in to make sure I had the best shot. *Perfect.* She wasn't looking directly at the camera, and had the vague, disinterested look of an Armani model.

"May I approach?" I asked.

But at a gesture from Cleopatra's slave, one of the guards took the phone. He held it gently, on the palms of two hands, like he was transporting the queen's jewels.

Cleopatra leaned over, blinking in surprise when she saw the photo.

"Extraordinary," she said. "No doubt the mother goddess gave you such gifts that you might, one day, give them to me. I will therefore keep the stylus, your sound and picture machine, and the remaining gift you are transporting using the...wrinkles...of your garment."

A snicker rose from the crowd. Not that their clothes were

Perceptible - Able to be seen or noticed

Belied - Contradicted; failed to give a true impression of something

Rapt - Fascinated

much of an improvement over mine, singed and dirty as I was, but apparently laughing at the appearance of others is a universal human pastime.

My hand went to my waist. I'd almost forgotten about the pepper spray, hooked around the same tie that held the pen.

I had no use for the items now, except maybe the pepper spray. Bartering them in exchange for Cleopatra's favor was the right choice.

Yet I found myself oddly reluctant to part with the phone. It was hardly glued to my hand, Caitlyn-style, but when I thought of the years of messages and memories it held... Seeing it in the hands of a stranger made me feel uncomfortably exposed, like when the TSA searches your bag by hand at an island airport.

It has no signal, I firmly reminded myself. *It's password-protected, and it's going to die soon anyway.*

Blast. *What would happen when the blasted phone ran out of battery?*

"I gladly surrender my gifts to Your Highness. Though, if I may, to extend the life..."

Cleopatra cut off my explanation of airplane mode with a wave of her bejeweled hand. "As for the accusations leveled against you, they are too serious to be purchased away, even with gifts fine as these. Take her to the dungeons while I consider the case."

And that was that. Two of Cleopatra's guards seized me by the arms, and I locked eyes with Marcus in a moment of panic. He

---

Apparently - As far as one can tell
Bartering - Trading
Reluctant - Unwilling

shrugged. *Nothing I can do about it,* his shoulders seemed to say.

Like the guards in the library, the men who approached were shirtless and heavily muscled. They were clearly of higher rank than Bruno and his partner, though, wearing striped headdresses, golden necklaces, and cuffs around their bulging biceps.

Instinctively I tried to tug my arms away, but neither man was even thrown off balance. I probably looked like a raccoon fending off two lions. The snickering peasants parted before us like the Red Sea, simultaneously giving us a respectful distance while jostling for a better view.

I peered up at my captors, wondering if I could forge any connection, but apparently one doesn't win a Marcus more than once every five guards. These men were thoroughly loyal to Cleopatra, and she'd ordered me thrown in the dungeons. To the dungeons I was going.

"Let me *go!*" I squirmed nonetheless, and guard number two let out a chuckle.

"Energetic little creature, isn't she?"

Then he punched me in the jaw. As I crumpled to the floor, he tucked me under his arm as neatly as if I were a newspaper.

In my half-conscious state, I was poignantly reminded of why the ancients were so fond of scented oils. His outstretched arm was releasing toxic fumes extremely close to my nose.

Bruno smirked as I gave one last kick, but it was no use. I had lost.

Fending (off) - Defending oneself
Simultaneously - At the same time
Jostling - Push or shove, especially in a crowd

HARVEY'S FIELD NOTES

Nov. 16:

She left. Without saying a word, Noor up and went back to Cairo. I didn't even hear her go. There can be no question she left of her own free will, though; her bag went with her.

Shouldn't be surprised. She's done far more impetuous things than board a train. Was probably feeling awkward about last night.

Must make things right when I see her. For now, have hands full with the professor. He's raving that the "sacred inscription" is gone; convinced one of his professional rivals is onto him. Hope to God I can calm him down before break ends.

Nov. 22:

Don't think I've ever seen Noor this angry. She forgave me quicker when I ratted her out to Frank and Mary during the Ne-

---

Impetuous - Impulsive; prone to acting quickly without thought or care

fertiti Bust affair. Though how she ever thought she could "liberate" one of the most heavily guarded artifacts in Germany is beyond me...

Been back in Cairo 3 days, but she's sent all my calls to voicemail. Due to blasted gender-segregated dorms, can't just knock on her door.

NOV. 25:

Forced self to make small talk with Viviana today for the sake of making contact with Noor. Sat next to her in "Roots of Arab-Israeli Conflict" course, and convo went something like:

"Viviana, it's good to see you again..."

"Hmph!" Nose in the air. Hair flick.

"Right. So, next time you see Noor, will you tell her to call me? I haven't been able to get through."

"Noor?" That got Viviana's attention. "I believed she was with you, in Alexandria."

"She was," I patiently reminded her, "for Eid. But she came back early, well over a week ago now."

"Harvey, I thought you — what you say? — extended your vacation. Noor never came back from Alexandria."

??????

NOV. 25 (LATER THAT DAY)

Considered immediately phoning embassy, but decided to call Mitzi before launching international manhunt.

Have sickening feeling that something is deeply amiss, but

Amiss - Wrong

138

embassy won't do anything before talking to Mitzi anyway. And M's more likely to answer *my* call at 7:00 a.m. than some restricted gov't #, so we'll get answers faster this way.

Praying to God Noor was just so upset about the prof's ravings that she decided to spend the rest of break with M, then extended her stay.

Must have stern conversation about informing loved ones — i.e. me — of whereabouts. Lord knows I bailed her out often enough growing up, but it wasn't through telepathy. We were joined at the hip, so I always knew what she was scheming.

Telepathy - The ability to communicate through psychic means

CHAPTER TEN

THEY'RE GOING TO *mummify me alive.* My brain recoiled at what I was seeing. We were descending deep into the bowels of the palace. Gone were the paintings of dancing girls in transparent dresses and men spearing fish. The walls down here were bare and dank, the humidity from the Mediterranean seeping in. Don't panic. Breathe. Think.

By the time we approached a heavy wooden door, I'd stopped struggling entirely. Resisting these two was futile. I was better off saving my energy, pretending to be docile and innocent, to lower the guard of whomever they were transferring me to.

A wiry old man answered the door and hopped aside to let us in. His hair stood in white tufts and his clothes were streaked with what I told myself was just dirt. Red dirt.

Recoiled - Sprang back in horror, fear, disgust
Dank - Unpleasantly damp and musty
Docile - Submissive

"Another one?" he asked. "How long?"

"Until she says so," the guard replied.

Leaving his partner behind, he carried me down a dark, earthen hallway, lit only with smoking torches. Five wooden doors opened up to either side, presumably marking the entrance to different cells. Chagrined, I mentally discarded one of my escape tactics. There wouldn't be nearly enough people to stage an insurrection.

When we arrived, the guard tossed me on the floor in the far corner. My knees and elbows received more scrapes on the wet, jagged stone, and the pungent odor left no doubt that the corner had been used as a urinal by at least one former cellmate.

I hastily scrambled to my feet.

"I'm going to be sick," I said plainly. "You *cannot* leave me down here."

But he was already on his way out. The door closed with a heavy *thump*, and the rattle of locks was the last thing I heard.

DON'T PANIC. *DON'T* PANIC. I paced in circles around the little cell. Maybe 10 feet by the same, it had stone walls and an arched ceiling. A small, barred window provided a modicum of air, but the only real opening to the outside world was the petrified

---

Chagrined - Distressed

Insurrection - Uprising

Pungent - A sharp smell

Hastily - Quickly

Modicum - A small amount

Petrified - Changed into a stony substance

wooden door through which I'd been thrown.

Occasionally I paused to investigate a smaller stone that looked wobbly. Surely former prisoners had made escape attempts, and I could take advantage of the groundwork they laid?

But none of the rocks gave way to reveal a convenient tunnel dug with wooden spoons to the outside world. No one had even attempted to begin the process.

Lazy jerks.

I sat down — far from the smelly corner where I'd been dropped — and used the inside of my sheet to wipe my eyes. No need to add pink eye to my growing list of cuts, scrapes, and bruises.

Inhaling deeply, I considered my situation. I wouldn't be locked up forever, at least. Unlike our modern practice of letting criminals languish in jail for years upon end, ancient "justice" was simpler. You were either freed, executed, or allowed to fight for your life in the arena.

Considering the third option, I grew uncomfortably lightheaded. *They're never going to make you a gladiator, so don't start worrying about that, too. This is Egypt, not Rome, and...*

At that moment, a pair of glowing, red eyes appeared at the base of the wall in front of me. I stopped breathing, afraid that any movement prompt it to attack. Slowly leaning forward, I attempted to ascertain what I was up against.

It's just a rat. *Just a little rat!* You've seen plenty of them in the

---

Languish - Suffer from being forced to remain somewhere unpleasant
Ascertain - Figure out; make certain of something

back alleys of Cairo…

My mind had taken on two personae, and they were arguing.

Yes, but I wear boots in Cairo for that exact reason! Besides, ancient dungeon rats probably have the plague!

I put my head between my knees and fought to regain control.

Snap out of it, Noor. Inhale, exhale.

I could no longer deny the reality of my situation. At this point, any additional talk of this being a dream would be irresponsible. It was time to reckon with the facts.

Yes, you burned down the Library of Alexandria. Yes, your role model threw you in prison. And no, you haven't found any trace of your parents. But you can survive this!

Questionable pep talk notwithstanding, another part of me recognized a more pressing, immediate dilemma: having accepted the reality of my situation, my mental state was quickly deteriorating.

I'd only been locked up a few hours, and I was already working myself into a state of utter hysterics. Spending the night in that wretched little cell was unfathomable. What would happen to me after a few weeks?

Re-frame the situation, I told myself.

I'd gotten to meet one of my role models. I'd seen her palace in its original state. I hadn't found any breadcrumbs from my parents, but I hadn't been here long. There was every chance I still could, if I was ever released.

The rattle of chains sent me leaping to my feet. I flew to the

---

Deteriorating - Becoming worse

Unfathomable - Unable to be explored or understood

side of the door, determined to attack whomever appeared. If it was the guard from before, I would go straight for the curved sword at his belt. I didn't doubt he could kill me with his bare hands, but this way I could keep those hands at a distance.

The door opened. I froze in a classic boxing stance, on the balls of my feet with my fists before my face. Marcus stood in the entryway, holding a tray of food.

"If you're planning to kill me, you might let me put down your dinner first," he said, a smile quirking the edge of his lips.

I lowered my hands. I wanted to hurl questions at him with machine gun rapidity, but forced myself to emulate his cool tone. If I wanted his help, I needed to keep his respect. Revealing my true state of panic would be a grave tactical error.

"Kind of you to check in on me," I said coolly. "Judging by the food, I don't suppose you bring official news of my release?"

"Unfortunately not, but the queen is intrigued." He eyed the little cell, as if deciding where to put down the tray, then passed it into my hands. "She ordered her sorcerers to investigate your gifts, though they will undoubtedly say they are nothing special."

"What? *Why?*"

"Any admission to the contrary would imply you are more powerful than they are, and such creatures live only for power."

He spoke with distaste, as only someone born into irrevocable power could.

"So that's it?" I squeezed the edges of the tray. "They'll say they

---

Quirking - Twisting or turning to express amusement
Imply - Indicate or suggest without being explicitly stated
Irrevocable - Unable to be taken away or reversed

can do everything I can, and I'll be, what — freed? Executed?"

"Unclear. The queen is hosting a gathering tonight, so she'll have other matters to attend to. She might send for you tomorrow, though."

"*Might?*"

"There *is* a chance she'll simply forget about you. Poor bloke in the cell next door has been there for weeks. But the allegations against you are far more severe, and you made a sufficient spectacle of yourself being dragged out, so I suspect she'll remember. And if she doesn't, I'll remind her."

Marcus gave me a wink and backed out the door.

"Rest well, priestess."

I AWOKE THE NEXT MORNING stiff as a corpse. A horrific smell had roused me — a nauseating combination of B.O., old urine, smoke, adrenaline, and terror. I lifted my right arm, tentatively taking a sniff, and gagged. The smell was coming from me.

Great. Just great. Now you get to make your case looking a hermit who eats locusts in the desert — and smelling like one too!

Eau de toilette, indeed.

With nowhere to go, I smoothed my tangled tresses, wrapped my arms around my knees, and passed the time by analyzing Marcus's accent.

His pronunciation of Latin wasn't the form taught in schools,

---

Allegations - Accusations

Spectacle - A show; a visually striking performance

Tresses - Long locks of hair

with hard consonants and a monotonous inflection. As I'd long suspected, it sounded more like Italian, with rolled r's and a slightly sing-songy delivery.

Next, I tried to recall anything about Cleopatra that I could use to my advantage. She and Caesar were already an item — that much was clear — but now that she was on the throne, he would have to return to Rome. He still had to become "dictator for life," after all.

And as everyone with a rudimentary education knew, Caesar would be assassinated upon his return to Rome, on the Ides of March.

I grimaced, secretly hoping I'd never get to meet him. He would face a terrible death at the hands of his friends and the man he loved like a son. His last words might not have been "*Et tu, Brute?*" but Shakespeare's imagining of the scene certainly left a mark.

Loosely translated to, "Even you, Brutus?" one couldn't help but see Caesar wounded, dying, and crumpling to the floor, looking up at the man he'd cared for since he was a child.

Caesar's legacy, like Cleopatra's, would resonate for thousands of years. How much more would it affect me if I knew him personally?

Monotonous - Having one tone or pitch
Inflection - The intonation or pitch of the voice
Rudimentary - Basic
Ides - The 15th of the month
Resonate - Evoke emotions

Could I warn him, averting the crime and earning his goodwill in the process? But what kind of butterfly effect would that cause? If Caesar didn't die, would his nephew Octavian still become Rome's first emperor?

Rome had three phases: monarchy, republic, and empire. And a world in which the Roman empire hadn't existed would be a different world indeed...

Not only that, but if I did warn Caesar, would he even believe me? According to legend, a soothsayer *did* warn him, and he didn't take the threat seriously.

I switched my attention to Cleopatra. There was plenty I could "predict" about her future. She would fall in love with Marc Antony, Caesar's top general, after Caesar's death. She and Antony would fight Octavian for control of Rome. They would lose. Not exactly the type of fortune a queen wants to hear.

It all came back to my gadgets. I just had to hope I could impress the queen enough, and that a *deny, deny, deny* approach would work when it came to my involvement with the library.

I choked back another wave of nausea. I felt physically ill anytime I thought about what I'd done, even if it was an accident.

The library would've burned either way, I told myself. History had shown that. And I saw with my own eyes that Caesar's fire had nearly reached the building by the time we escaped. My actions just accelerated the timetable a little.

But would it have destroyed as much? Probably. Maybe not.

At that moment, I once again heard the rattle of chains at the

Averting - Preventing

door.

When the wiry, old white-haired man appeared, I was at the back of the cell, holding the tray like a baseball bat. Tactically speaking, standing by the side of the door and blindly whacking the entrant as they passed through would have made more sense, but I didn't want to hurt Marcus or someone who might be announcing my release.

The white-haired man and I stared at each other for a long moment, testing each other's will. Just looking at him made my skin crawl.

I'm typically not a violent person, but I actually think I would've whacked him over the head and climbed over his unconscious body in a wild bid for freedom had he not spoken at that moment.

"The queen wishes to see you."

To MY CHAGRIN, I was not given the opportunity to freshen up before being led back to the Great Hall.

Unlike the day before, no onlookers from the public were in attendance. Instead, three sorcerers stood in the center of the room. They were bald, with enough eyeliner to make Viviana jealous, wearing loose, glittering robes that belted at the waist.

An entourage of slaves and guards stood on a step at the back of the room. Behind them, several feet above, Cleopatra sat on her elevated throne.

But this time, Caesar — it could only be Caesar — stood beside

---

Chagrin - Distress; disappointment

her, arms crossed and stance domineering.

He looked just like his bust in the Vatican Museum — short, cropped hair, a powerful but straight nose, and cheeks that, even in marble, somehow looked tan and muscular.

The layout of the room gave the distinct impression that Caesar and Cleopatra were gods, and we should be grateful they were looking down at us mortals. Her throne was completely gilded, if not made of solid gold, as was the wall behind them. Engraved on the wall was the goddess Isis with giant, multicolored wings stretched out to either side.

A low table, black with gold accents, had been brought before the sorcerers. My belongings were neatly laid out upon it.

One of the guards escorted me to the table, then Cleopatra's slave — the same one who spoke on her behalf the day before — decreed, "Her Royal Highness Queen Cleopatra Philopator, Mistress of Upper and Lower Egypt, orders you to provide more information on the gifts you received from the mother goddess."

I bowed my head in the direction of the queen. "I would be honored, Your Majesty. Where would you like me to begin?"

"With this," one of the sorcerers lifted the pepper spray with two fingers. "We all know what the other items do, and I have attempted to explain to the queen—"

"Silence," Cleopatra said. "Priestess, proceed."

"It's, well, a poison," I said. "An extremely potent, but temporary, poison. It will incapacitate your enemies long enough for

---

Domineering - Dominating; asserting one's will over others in an arrogant way

Potent - Powerful

Incapacitate - Prevent from functioning normally

you to escape, but not kill them."

"Show me."

"*Show* you, Your Majesty? You wish that I poison someone?"

"Him," Cleopatra gestured to the sorcerer. "Ahmes believes the object is of no importance, valuable only because of the foreign material encasing it. We shall see which of you is telling the truth."

The sorcerer gave me a look of sheer terror, then dropped to his knees before the queen.

"Your Majesty, how could I know what was inside the object? With more time—"

"Is seeing the unknown not one of your talents? Do as I say, or execution will follow poison."

His two companions went a sickly pale, and were inching themselves behind the table, far from their spokesman.

I slowly approached the sorcerer, still genuflecting before his queen. He was trembling; his bald head shone with perspiration.

Holding my breath, I covered my eyes with my forearm and unloaded a wave of capsicum. As a precaution, I took a few steps back before opening my eyes. The sorcerer was shrieking and crying, writhing on the palace floor in anguish.

"I'm so sorry!" I said softly. "Water...rinse your eyes..."

Caesar looked impressed. His eyes were working and a hand stroked his chin, but he said nothing.

"Escort Ahmes to his quarters," Cleopatra gestured to one of

Encasing - Enclosing; holding

Genuflecting - Kneeling

Anguish - Pain; suffering

the guards, speaking with as little emotion as if she'd just asked for a glass of water. Nodding in the direction of the other two sorcerers, she added, "You may go."

"Thank you, Your Highness. You are most merciful!" The sorcerers continued bowing and scraping as they left the room.

When they were gone, Caesar spoke for the first time. "Your story interests me, priestess. The gods have clearly blessed you, else you could not have their gifts. Equally clearly, you are not a liar. But half the city saw the fire spread from my boats to the library. It would be unjust for you to take the blame. Not to mention, to be seen scapegoating an obscure young priestess would look ill with the people."

"You are wise and merciful, sir." I blushed, embarrassed to sound like one of the obsequious sorcerers, but I didn't know what else to say.

Cleopatra nodded at Caesar, then turned to me. "Very well. You will remain as a member of my court. You are dismissed."

(Bowing and) Scraping - Make deep bows; backing out of the room in reverse

Obscure - Not well-known

Obsequious - Excessively obedient or attentive

CHAPTER ELEVEN

I WAS GIVEN ROOMS overlooking the sea, but wasn't sure if I should interpret the location as a position of prestige, like an oceanfront suite on cruise ships, or if sea views were the norm on an island palace.

The suite reminded me of a nice European hotel — elegantly appointed, with exquisite attention to detail. In addition to the bedroom, a sitting room boasted two divans across a leather ottoman, and an intricately carved (if uncomfortable-looking) wooden chair to the side.

The view from the balcony was one that few throughout history would have the opportunity to admire. The island would disappear in a few hundred years, after all.

Upon exiting the throne room, I'd been passed from the guards to the slaves. The girl who led me through grand, open-air hall-

---

Intricately - In a complicated or detailed manner

ways to my new quarters was young, around my age, with big brown eyes and shiny black hair. Her name was Mentit, and she'd just arrived at court, too.

"My mother is the queen's cousin," Mentit explained, to my surprise. "Her Majesty believes my family could have been more...supportive...of her cause during the war. We have not been sold into slavery, but we may as well have. Our role at court is the same."

Mentit's lower lip wobbled, and I put a supportive hand on her forearm.

"Like ladies-in-waiting," I said, receiving a fishy stare in response. "During the Wars of the Roses...Well, there's a saying. 'Keep your friends close and your enemies closer.' Over time, people often forgot why the ladies were there. And since they did everything with the queen, they sometimes become her closest friends."

"You really think so?" Mentit's eyes filled with hope. "My mother is serving Queen Cleopatra herself. If she can show we never meant any harm—"

"I'm sure it will all work out."

"Not that I'll be of much use, serving a beggar priestess," Mentit appeared to be talking to herself now.

"Erm, yes, quite. On that note, can you show me where I can take a bath?"

IT WOULD BE IMPOSSIBLE to fully describe Cleopatra's bathhouse, so I won't try. Suffice it to say that the "bath" more closely resembled a giant, heated pool than anything else. Glimmering torches provided spa-like light amid the colossal columns. Carved paintings of girls gossiping, smelling giant lotus flowers, and doing each other's hair graced the walls.

Four slaves were assigned to each person. They scrubbed you, rubbed you, oiled you, and dried you with a dizzying mixture of luxury and efficiency. They even put ointment on my scrapes, pressing a jar of it into my hands as I left, assuring me the wounds would heal without scarring if I used it each night.

By early afternoon I was back in my room, dazed and looking like a new woman — or, at least, the woman I'd been before arriving in ancient Egypt.

Mentit was sitting at my vanity, examining her nails when I returned.

"Ye gods!" she cried. "Is it you? It is you!"

"It is I!" I agreed. "Restored, but not quite revitalized. Would you mind terribly if I went to sleep? I know it's only midday, but..."

She snorted. "It is not for you to ask permission from me. If you want to sleep, sleep. I'll see if I can get you some new clothes, eh? I believe we're about the same size."

"That would be wonderful."

And with that, I enjoyed a contented sleep for the first time

---

Suffice (it to say) - Saying enough to make one's meaning clear, without going on about it

Revitalized - Brought back to life; given new life

Contented - Happy and at ease

since leaving Cairo. I was covered in the finest Egyptian cotton, but had no pillow, only a firm wooden headrest shaped like the letter "c" at the top of the bed. Yet for all I knew, I'd been taken to heaven on gossamer wings.

As I drifted into oblivion, I wondered what was happening in my own time.

The professor and Mitzi would soon work out the truth, I was sure. Between my phone call with Mitzi, the stolen text, and the missing coins, there was really only one plausible explanation.

Would Harvey believe them, or would he cling stubbornly to his doubts? A second wind swept through me as his name entered my mind, but I turned on my side, trying to continue a rational train of thought.

What would Shira and Viviana think when I didn't come back to school? Would I be reported missing to the authorities, even if Mitzi and the professor thought I was safe?

The questions swirled in my subconscious, rocking me into a gentle slumber.

* * *

I DIDN'T WAKE until the next morning, when the gentle sun and lapping of the sea nudged my eyelids open. I was alone in my room, but happy to see that someone had left bread and water on the nightstand. The wooden armoire in the bedroom had four

---

Gossamer - Very light, thin, delicate

Plausible - Probable; reasonable

new dresses in it, as well as a pair of sandals.

I got dressed, scrubbing my fuzzy teeth with a washcloth and some of the leftover drinking water, then decided now was as good a time as any to greet the day.

I'd scarcely gone three steps before Mentit appeared. She must have stationed herself outside my door, waiting for me to wake up.

"Priestess! Your presence has been requested in the throne room."

"Requested? When?"

"You shouldn't delay much longer," she shrugged, avoiding a direct answer with the ineffable ease of someone who's never owned a watch. "Caesar wants a portrait of himself with the queen before he goes back to Rome."

My head spun. "Next time I receive a royal summons, wake me up, okay?" Then I turned on my heel and began making my way to the throne room, silently cursing and strategizing.

The phone hadn't been charged in days. Working twice as hard to find a signal, there was no way it still had battery. I could only hope that someone had lost it. I truly saw no other way out.

"Ah, priestess." Caesar broke off conversation with his slave, turning to greet me as I entered the throne room. After repeating the request Mentit conveyed, he added: "This won't be a problem, I trust?"

"Of course not. I'll just need the device, of course. Unless—"

Scarcely - Hardly; barely

Ineffable - Too great to be expressed in words

Conveyed - Communicated

"Naturally." Caesar waved a finger and the phone was brought to me, resting in the center of a golden tray. "I've been told you need only a moment to capture the portrait. Is it so?"

"It is, sir."

I clicked the home button, distraught but not surprised to find the phone wasn't lighting up. In a last-ditch attempt, I jabbed the power button in the futile hope it would turn on.

It did! My God, I could've kissed that glowing apple.

"Does something surprise you?" Caesar asked.

"Not at all, sir. I was just, um, concerned that the gift might not function as it once did, being in the sorcerers' hands for so long."

Yet the sorcerers had saved me. They must have accidentally turned off the phone when they were playing with the buttons, trying to figure out how to make it work.

I suppressed a laugh, imagining the device powering down before them. They must have been horrified at receiving such a clear message of disfavor from the gods.

"Ah, my love," Caesar addressed Cleopatra, who was gliding into the throne room. She was in all-out queen mode. Gold and jewels dripped from every limb, and her headdress must've weighed 15 pounds. No wonder her steps were so graceful. Any sudden movements and her crown might fall off.

It was the first time I'd seen her standing, and — though I'm ashamed to admit it — I was a little surprised by her weight. I'd

---

Distraught - Devastated; deeply upset

Suppressed - Held back; repressed

grown so accustomed to the modern standards of beauty, with the general mantra of "the skinnier the better," that seeing her curved hips and slightly rounded stomach were a bit of a surprise.

Not that she was large, by any means, and Lord knew she walked with the confidence of a supermodel, but for some reason I'd always had a different image in my head when picturing the timeless beauty icon. Who knew I'd been so brainwashed?

Cleopatra took Caesar's arm, then addressed me directly. "I am unfamiliar with how to pose for an instantaneous portrait, priestess. The result seems more Greek than Egyptian. It is so dynamic, so lively, capturing the spirit of the individual. Yet I do not wish to break with the Egyptian canon."

"I understand," I nodded. "How do you feel about doing something entirely different? Setting your own tone, rather than emulating Greek or Egyptian art?"

She would look ridiculous trying to stand like an Egyptian wall painting anyway. I wasn't even sure the human body could stand like that, with feet facing sideways and torso facing the front. Similarly, she didn't need to strip half-naked and hurl a discus, or anything so typically Greek.

"I am willing to try, priestess, as long as we are pleased with the outcome."

Noted. I asked them to stand near Cleopatra's throne, thinking the golden wall would make a nice backdrop. The two stood awkwardly next to one another, hands at their sides, and I took a

---

Instantaneous - Happening instantly

Canon - Model; something that is generally accepted or recognized

few photos. They looked terrible, like blind dates on Halloween.

"Caesar, perhaps you could, um, put your arm around Cleopatra? Or hold hands? Some gesture of affection would be nice, I think."

I waited for one of them to announce my imminent execution, but Cleopatra just smiled. She clasped a hennaed hand around his, leaning her head on his shoulder.

"Much better." I snapped photos like the inane photographer Mitzi hired when I graduated. "If you could look over here," I held a hand to the side. "And now look at each other. Take just one step back...perfect."

Within a few minutes they were more at ease. Both were naturally photogenic, and hardly shy of the spotlight.

"There is another portrait you might appreciate," I said tentatively. "It would just be for the two of you, though. Not for the people, you understand."

"Yes?" Cleopatra raised an inquiring eyebrow.

"The scenery in Antirhodos is so beautiful. Should we take a few by the beach?" I was thinking of a typical family photo, something Cleopatra could remember her husband by.

"The beach is not suitable for Her Majesty," Cleopatra's slave interjected. "It is rocky, and the tides are unpredictable."

"I understand." I bowed and began to back away, assuming my job was done, when Cleopatra's slave offered an alternative.

"Perhaps Her Majesty's private balcony? The view is the same,

---

Imminent - Happening very soon

Inane - Silly or stupid to the point of annoyance

Inquiring - Seeking information

but the surroundings are more fitting."

IF I LIVE TO BE 110, I will never again behold anything like Cleopatra's bedroom. For starters, everything was custom-made. One gets used to seeing furniture in certain sizes — beds in a twin, queen, or king, for instance.

Cleopatra's bed was the size of a small basketball court, with gauzy drapes billowing from a canopy above. Dozens of pillows rested lazily on the rumpled sheets inside.

The walls were hand-painted with "every good thing" as one ancient inscription put it — beautiful people eating at fine banquets, music players providing an unheard ambiance. Greek and Egyptian sculptures graced niches in the walls.

Cleopatra walked past all of it without a second glance, her skirts revealing a hint of leg with each step. She led us to the balcony and I snapped a few more photos, letting them choose their poses now that they were more comfortable. In one, Cleopatra placed Caesar's hand on her stomach.

It hit me like a sucker punch to the gut.

Of course. Cleopatra would be devastated by Caesar's assassination, but I forgot one crucial detail of the story. She was pregnant with Caesar's son, little Caesarion.

And here I was, thinking she looked fat.

I turned away, unable to look at them for a moment. *There's nothing you can do,* I reminded myself. *He wouldn't listen even if you warned him, and it's not your place to change history.*

Ambiance - Mood; atmosphere

But what about saving the library? My other half asked. *You were fine changing history there.*

I gave my head a small shake, telling the couple: "I think we have everything we need. Would you like to see the photos?"

I let them scroll through the images while there was still battery left. Heads together, they pointed at the ones they liked and laughed at the ones they didn't.

It was the last time I saw Julius Caesar.

HARVEY'S FIELD NOTES

Nov. 25:

Thank God. Noor is in CT with Mitzi. Hasn't gotten a new SIM yet, which explains why my calls are going straight to voicemail.

She was getting groceries when I phoned, but have every intention of reading her the Riot Act when we next speak.

Infernal girl will be the death of me.

[...]

Dec. 13:

Winter break starts today. Have four glorious weeks off.

Things are absolutely ridiculous with Noor. Still haven't spoken, and I can only imagine what she's told her professors. She's been out over a month!

Infernal - Fiendish; diabolical

Hadn't realized how immature she is. The silent treatment? Really? Mitzi says Noor will be in CT through the end of break. Just "give her time."

CHAPTER TWELVE

LIFE SETTLED INTO a precarious routine in the days following my acceptance at court. The primary activities were the queen's daily levee, when she arbitrated the disputes of the commoners, and the lavish dinners she hosted every evening.

I'd been invited to eat with the other members of court — an eclectic group that included certain of the queen's relatives, viziers, and people whose only function seemed to be that they were beautiful and/or entertaining.

Some 30 of us made up the royal entourage, but since everyone had multiple slaves and attendants of their own, the banquet hall fairly teemed with people each night.

Precarious - Uncertain; dependent on chance
Levee - A formal reception of visitors or guests
Arbitrated - Settled; judged
Viziers - Advisors
Teemed - Swarmed with; was filled with

Mentit joined us, as well. It was difficult to discern her exact status — she obviously ranked higher than a "normal" slave, for she had no problem bossing them around, but she was also expected to wait on me.

Not that I'd treat her differently one way or the other. I always sought to make her job easier, donning the palace-provided dresses and jewels in the morning and dismissing her early at night.

And, truthfully, life was just easier when she wasn't around. On the second morning, she brought up a slave from the baths.

I sat down, then leaped to my feet when the woman unsheathed a giant knife. Turning on the assassin, I grabbed a heavy statuette of a cat to defend myself.

"What are you doing?" Mentit cried. "She is here to help you, to rid of that disgusting hair!"

"What?" I lowered the cat.

"Your hair! Why do you have it?"

"Umm..."

Of course. The ancient Egyptians cut their hair short, or shaved it off entirely, to keep cool. When in public, they wore wigs.

The slave cowered between us, afraid to look up.

"I'm so sorry," I said to the slave. "It's been a weird couple of days. I saw the knife..."

"Are you apologizing to it?" Mentit said.

I gave Mentit a sharp look, and she shrugged.

Discern - Determine; figure out
Donning - Putting on

"You may go," Mentit told the slave.

"So can you," I told Mentit.

On the third day, a quorum of Romans was invited to join us at dinner. Caesar had left a small contingent behind to maintain the peace, and as we entered the banquet hall, I recognized a familiar profile.

Turning, Marcus saw me at the same time. He gestured to his friends to go on, then came to join me near the window.

"I'd heard of your miraculous transformation, but—" Marcus let out a low whistle. "Did you know you're the talk of court? Even the Romans are fascinated by the mendicant priestess who poisoned a sorcerer, then reinvented herself as the goddess of beauty."

He took my hand and spun me in an admiring circle. I blushed.

"Nice to see you too, Marcus."

"You two know each other?" Mentit interrupted.

"Sure we do," Marcus said. "Old friends. And you are?"

"Mentit, beloved of Ra, daughter of Arsinoe V. We met on the night of your arrival."

"Of course, the welcome dinner," Marcus said with the utmost politeness. "You'll have to forgive me. It was a long journey, and I wasn't myself."

Mentit sniffed. I doubted men often forgot her.

Quorum - A group of people

Contingent - A group of people united by a common feature

Mendicant - Poor; relying on charity

Utmost - The most extreme; the greatest

"Everyone!" a voice called. "To your seats, please."

We were dining Egyptian-style, seated in chairs rather than the lounging divans preferred by Romans. The seats weren't assigned, and Marcus sat next to me at a long wooden table, Mentit across.

Heaping platters of wild fowl and Nile fish covered center of the table, interspersed with side dishes and enormous vats of wine. Glimmering candles set the gold in the palace walls to shining.

"How are you adjusting to life at court?" Marcus asked, reaching for the olives.

"Quite nicely, I should think," I responded. "Though I had no idea I was amassing such a reputation."

"Look around, priestess."

I did as he suggested. Among the countless little circles of conversation, there was usually at least one person looking at me. They quickly looked away when I glanced in their direction.

"I just thought it was that I was new, and maybe that I have fair hair."

"That's part of it." Marcus glanced at my hair admiringly, like it was some sort of halo.

"She's not *that* special," Mentit muttered. "She didn't even know how to brush her teeth until I taught her."

Marcus' gaze moved to my mouth, no doubt struggling to reconcile this revelation with the white smile 21st century dentistry

---

Interspersed - Mixed in with something else

Amassing - Gathering; accumulating

Reconcile - To make different things compatible

provided.

I gave Mentit a "thanks for that" look, then admitted: "It is true. Where I come from, we do not clean our mouths with frayed twigs."

"Really?" Marcus asked. "And yet I've always found Egyptian dentistry quite advanced. The paste is much more pleasant. It's made of salt and crushed flowers, no?"

"More or less," Mentit said. "What do you use in Rome?"

"Ground animal bones, mostly."

Mentit stopped chewing, and my face held a similar note of disgust. Animal bone toothpaste?

Marcus laughed, and the night continued to progress in pleasant conversation, the mingling of cultures on full display.

* * *

I SAW MORE OF MARCUS than expected in the following weeks. With Caesar gone, I assumed his responsibilities would increase. He'd become one of the most powerful men in Egypt, after all, in his position as Roman plenipotentiary.

And yet he always seemed to be delivering some missive or another to Cleopatra. Since I was expected to hold court with her, we inevitably made eye contact on his way out.

"Fancy a stroll, priestess?" he'd ask.

The first time this happened, I looked to the queen for permis-

---

Plenipotentiary - Diplomat; someone who has the full power of their government

Missive - Message

Inevitably - Unavoidably

168

sion. Finding her absorbed in the scroll Marcus delivered, my gaze fell to the slave who often spoke for her. Receiving a brusque nod, I joined him.

The women around me twittered like a flock of birds. Normally they just sat there, but at the sight of him, they all seemed to be fanning themselves and seductively pouting in his general direction.

The next time Marcus arrived, Mentit and one of her innumerable cousins were playing a fierce game of *senet* (essentially Egyptian chess). By then I'd realized Cleopatra didn't much care what we did, as long as there were enough people around to maintain a lively atmosphere.

"Don't you have to, you know...work?" I asked him, my attention still half on the game of *senet*.

"Keeping tabs on you is a matter of public safety," he explained with mock solemnity. "Have to make sure the old prisoner has really reformed."

On a few hair-raising occasions, I was called to Cleopatra's private chambers. The terror of having no idea what to expect was ever at war with my historical fascination. *So this is what Cleopatra looks like when there's no one around!*

Wigless, her dark hair was cut short. Her heavy, jeweled garments were replaced by a simple cotton dress, cut low in the front and billowing around the stomach. She reclined on a mountain of pillows in her enormous bed, exotic fur blankets thrown hither

---

Brusque - Abrupt; perfunctory
Solemnity - The state of being intensely serious or dignified

and thither like some kind of horrible, lifeless zoo.

"Tell me about the child," she said, hands on her stomach.

"Mmmm," I replied in a humming tone, trying to look mystical. Did she expect me to read her fortune on the spot? Go consult someone at a temple?

But she was looking at me so expectantly I decided to go for it, adding a little drama to lend verisimilitude to the charade. I closed my eyes and took exaggerated breaths, my palms turned heavenward. While pretending to commune with her gods, I sent up a plea to my own.

"Your boy, Caesarion," I intoned, "will be strong as his father and beautiful as his mother."

"A boy? Caesarion?" she sat up straighter.

I sat beside her and gently placed a hand on her arm. "Without question."

My body froze, hand still in its compromising position. *What was I thinking?* Sitting on a stranger's bed is such an invasion of privacy! *And to touch the queen of Egypt?*

I'd been so busy channeling some random, old-lady fortune teller that I'd forgotten to filter her actions. Cleopatra moved; her lips parted.

Just when I expected her to call for the guards, she clasped a hand over mine and remarked, "Not that I had any doubts, of course. But I am happy to have my own messages confirmed."

My heart fell back into my chest, and I sent up a prayer of

Verisimilitude - The appearance of being true or real

Commune - Communicate, especially on a spiritual level

Intoned - Said melodically, with a rise and fall of the voice

thanks that I'd managed to survive another perilous encounter.

* * *

AND YET DESPITE my seemingly auspicious circumstances, I woke up in a panicked sweat roughly one month after my arrival.

It was sometime in December — I'd lost track of the exact date — and the sea air carried a chill that burrowed deep into the bones. There was no reason for me to be sweating. Except for the dream.

My parents clung to life on a small inflatable raft, so far from shore that I could scarcely see their silhouetted forms. My dad was waging a vicious battle with the water, sending long powerful strokes of the oar into the sea. My mom, never content to sit on the sidelines, dove into the waves, then re-emerged at the back of the boat, kicking and pushing.

But their efforts were in vain. The current was dragging them back towards the setting sun until, to my horror, I couldn't tell them from a flock of birds. I looked for anything I could use to save them, but no one had conveniently misplaced a helicopter or float plane.

There was no misinterpreting the dream. With my own sur-

Perilous - Dangerous

Auspicious - Favorable; good

Burrowed - Dug

Re-emerged - Came back into view

(In) Vain - Useless; producing no result

Misinterpreting - Understanding something the wrong way

vival now (more or less) secured, it was time to find my parents.

* * *

WHEN MENTIT ARRIVED for "work," I told her I'd been blessed with a vision. "There is a couple in grave danger, whose help we will need in the seasons to come."

Unperturbed, Mentit sank into the divan opposite me and put up her feet. "Who are they, this couple?"

"They're — they're my parents."

I'd already decided not to lie about their identity. Pretending to speak for a goddess was bad enough. Adding another lie on top of it would not only be immoral; it would be stupid.

Anyone with half a brain could put two and two together once I described them. *They look like me, mispronounce words like me, dress funny like me...*Lying would only cast an unnecessary layer of suspicion over my quest. And as my mother always said, "If you're going to be stupid, at least be smart about it."

"Your parents? They're not back in America?"

"No."

She didn't press me for details. Rubbing her chin, she remarked, "To find someone in a city like Alexandria..."

"I know. It's a needle in a haystack."

"What?"

"That is, it will be extremely difficult."

There was a long pause before Mentit responded. "I know

someone who may be able to help, but he's wary of strangers."

"Ah. Not the most reputable person, then?"

"Unfortunately, no. You will tell me everything about your parents, and I will see that the message is delivered."

We spoke until the morning levee. By then, Mentit knew their appearance down to the freckle above my mom's right eye.

"And your parents, *Frank* and *Mary*," she pronounced the names slowly, her tongue struggling to wrap itself around the "r's." "The way you describe them, it's hard to believe they haven't been noticed."

"Right? I mean, look at the mess I made, and there's only one of me. Even if they're going by different names, *someone* must have seen them!"

"Maybe," she said. "But I was thinking the opposite."

"What do you mean?"

"Well, there are people who are known, and then there's everyone else," Mentit waved a dismissive hand. "You and I, we are known. Even if the gossips now speak of someone else, everyone knows that a blonde priestess from America is now in the confidence of the queen."

"What are you saying?"

"Your parents — it is impossible that they would fade into obscurity as farmers or craftsmen. Such communities are tight-knit; they are families. And if they are not living in obscurity among the vulgars, they must be known, amid the upper classes. And yet they are not. So where are they?"

Vulgars - A rude way to describe average people; the masses

* * *

MENTIT WAS ADAMANT that I not partake in the back-alley meeting with her mysterious informant. I didn't press her for details about his identity, or how she came to know such a character. Even noble families have their problems, and the loyal men who quietly make those problems disappear.

"He will make the necessary inquiries," Mentit said. "But his price is not inexpensive."

"How much?"

The number made my jaw drop. A rough mental calculation told me it was some $5,000 — far more than I would've possessed even if my backpack hadn't been incinerated.

"If this is a problem..."

"No problem," I assured her, racking my brains. "What about a trade? I don't have much money, but I've been blessed by the gods in other ways. The queen did not take all of my gifts."

"Oh?"

I gestured to my shoes, waving a hand above them like a shopkeeper.

"And, what are we looking at?"

"My shoes! Haven't you noticed how fine the craftsmanship is?"

"I've noticed how dirty they are."

I unzipped the back of one of my gladiators, and from her seat-

---

Adamant - Determined; unwilling to change his/her mind

Partake - Take part in

Incinerated - Destroyed by burning

ed position opposite me, I could see her interest pique.

"How did you do that?"

"The shoes only *appear* to be intricately wrapped, but because of this device, they never lose their position," I lifted the little flap to show her the zipper. "Everything is fixed, before coming together here."

She reached for the shoe, her slender fingers playing with the metal. "I'd never noticed. And it's made of silver! So fine!"

"Mmmm," I agreed. Silver was extremely rare in ancient Egypt, and thus, extremely valuable. "Very fine, indeed," I said. "He could strip the silver from the shoes and turn quite a profit. Or he could polish up the leather, sell the shoes to someone wealthy..."

I could see her brain working. "I will see what he says. But silver-encrusted sandals...I imagine they will fetch a very fine price."

"Take them," I unzipped the back of other shoe and passed it over.

"Yet...it may not be enough."

Mentit eyed my snake ring.

"My ring?"

"Do you wish to find your parents?"

"Of course! It's just..."

The ring was all I had left of Harvey. My photo burned with the library; my phone was locked in a royal vault. I'd done my best not to think of him or Mitzi, since my experience in Connecticut showed me how painful homesickness can be. But to part with the last physical connection...

Pique - Awaken; grow greater

"Are you sure the shoes alone won't do it?"

Mentit hesitated, then said, "Quite sure. The shoes will not cover his fee. The ring, too."

She held out an expectant hand. I looked down, remembering how Harvey bought it for me on my first day back in Egypt when I said snake rings reminded me of Cleopatra. Oh, the irony.

Taking a deep breath, I wriggled it off. Mentit's fist closed and, without a word, she turned and walked out the door.

As her steps faded, I realized I hadn't just handed over my last physical connection to Harvey. I'd surrendered the last of my worldly possessions.

Irony - When the full significance of someone's words are not known to them

HARVEY'S FIELD NOTES

JAN 4:

Living in heart of the news cycle as Middle East gripped by protests. One can barely drive through the streets of Cairo for all the riots.

Start of spring semester temporarily postponed.

JAN 14:

Tunisian president forced to flee the country! Protesters want the same for President Mubarak in Egypt.

Thousands taking to Tahrir Square each night. Lots of tires/ flags being set on fire. One can smell the tear gas, hear the chanting a mile away.

FEBRUARY 2:

Foreign students ordered to evacuate. Escorted Shira and Viviana to their respective embassies, though don't know why. Shira could do a far better job of protecting them than I ever could.

Spring semester *still* hasn't begun. Attempted to get more information from father about when they'll start classes.

He just shrugged and looked nervously out the window.

On the bright side, protests have distracted him from time travel nonsense.

FEBRUARY 11:

My God, they did it! Cannot believe it, but Egyptian President Hosni Mubarak has been ousted after 30 years!

Future remains uncertain. Military effectively in charge now. Not sure if that's an improvement over Mubarak, but we'll see.

FEBRUARY 14:

Still no classes. Dorms feel empty, though I don't mind having a double room to myself.

Had the oddest conversation with Mitzi today. Had given up calling, but she phoned me. Asked if I'd noticed anything unusual lately.

Besides the government being overthrown, of course.

Not a clue what she was going on about.

FEBRUARY 27:

Jesus. Pen shaking so badly I can barely write.

Noor isn't in Connecticut. Never has been.

Mitzi told me she wanted to give Noor time to explore the

Respective - Belonging to separate people

Ousted - Driven out; removed

TIME TRAVEL theorem (has everyone but me lost their bloody minds?), but got worried that she hasn't come back by now.

I already contacted the American and British embassies. They warned me of the "difficulties" in finding someone who's been gone so long. Criminals and extremists take advantage of the power vacuum, they said. Large spike in kidnappings recently.

Noor has been missing THREE MONTHS in a country gripped by revolution, and no one has even been looking for her.

And I was mad at her for not answering her phone.

Feel ill.

CHAPTER THIRTEEN

THOUGH MENTIT'S INFORMANT accepted my shoes and ring immediately, he took his sweet time providing any information.

Every time I tried to follow up, Mentit brushed me off with a comment like, "Don't worry! These things take time."

Then she'd change the subject or go back to brushing her hair while I nursed my aching feet. The palace-provided sandals gave me so many blisters, I'd have rather gone barefoot.

By the Ides of March, I was a bag of nerves. Marcus had chosen that day to stop by, unaware that Caesar was being brutally assassinated in Rome. In desperate need of something to lift my spirits, I suggested we take a stroll through the palace gardens.

To my surprise, it worked, to an extent. Countless perennials bloomed in delicate shades of pink, purple, and white, winding around pathways, benches, and the columns marking the entrance

---

Perennials - Remaining active all year

to the palace. The sea provided a stunning backdrop, its breeze catching the gentle scent of the flowers. Even Marcus was moved.

"There's nothing like this in Rome," he said. "To think, I might actually miss Egypt when Caesar calls us back."

I turned to him. "Are you leaving?"

"No. Just, eventually."

We walked in silence for a few minutes — a rarity, for the two of us — before I decided it was time to widen my net. Mentit's informant wasn't getting the results I was after.

I'd have to be more tactful with Marcus, though. As a Roman, he didn't hold the same reverence for Isis as the Egyptians. He called me "priestess," but it always felt somewhat tongue-in-cheek, like he was amused by the title.

No, the old "Isis gave me a message" line wouldn't work this time. I decided to approach the subject laterally, like a sailor traveling into the wind.

We sat on one of the benches facing the sea, and I remarked, "So, Marcus, tell me more about your family. What are your parents like?"

He raised a brow, but I just waited with a patient smile for him to answer.

"Well, my parents are...my parents. My dad's a senator, but you probably already knew that."

"Why would I know that?"

"Most girls do," he grinned.

Reverence - Deep respect

Laterally - Sideways

"Easy, Casanova. Are you guys close?"

He shrugged, no longer surprised by my strange phrases. "My parents have high expectations for me. I'm their only son."

I puzzled this response for a moment before he returned the question to me, as I hoped he would.

"My parents and I are very close. Or, *were* close, I should say."

"What do you mean?"

"My parents disappeared almost two years ago. They came to Alexandria and haven't been seen since."

When you say things like that in modern times, people go all red and flustery. Marcus held my gaze and said a soulful, "I'm sorry, truly."

"I'm looking for them," I continued. "I think they might be here, somewhere."

That's when my brilliant plan fell apart.

I'd counted on Marcus' skepticism. It's why I decided not to play the "priestess of Isis" card once more — I didn't want to push the bounds of his credibility.

But as clearly as if I were inside his skull, I saw something terrible click.

"That's why you're here!" he bellowed. "Not this priestess of Isis, here-to-save-the-library story."

I grabbed him by the armor and yanked him behind a tree. "Are you trying to get me killed?" I hissed. "No. I am! I was! Trying to save the library, that is. But I think my parents were on the same trail, and something happened to them."

Marcus looked sheepish, or as sheepish as a Roman warrior in full battle armor can. "Sorry. I'd hate to be the reason you were executed. I've grown rather fond of you, you know."

"Believe me, I'd be equally displeased. But I've hit a wall in looking for them, and was hoping you might be able to help."

Marcus didn't say anything for a moment. "Your parents," he began. "They'd be...eccentric...like you? Look like you?"

"Certainly. My mom especially."

His brow furrowed as he stared into the horizon. "There was someone, I don't know how long ago, who looked like you," he said finally. "Natural blondes are rare here, or she wouldn't be so well-remembered. She..."

Marcus squinted as he tried to remember the details. "Ah, that was it! She was with someone, and their clothes — brightly colored and *utterly* barbaric. She was wearing pants, *pants*! And they were cut off above the knee!"

I resisted the urge to laugh. The Romans hated pants (in the American sense of the word, not the British). Northerners wore them, and therefore they were inherently uncivilized. Skirts, dresses, togas — a person of character wouldn't be caught dead in anything else.

To see a woman wearing garishly-colored pants, *and* to have them be short...the *scandal*! I couldn't remember what my mom was wearing the night of her disappearance, but most of her pajamas had floral patterns or something similar. Definitely unique enough to stand out.

"That must be them!" I exclaimed. "What happened to them?

Eccentric - Unconventional; slightly strange

Inherently - Permanently; in an essential way

Garishly - Excessively bright and showy

Where are they now?"

Marcus cocked his head to the side. "I don't know all the details, but the story is that they were arrested. Vandalism."

"*Arrested?* Have they been freed?"

"Not that I'm aware of, but I hardly keep track of every prisoner in Egypt."

"Well, when did you meet them? *How* did you meet them?"

"I didn't," Marcus said. "This all happened before Caesar came to Egypt. When you arrived, talk of them resurfaced. I just happened to hear the story."

"*What?* People have been talking about this?"

"Not much, but those who have met you drew connections between your accents, your appearance."

I clenched my jaw. Either Mentit's informant was incompetent, or he was a crook. I vowed to get my hands on his throat at the earliest opportunity, but there were more pressing matters to deal with at the moment.

"But surely they can be located," I said. "You could put in a call, a request?"

"Why should I do that?"

"With Caesar in Rome, you're the ranking officer left behind. You speak for Rome. No one would say no!"

"You've explained why I *could* find them, not why I should."

Marcus leaned back on the bench, stretching out his arms out to either side. The movement sent muscles rippling.

I scooted forward, out of their tempting grasp, though the

Incompetent - Unskilled; unqualified

same inexorable draw I'd felt that night with Harvey seemed to be pulling me in.

"You'll do it because you'd have my eternal gratitude," I stood, primly wiping the dust off my dress.

Marcus chuckled, withdrawing his arms. "For that, I'd give you the sun and stars."

* * *

I COULDN'T WAIT for the next time Mentit wandered into my room, pretending to offer help, but I didn't know where her rooms were.

I was slightly ashamed at the realization. How long had I known the girl, yet I hadn't even had the decency to make sure she had a clean place to sleep?

A few inquiries on the way back from the gardens gave me the answer. Her rooms were near mine, to my relief, which implied they were of similar quality.

I knocked on the tall, wooden door. When no one answered, I opened it slightly.

"Mentit?" I called. "I'm sorry to interrupt, but it's quite urgent."

Her quarters were smaller than mine, more like a dorm room than a hotel suite. It was one room, rather than several, with a bed in the left corner, a window at the back wall, and an armoire to the side. Yet everything was clean and of the highest quality, the

---

Inexorable - Unable to stop or escape

view impeccable.

A quick glance left no doubt the room was unoccupied. I took a moment to admire how organized she was — her shoes were neatly lined up to the side of her dresser, her jewelry above — when my breath caught.

MY shoes were neatly lined up among them.

I charged inside and made a beeline for the gladiators. Picking them up, I took a closer look. There was no doubt they were mine.

Suspicion sent my eye to the jewelry above. Sure enough, my snake ring was nestled among the rest, easy to distinguish because of its size.

Rage pulsed through me, the kind I hadn't experienced since my 17th birthday. Mentit's actions weren't quite as wicked as Caitlyn's, but how *dare* she?

Not only had she robbed me, but I could've been reunited with my parents a month sooner if not for her! Here I was twiddling my thumbs, waiting for her mysterious "informant" to track down my parents, when the connection between us was common knowledge!

The thought made me sick. I sat on her bed, my belongings next to me, waiting for her to return. She took a good twenty minutes. By that time I was in such a state of rage, I could've strangled a rhinoceros.

"Noor! What a surprise..." Mentit opened the door, her eyes falling to the items at my side.

Impeccable - Perfect; faultless

"Care to explain this?" I asked.

"I, um, well—"

"You, um, well what?"

She looked around, making sure no one was around, before stepping inside and closing the door. "I *did* meet with our family's...fixer."

"And?"

"And he told me the price, and I told you! But once you gave me the shoes and the ring—"

"You decided to keep them for yourself?"

"He was never going to find your parents!" she protested. "In a city like Alexandria, it's an impossible task. If no one has seen them by now—"

"First of all, that wasn't your call to make. Second of all, I found them! Today! After one day of asking! And I could've been with them a month ago if you hadn't been making me wait!"

Her cheeks turned a mottled pink, defiance rising in her voice. "What's the problem then? You found your parents. Take your perfect gifts and your perfect soldier and your perfect parents and leave!"

"So that's what this is about? You're jealous?"

"I am *not* jealous."

"Whatever." I grabbed my belongings and pushed past her. "You're a catty, stupid girl, and I hope Ammit eats your heart."

A prominent (if puzzling-looking) figure in ancient Egyptian

Mottled - Blotchy

Defiance - Open resistance; stubbornness

mythology, Ammit had the face of a crocodile, the torso of a lion, and the hindquarters of a hippo. He dwelled in the underworld, devouring the souls of the wicked.

It wasn't the nicest comment to leave her with, but at that point, I didn't much care.

Hindquarters - Back legs
Dwelled - Lived

HARVEY'S FIELD NOTES

MARCH 3:

Nearly got Mitzi arrested this morning. She booked the first flight out of CT, but due to layovers/time change, only just arrived.

A sandy-haired Interpol agent was taking our statements at the American embassy, and (understandably) asked why no one noticed Noor's absence before now.

"We thought she was in Connecticut, with Mitzi," I explained.

"Oh?" his thick eyebrows raised. "Why did you think that?"

"Because she told me..."

Seeing Mitzi's panicked expression, I hastily reworded the back half of the sentence. "That is, *Noor* told me that she loved Connecticut. We figured if she wasn't here, she'd gone to spend

---

Interpol - International police; a force made up of law enforcement from different countries to tackle crimes with an international dimension

Hastily - Quickly

time with family."

I was rather proud of my quick thinking. It released Mitzi from her lie, but didn't make any claims about Noor's true plans.

But the Interpol agent didn't miss the panicked look Mitzi shot me, or the relief on her face when my sentence concluded.

He leaned back in the metal chair, blue windbreaker crinkling, and folded his hands across his paunch. "And yet, it still feels like I'm missing something."

Mitzi's gaze fell, and I intervened. "Mr. Smith, if we could return..."

But he'd conducted enough of these interviews — interrogations? — to know guilt when he saw it. In fact, I was willing to bet he was the top missing persons locator the agency had.

Having cute blonde girls abducted would be a nightmare for Egypt's tourism industry, and neither America nor England wanted to deal with hostage negotiations while trying to find their footing with a new government. No, it would be in everyone's best interests for Noor to be recovered quickly and quietly.

The agent zeroed in on Mitzi. "You know the consequences of lying to an Interpol agent, don't you, Ms. Forth?"

Mitzi's nails clenched the straps of her designer handbag, but she raised her gaze to meet his. "I would never do such a thing. I've lost far too much not to cooperate."

"Yes," he leaned forward, flipping through the papers on his clipboard. "This is the third member of your immediate family to go missing in as many years. Is that correct?"

Intervened - Interrupted; came between people to change something

"It is."

"And you see how that strikes me as suspicious, from the outside looking in?"

Mitzi's jaw dropped.

I stood up. "Alright, that's enough."

But Mr. Smith continued, his eyes never leaving Mitzi's face. "I wonder how many years they'd give you, an accessory to three different kidnappings...Or was it murders? Either way, I doubt you'd live to see the end of your sentence."

I yanked Mitzi to her feet. "We're leaving. Now."

"How much did you collect off Frank and Mary's life insurance?" he called after us, eyeing the "Prada" label on Mitzi's bag.

I shook my head in disgust, and he left us with a cool, "I'll be in touch."

CHAPTER FOURTEEN

MENTIT DIDN'T SHOW UP for "work" the next day, or the day after that. After a week had passed, it was safe to assume she wasn't coming back.

I hadn't said anything bad to whomever managed the slaves, or ladies-in-waiting, or whatever she was. First of all, I didn't know whom she reported to. Second of all, I wasn't trying to get her in trouble. I just wanted her to know how wrong she was to rob me, lie to me, and string me along about my parents' disappearance.

Phrased like that, I thought, maybe she deserved a bit of trouble.

I didn't see her at Cleopatra's daily levee, an event I now attended in body only, or any of our other regularly-scheduled events. I briefly wondered whether she was still at court, and how she was explaining her unusual whereabouts, but soon decided I didn't care.

A lot of that was because Marcus had sent a message. He had

news to share, and wanted to meet me in the hypostyle hall that evening.

This is it! I thought. *What would it be like to see them again? Would they look different? Two years might not age a person under normal circumstances, but two years in an Egyptian prison...*

A tiny voice in my head struggled to make itself heard, but I refused to listen. A spring in my step, I went down to the magnificent gallery to meet Marcus.

Massive columns supported the roof above, casting long shadows out to sea. It should have felt cold and forbidding, but with dusk settling in, fires burned bright in elevated braziers. Dancing flames brought the carvings to life.

The slap of sandals told me Marcus was coming. "It wasn't easy to acquire this information, priestess," he said. "I had to make many inquiries, follow many trails..."

"Yes, yes, and I am eternally grateful."

"You'll be more than grateful when you hear what I found out."

"Which is?"

"I found out where they are."

My breath came out in a wave of relief. The small voice in my head kept trying to remind me that, in ancient times, people were rarely left to languish in prison. But my parents? Executed? I refused to consider the thought.

But Marcus spoke in the present tense. They were alive! And I was going to see them!

Hypostyle - A building with a roof supported by large pillars

Brazier - A portable heater with a pan or stand for holding lighted coals

Acquire - Get; obtain

"You are amazing," I put a hand on his arm. "Where are they? When can I see them?"

"As soon as you come with me to Italy," he responded.

I stopped in front of one of the columns. "What are you talking about?"

Marcus smiled and stretched out an arm against the column behind me. His face was so close I could smell him. Earth and olive oil, I thought, mixed with a hearty dash of something more primitive I couldn't help but appreciate.

His breathing was coming a little faster than normal too, I was pleased to see.

"My parents have been trying to arrange a wedding for years now, but having met you...You're beautiful and ridiculous and I've never met a girl like you. When I learned your parents were in Rome, I knew it was a sign. Come with me when I go back."

"A wedding?" I squeaked. "You mean you want me to—"

"Marry me, Noor. Our wedding will be the finest in Rome. You will want for nothing."

"Oh! I, ah—" I stammered incoherently. "I really *do* like you, Marcus..."

Two declarations of love in one year. I really needed to learn how to respond to these. More importantly, I needed to figure out how I *felt* about these.

Apparently, some clichés are timeless. Marcus saw right through mine.

Incoherently - Spoken in a confusing or unclear way
Cliches - An unoriginal phrase or idea

"You really *like* me," he said. "I take it 'really liking' someone isn't enough to win your hand?"

"Well, it's just that I'm so young…"

"You're not *that* young. Most girls your age would have been plucked summers ago."

"Right," I nodded, forgetting how much younger people married in ancient times. "But I really must find my parents first. Have them attend the wedding and all that."

I couldn't put him off entirely. He was my greatest ally, and besides, I really *did* like him. If I stayed here long enough, who knew what the future might hold?

Marcus nodded and narrowed his eyes like I was an elusive bird of prey. "Sounds like I'll have to redouble my efforts, then."

He started to lean in for a kiss, but I neatly ducked out from under his arm. "You can start by telling me everything you found out."

IT WASN'T A LONG STORY. They escaped from prison sometime last year, and a couple matching their description was seen boarding a ship to Civitavecchia, the port nearest to Rome.

"By the time the authorities put it together," Marcus concluded, "they were too far ahead for us to catch."

"Escaped? Go team! That's definitely my parents."

"If prison stints are hereditary, I may have to reconsider my proposal."

Redouble - Double down on; make greater or more intense
Hereditary - In the genes; passed from parents to children

I swatted him in the arm, trying to distract him from my dubious origins. "Do you know where they went next?"

"Not a clue. But if I were them, I'd stay in Italy. Civitavecchia is near enough to Rome. No one is looking for them there, and there are plenty of opportunities for a clever man to reinvent himself."

I didn't say anything for a moment. I was making progress, yes, but it felt like one step forward, two steps back. I thought I'd be able to see them within days, just pop down to the local prison and arrange their release.

My hopes had been terribly simplistic, but finding them in a city like Rome would be as hard as finding them in Alexandria. I'd be starting over, and I still had to get to Rome before the search could commence.

As though he could sense my mood, Marcus remarked. "I thought you'd be happy! If your parents are anything like you, they'll do well for themselves in Rome. They'll stay away from this vandalism business. Won't make the same mistake twice, them."

I sniffed. "You're right, but that's not the point. I...I *miss* them."

Marcus took my hand, and when I didn't resist, brought my head to his chest. "They must've been good parents for you to miss them so."

"They were." My tears were leaving marks in the leather of his breastplate. I rubbed my eyes and pulled away.

"Marcus, even if I did go with you to Italy, you were just saying

---

Dubious - Suspicious; unable to be relied upon

Commence - Begin

196

Caesar hasn't made any plans to call you back."

"My duties here can be assumed by another tribune," Marcus waved the matter away. "The war is won, my time is served. I do little except act as an official representative of Rome. Any Roman with sense can fill the role."

I smiled. "Your presence would certainly make the journey easier."

"No sea voyage is luxurious, but I'll keep an eye on you. I can promise you that."

But our trip wasn't meant to be, for amid preparations for the voyage, news of Caesar's death reached the palace.

Surrounded by a horde of murderous senators, he was stabbed 23 times.

* * *

CLEOPATRA'S WAILS could be heard a mile away. She screamed, threw vases at slaves, and rubbed her eyes until mascara reached her lips. When her slaves tried to remove the makeup mustache, she swatted them away.

"Majesty, the baby..." Iras cautioned.

By now, I knew Iras by name. She was Cleopatra's head slave (or whatever the terminology was) — the one who spoke for the queen at court, or whenever a response from the royal lips wasn't suitable.

The two could have passed for sisters, except for their wildly

---

Terminology - The terms used in a specific field

different wardrobes and Iras' more sensible demeanor.

With great shame, I'll admit I had a difficult time remembering some of the other slaves' names. They hailed from across the known world, from Europe to Africa, but often stared straight ahead or down at their feet, making it difficult to distinguish their personalities.

Iras was different, though. She spoke for the queen, and carried herself as such.

At the mention of the baby, Cleopatra just clutched her stomach and cried harder.

She'd invited everyone of rank to the throne room, perhaps hoping we could distract her. But no one approached her with anything but condolences. For the most part, people kept their distance.

"She's hysterical," Marcus said in tones of deep disapproval. We were towards the back of the throne room, sitting on floor cushions before a low table. He spoke quietly, but I still gave him a wide-eyed, "watch what you say" look.

"Her husband was just foully assassinated — and by fellow Romans, no less!" I whispered. "Wouldn't you be a little upset?"

"I *am* upset, but vengeance is the only fitting response. How can she lead like this? This is precisely why women cannot be elected consul in Rome."

"Yes, and Rome's affairs are swimming smoothly, aren't they?"

Demeanor - Behavior; personality

Vengeance - Revenge

I retorted in saccharine tones. "Tell me, who's in charge of your government at the moment?"

Marcus scowled, relapsing into a moody silence.

I glanced up just as a messenger arrived for the queen. He carried in the scroll on a tray, like it was a gourmet meal, bowing as Iras took it. Iras broke the seal and scanned the document, then murmured something to Cleopatra.

Immediately, the queen's gaze cleared.

I stood up, circumventing dancers and loungers in an attempt to edge closer to the platform.

"Battle...Antony and Octavian are certain to succeed..." Iras murmured.

"But this is joyous news!" Cleopatra hiccupped, then continued, "I hope they feed Brutus to wild dogs. What can we do?"

"They are already in pursuit, Your Majesty. They will have left many weeks ago, and by the time we can gather an army..."

"Who knows where they'll be," Cleopatra finished. "Then we must make an offering to the gods."

She gathered her dress and floated away, Iras close on her heels, not saying a word of goodbye to the crowd she'd summoned.

Retorted - Said sharply/wittily in response

Saccharine - Excessively sweet or sentimental

Relapsing - Falling back into

Circumventing - Finding a way around

CHAPTER FIFTEEN

CAESAR'S MURDERERS raised an impressive army, but were vanquished at the Battle of Philippi. Predictably, however, the victors soon began to squabble among themselves.

Marc Antony, Caesar's top general, believed he was Caesar's logical successor.

Octavian, Caesar's nephew and heir, believed the privilege should be his.

Without a common enemy to unite them, the two quickly began scheming against one another, foreshadowing the war to come.

By some miracle of common sense, they agreed it would be better if they divided Rome's territories into spheres of influence and lived far, far apart. Antony got Egypt and most of the modern Middle East. Octavian got Rome (the capital, not the whole em-

---

Vanquished - Thoroughly defeated

Foreshadowing - Hinting at a future event

pire) and most of Europe.

A third general, Lepidus, got the rest of Roman-occupied Africa. He was only really included so they could call themselves "The Second Triumvirate," though, in honor of a three-person alliance Caesar once had.

In their haste to compare themselves to Caesar, they obviously forgot that The First Triumvirate ended in disaster. One of the men died, and the remaining two went to war.

Or maybe they didn't forget? After all, their "alliance" would end the same way.

Antony was due in Egypt any minute, and Cleopatra had planned a luxurious trip to the pyramids for when he arrived. The entire court would accompany her in the lap of luxury — an *embarrass des richesses*, so to speak, to show Antony how valuable Egypt was.

I, personally, had reservations about whether a man who's been on a boat for a month would fancy another trip so soon, but didn't deem it wise to point this out.

Everyone of importance — Egyptian and Roman — had gathered in Cleopatra's throne room for Antony's arrival. I'd barely seen Marcus since Caesar's death, and looked forward to the prospect of his company.

I understood his absence, of course, and wanted him to succeed in avenging Caesar, but felt slightly whiplashed at going straight from a proposal to a period of prolonged absence.

Embarrass des richesses - An overabundance of riches; literally translates to "an embarrassment of riches"

Deem - Decide; consider something a certain way

I couldn't help but wonder if Harvey felt the same way. He hadn't proposed, of course, but he'd professed something…love? Had he actually said "love"? It was certainly implied.

Harvey had it worse, even if he hadn't proposed. I knew where Marcus was. To Harvey…where was I?

In Marcus' absence, I'd been forced to diversify my acquaintances at court. My favorite new companion was a pleasant little man called Neby. He was related to Cleopatra by some convoluted extension of the family tree, but so far removed, and so utterly guileless, that he wasn't the slightest threat to her authority.

Waiting for Antony's ship to dock, he and I were standing to the side of the throne room.

"But the pyramids are Egypt's masterpiece!" Neby exclaimed in horror when I claimed I'd never been.

This wasn't true, of course, but how could I explain having visited them? Neby waved a hand before him, like the imposing landmarks were in front of us. "They are the oldest and the tallest structures in the world. Their age puts anything in Rome to shame."

I looked across the room at the Roman cohort, secretly pleased to so easily make eye contact with Marcus. He finished giving instructions to his men, then came over to join me.

Neby, unaware of the energy between us, just kept talking.

Diversify - Make more diverse or varied
Convoluted - Complex and difficult to follow
Guileless - Sincere; honest; without deception
Imposing - Grand and impressive

"You know, Egypt was already an ancient civilization when little Romulus founded Rome all those years ago."

Marcus gave him a good-natured grin. "'Little Romulus'? 'All those years ago'? I believe '722 years ago' is the phrase you're looking for."

Neby hardly came up to Marcus' chin, but he still managed to look down at him. "You Romans and your *obsession* with time. Why not make it easier on yourselves and start over at zero with each new ruler, like we do?"

"Because then we wouldn't know how many years have passed since our own founding. Do you?"

"Ha," Neby responded. "Of course I do. I can have the number in just a few hours, if you provide me the king's lists and the use of a good mathematics slave."

Marcus barely had time for a quick, "Are you well, priestess?" before Iras clapped, warning that Antony was approaching the palace. The soldiers, both Egyptian and Roman, went to stand at attention. The rest of us were supposed to go on with our business — playing games, chatting, what-have-you — like extras in a TV show.

I wasn't sure how Cleopatra rationalized her behavior, but gave her credit for being a more shrewd tactician than I. Her actions towards Antony were a baffling mixture of flattery — like arranging a luxury voyage to the pyramids in his honor — and apathy, like ordering her courtiers to ignore his arrival.

Shrewd - Clever; resourceful; astute

Tactician - A person who carefully plans a strategy to reach a specific end

Apathy - Lack of interest; not caring

Neby and I continued talking about the pyramids, but naturally, the conversation veered when Antony entered.

"What's he like?" I whispered in the low, gossipy voice I'd learned in Connecticut. Neby loved it when I talked like that.

"He was in Egypt before, you know, with Caesar," Neby replied, a mischievous glint in his eye. "All the rumors are true."

"What rumors?"

"The drinking, the gambling, the women...a thoroughbred soldier if I've ever seen one."

I tried to look shocked, though Antony's reputation had been faithfully passed down through history. He might have been Caesar's top general, but their personalities were nothing alike. Caesar was controlled and abstemious. Antony worked hard and played hard.

It was probably why Caesar had broken with tradition, naming his nephew Octavian his successor, rather than Antony, I thought.

I craned my neck to get a better look. Antony was younger than Caesar, closer to Cleopatra's age, and in fantastic shape (like every Roman soldier — I wondered when that would stop surprising me).

He had thick, dark hair, and the sort of smoldering look that made women blush. It was like you could tell his thoughts were indecent.

"Cleopatra Philopator, Queen of Upper and Lower Egypt," Antony inclined his head gracefully. "It is good to see you again."

Veered - Changed directions

Thoroughbred - Pure; complete; embodying the essence fully

Abstemious - Restrained; disciplined; not indulgent

"Have we met?" she politely looked down at him from her throne.

"Indeed," Antony responded. "I was here with Caesar."

I knew immediately that — unlike when Marcus genuinely forgot meeting Mentit — Cleopatra was playing a game of chess.

She was wearing more gold than ever, yet she looked at Antony with nothing more than polite curiosity. And though she'd given birth to Caesarion just months before, shortly after Caesar died, she'd worked with celebrity-like diligence to regain her figure before Antony arrived.

At the mention of her late husband, the queen's royal gaze softened. "In any case, you will find that Egypt welcomes you with open arms."

The two continued to exchange pleasantries, then Cleopatra shared her plan to show Antony the pyramids. "We'll set sail tomorrow. You will join me on the royal barge, of course."

I thought Antony turned a little green, but he manfully suppressed his queasiness. "It would be my pleasure, Highness. If we are to leave so soon, there are a number of things I must attend to. You'll forgive me if I excuse myself, and dine tonight with my men?"

"Of course," she said. "We'll meet in the morning."

Diligence - Determination; persistence

Barge - A large ornamental boat used for pleasure or ceremony

HARVEY'S FIELD NOTES

March 15:

Cavalry arrived today, thank God. After Mitzi's run-in with the law, her high-powered NY attorney wanted to be close at hand in case of unexpected developments. Unfortunately, nighttime arrests and "missing" detainees are far too common in Egypt.

Mitzi refuses to leave though, so the attorney did what she could to shield her. Got Interpol's overzealous Mr. Smith reassigned (something about "elder abuse"?), and authorities seem to have returned to the "kidnapped by terrorists" theory.

Shira and Viviana also came, opting to spend their spring breaks in Cairo to help with the search. Surprisingly, the British embassy has allowed me to help wade through anonymous tips — only after they've already been vetted and discarded by officials, of course.

Was initially surprised that they allowed me to help, but after

---

Detainees - People being held somewhere, especially for political reasons
Overzealous - Too eager or enthusiastic
Elder - A person of greater age
Wade - Walk through; get involved in

reading some of the "tips," I understood why.

Some nutter in New York believed Noor was abducted by aliens. In Washington, a girl swore she was torn to shreds by a werewolf during the last full moon. Honestly, some of the transcripts make dad's time travel ramblings sound positively sane.

Still had to sign about 1,000 non-disclosure agreements, though, and can't take anything out of the embassy. Shira's IDF credentials enabled her to join me, while Viviana flounced around getting everyone coffee and baklava.

She has a new boyfriend back in Italy, and really isn't that bad when her fake nails are dug into someone else...

[...]

Ramblings - Speaking in a lengthy and confused way

CHAPTER SIXTEEN

OUR VOYAGE TO THE PYRAMIDS began at dawn, since we had
to be ready to depart the moment Cleopatra's dainty feet chose to
board. It was unthinkable that she might have to wait while the
slaves finished loading the food, or the courtiers sorted themselves into their respective rooms.

Everyone of importance, Egyptian or Roman, had been invited
— ordered? — to join the tour. We made up a nine-barge
flotilla, each ship more opulent than the last.

As far as I could tell, Cleopatra wanted to show Antony that
she was firmly in control of Egypt, its treasury thriving under her
rule. He may hold a higher rank internationally, since Egypt was a

---

Flotilla - A fleet of ships
Opulent - Ostentatiously rich or lavish
Thriving - Flourishing; doing very well

vassal to Rome, but it would be unwise to tamper with her power.

Neby, who had made the voyage before, assured me that we would spend all our time admiring the view from the top deck, so it didn't matter which ship we chose. Nevertheless, I insisted on a tour before committing.

While I admired the crisply-polished wood and clean white sails, ogling artwork and hand-carved furniture, Neby scrutinized the passengers who had already settled in.

"Ugh, that's Ramose," he said, producing a fake smile and politely waving at a man some distance away. "He's the worst. Just keep walking!"

I laughed. "Moving on, then."

We eventually settled on ship number four. By then, I was willing to accept that they were all basically the same — except for Cleopatra's, of course. And while they were all docked side-by-side in one of the Nile inlets, my bag was starting to feel a little heavy from all the walking.

Telling his slave to deposit his luggage in a nearby room, Neby eyed my palace-provided linen carryall.

"Is it custom in America, to carry your own bags?"

"It is," I improvised. "But only before a sea voyage. It's — it's good luck."

Vassal - A person or country in a subordinate position to another

Tamper - Mess with; interfere with

Ogling - Stare at admiringly or covetously

Scrutinized - Closely examined; inspected

Inlet - A small part of a body of water

Mentit had taken care to avoid me in the months since our confrontation, and I hadn't gone out of my way to look for her. It didn't sit right with me to request a new slave, and most days, it simply wasn't an issue. I was quite capable of brushing my own hair and putting on my own clothes.

"What an unusual place, this *America*," Neby marveled.

I selected the room next to Neby's, though the word "room" might have been an overstatement. Roughly the size of my prison cell, the only furniture was a cot-sized bed and a small chair, both discreetly bolted to the floor. However, the room was clean and crisp, with linens of the highest quality.

Neby was right. It would be a waste of time to spend the voyage there. I made my way to the upper deck, where I knew he must be, and found him stretched out in contentment, feet resting on a footstool and eyes facing the sky.

"Nothing as peaceful as a Nile voyage," he sighed, taking a sip of his drink. I couldn't help but imagine that if he lived 2,000 years later, he'd be lathering on tanning oil and wearing $500 sunglasses.

Fetching a waiter, he ordered me the same drink — something unpronounceable but clearly pomegranate-flavored — and we rested under the gentle morning sun until the rest of the court was settled.

The trip would take around two days each way. I'd driven from Alexandria to Giza in just over two hours, but obviously that feat was impossible in ancient times.

Discreetly - In a not-obvious way; unobtrusively

Ironically, the journey we were about to attempt was impossible in the modern era, since the Aswan Dam prevents the river from rising enough to make the passage sailable. We were crossing through the Nile Delta, a glorified swamp most of the year, but every so often the annual floods produced a stunning, sailable landscape, with little islands peeking up from the waters and long-legged birds dotting the scenery.

When the sun rose too high to be comfortable, a pleasant shade was erected and food appeared on the tables before us. It was mostly finger-food — bread, oil, olives, and the like. We were no longer alone, but there was enough space to prevent us from feeling crowded.

It wasn't much longer before an assortment of Romans — a dozen or so in total, including Antony — approached. I knew Antony would sail aboard the royal barge, but assumed the rest of the Romans would stick together on a boat of their own.

When they began to disperse, I watched with moderate interest to see which ship Marcus would select. He appeared to be looking for something, and when he saw me sitting on the upper deck, made his way in our direction.

"Cold!" Neby shrieked.

"What?"

"You've just spilled your drink on me, woman. Or hadn't you noticed?"

"Oh! Sorry. Here, take this…"

Annual - Yearly

Disperse - Go out in different directions

"No matter, no matter," Neby blotted the wet patch on his bare leg with a humph, then returned to landscape-gazing.

By the time Marcus had chosen a room and arrived on the upper deck, Neby and I were once again composed. "Our paths do seem to keep crossing," I said. "Fancy a drink?"

"I'd love one." He sat on the reclining chair next to me, and I couldn't help but notice it was the first time I'd seen him out of uniform.

He was dressed for the trip in a loose *chiton*, a sort of dress that belts at the waist, and leather sandals that wound up his calves. He sighed and said, "I'll give you one thing. You Egyptians travel in style."

"Thank you," Neby said from my other side, as though he'd orchestrated every detail.

Conversation halted as Cleopatra arrived, resting in a gilded litter supported by eight slaves. The moment she was comfortably relocated, captains began to loosen the ropes and our ships fell into the gentle current.

Marcus' hands, which had been gripping the armrests of his chair since we set sail, slowly relaxed. "If this is the pace, the men will be bloody relieved. Far better than the sea, this."

Neby scoffed. "Romans and ships...Trust me, old boy, there's more to the water than those ramshackle row boats you call a navy. You'll never experience a journey more pleasant than one atop the Nile."

Marcus raised his brows in amusement. "'Ramshackle row

Scoffed - Made a scornful noise

boats,' you say?"

But since there was no denying the beauty of the sight before us, Marcus couldn't really rebut the back half of Neby's statement.

Instead, the three of us fell into a companionable silence as we plunged deeper into the Nile Delta, the landscape growing increasingly fertile as we moved further from the Mediterranean.

After a few hours of pleasant drinks, food, and small talk, I was jolted out of my reverie.

"Yeesh!" I said. "Those are crocodiles, aren't they?"

Neby looked in the direction of my outstretched finger, then recoiled, "At least a dozen, it looks like. Gods, I've never seen so many this close."

"Fascinating," Marcus followed our gaze. "We don't have crocodiles in Rome. Monstrous-looking creatures, aren't they? If we run aground here, I can't imagine all the slaves will make it back."

I couldn't tell if he meant that in a callous way, or a "let's hope that doesn't happen" way, so I chose to give him the benefit of the doubt.

I stood, edging closer to the railing to get a better look. The crocodiles were enormous, twice the size of a grown man, their muddy bodies blending in with the marshy water below. Even with their mouths closed, jagged teeth protruded from their overbites.

A cute little gull was hopping around the rocks in the middle

---

Rebut - Refute; make a comeback against

Fertile - Lush; green; growing abundant crops

Callous - Insensitive; showing a cruel disregard for others

Protruded - Stuck out

of their feeding ground. The poor creature had absolutely no survival instincts. It was still energetically flapping its wings, blissfully unaware of its impending demise when a crocodile lurched from the water, mouth open. I averted my eyes as three other crocodiles closed in, jaws snapping over the scraps.

Marcus let out a low whistle and clapped. I gave him a severe look.

"Are you cheering for the *crocodile?*"

"It was a spectacular performance," Marcus insisted. "The crocodile laid in wait, letting the bird believe it was part of the scenery until the time was right. Then it struck with speed and utter ruthlessness."

"Those are traits you value, then? Deception, speed, and ruthlessness?"

"Of course not. But there are times — in war, for instance — when deception is necessary. To a crocodile, life is war."

His premise was technically correct. I couldn't blame an animal for eating. But his anthropomorphic view of the situation — assigning wicked human traits to the villainous creatures, then cheering for them — displeased me.

"I think I'll go freshen up," I said abruptly. Despite the sunshade, my nose was starting to burn; I wanted to get out of the sun anyway.

"As you wish, priestess," Marcus grinned.

Demise - Death

Premise - Point; a statement that forms the basis of a theory

Anthropomorphic - Assigning human characteristics to something not human

214

***

BY THE TIME I re-emerged several hours later, after a thoroughly restorative nap, the upper deck had been transformed.

Tables lit by the fading light of Ra boasted heavy platters of food. The main course was freshly-caught fish, which made sense, considering there wasn't a refrigeration unit aboard. Other, less perishable products had clearly been brought from the palace — nuts, oils, breads.

The waves were gentle, but still, I wondered how nothing was sliding around on the tables.

I dropped a hand to the heavy tablecloth, expecting something sticky, but it was wet — just wet, with water. The extra weight and friction must help prevent the items from moving!

How clever, I thought with admiration, while also reminding myself not to eat anything that fell on the tablecloth. Even ancient Nile water — unpolluted by modern factories and chemicals — carried a host of parasites potent enough to leave me bedridden for weeks.

A miniature band had assembled at the front of the ship, playing everything from flutes and harps to the sistrum to provide a peaceful, yet festive, ambiance. Torches danced with their reflections in the water, and many humans were doing the same.

Someone was pouring drinks by the back railing. I joined the line, and was making the requisite small talk with another of

---

Restorative - Restoring strength and well-being

Potent - Powerful

Requisite - Required; necessary

Cleopatra's cousins when a familiar voice said, "You aren't still angry about my little crocodile comment, are you? I take it all back."

"Marcus," I nodded in his direction.

Cleopatra's cousin, an older woman with an eye for the formalities, interrupted in an admonishing tone. "*Tribune* Camillus, I have a daughter I'd like to—"

"And I would be *delighted* to meet her," Marcus said. "But for now, I really must finish this conversation."

Marcus took my drink from the bartender and steered me to one of the empty tables on the upper deck, then gave me the same smoldering look I'd already come to recognize on Antony.

"I'm not angry," I said, tearing my gaze away with some difficulty. "Your views just seemed a little...harsh."

"Harsh? And yet I've often been told I'm too soft. One of my father's favorite faults of mine."

I rubbed my arm. "I suppose people are softer where I come from, so my standards might be different."

"In America, you mean?"

"Perhaps."

Or modern people in general.

"You never cease to amaze me," Marcus murmured. "For a girl to travel to Egypt — alone! — you must have a streak of steel in you. And yet you mourn for a bird!"

Marcus scooted closer to me, his voice lowering. "You have other attractions, too, of course."

Admonishing - Scolding

Was I being too hard on him? It was one comment, its origins understandable given his upbringing, and he'd apologized...

I threw caution to the wind and emulated his purring tone. "Do I, now? And what are those attractions?"

He smiled, gently tucking a tendril of hair behind my ear. Then he kissed me on the cheek, slowly working his way down my neck.

"There's one here...and here."

I struggled to keep my breathing even. "I'll not deny you have attractions of your own..."

"Ahem," Neby said. "*AHEM!*"

"Jupiter's stone!" Marcus cursed. I deduced that Neby had kicked him in the shin, since he was rubbing that part of his anatomy in surprise.

"Thank you," Neby said with insufferable politeness. "Not that I mind your budding romance. On the contrary, I find it quite heartwarming. But perhaps such demonstrations of affection would be better conducted *not* in the middle of dinner? Neither of you even noticed when I sat down."

I blushed furiously, having forgotten that anyone else was on the ship. Marcus just smiled and ate an olive.

* * *

I TOSSED AND TURNED the entire night, a ridiculous grin plas-

---

Emulated - Copied

Deduced - Concluded; arrived at the fact based on reasoning

Anatomy - Body

tered on my face.

And yet there was a part of me that felt...strange, somehow. I'd experienced so much, but couldn't truly share it with anyone.

Even in Connecticut I had Mitzi, and Harvey was just a phone call away. *What he would've given to see the library before it burned!* Harvey's name was the one I fought to keep at bay the most, but now that it entered my mind, it was impossible not to think of him.

What would he make of my disappearance? Would he draw the logical conclusion that I'd followed my parents, or would he obdurately refuse to believe something so out of the ordinary?

I wished there was some way I could leave him a message, just to let him know I was OK. It didn't seem wise, though, considering the consequences my parents suffered for doing the same.

Yet even as I dismissed the thought, my brain schemed other ways of communicating through the ages.

What about authors? Could I get myself included in Cleopatra's memoirs?

But most of the historians who wrote about Cleopatra never actually met her. They'd pull together accounts from secondhand sources, and whomever they included landed there by chance.

No. There was no way I could safely get a message to Harvey this many years removed.

I turned on my side, trying to get comfortable in my little cot.

Of course, after that last night in Alexandria, Harvey was more than just my other half, my lifelong confidant. It was impossible

---

Obdurately - Stubbornly refusing to change one's mind
Confidant - A person you confide in, share secrets with

not to compare him to Marcus.

At face value, Harvey was long and lean, a little over six feet tall. Marcus was pure muscle, and perfectly proportioned, but a good few inches shorter.

Personality-wise, both men were clever, possessing a strong sarcastic streak I appreciated.

But...even though appearance and personality theoretically make a person, reducing them to such descriptions felt woefully inadequate.

Harvey was comfortable. We shared a history, a language more complex than anything spoken at the United Nations. I loved him, certainly, but in what way?

Marcus was another matter entirely. I was constantly on my toes in his presence, excited for the verbal spar that would inevitably ensue. I didn't love him, but did that mean I would never?

I threw the covers over my head, tossing and turning until dawn.

* * *

BY THE TIME I'd taken a sponge bath and prepared for the day, it was nearly time for lunch.

"Good morning," Marcus said, eyes positively twinkling.

Spar - Fast-paced banter
Inevitably - Certainly; unavoidably
Ensue - Happen

"Good morning yourself," I replied, wishing I could control the color of my cheeks. "Do you know where we are?"

"Not a clue," Marcus patted the seat next to him, and I willingly sat.

This time when he put his arm around me, I didn't object. Regardless of how everything turned out, how could I resist such a moment? I was a guest on Cleopatra's boat with a Roman soldier, comfortably admiring the view of the Nile. Could life get any better?

Miraculously, it did. Right after lunch, we rounded a curve in the river and beheld the Great Pyramids of Giza, rising from the sands in all their glory.

I gasped and freed myself from Marcus' grasp, stumbling to the ship's railing. Neby wasn't lying when he said they were ancient. From when I stood, they were already more than 2,000 years old.

They'd fared far better in their first 2,000 years of their existence than the second, though. I silently cursed whichever megalomaniacal sultan removed the limestone exterior for his own use.

Unlike today, when one can see the contour of every block, the slopes were so smooth, so polished, they glimmered in the sunlight. The sight before me was so beautiful, my heart ached.

"Magnificent, aren't they?" Neby asked.

"The word can't do them justice."

"Quite nice, my friend," Marcus admitted. "Quite nice."

Beheld - Saw something remarkable

Megalomaniacal - Being obsessed with your own power

When we arrived, everyone made their way into gilded litters. Most fit only two to four people, but Antony and Cleopatra's was the size of a small bedroom. At least twenty muscled slaves supported it, holding large spokes extending from the edges.

"Oh!" I remarked, as Marcus and Neby made their way to one of the litters provided for our boat. "Honestly, after all that travel, don't you think we should walk?"

I continued talking as I spoke, this time addressing the slaves. "Is there anything we can help you carry?"

The slaves stared at me with abject horror, then looked back at their feet.

"I'm trying to help you!" I explained. "I know it's not conventional, but..."

Neby chuckled. "Where *do* you get these notions? Carrying food for a slave! Walk all you like, but I'll not blister my feet like a peasant."

Neby climbed into the litter without a second thought.

"Marcus?" I asked. "It's not far. We can see the pyramids."

"If it makes you happy," he responded. "I'm not above using my own two feet."

We set off immediately, without waiting for the others. We wouldn't be able to outstrip them by far, but I think we were both secretly looking forward to a little alone time.

The weather was perfect. The Egyptians used a different calendar, but it must've been... oh, late April or early May by that

---

Litter - A bed or seat that is enclosed by curtains and carried by people

Abject - Total; to the maximum degree

point? The sun shone softly on the sands, a gentle breeze prevented our garments from sticking to us, and sunglasses were the only amenity I missed from my previous life.

"Have you ever wondered," I mused, "what's inside the pyramids?"

"I heard they were tombs," Marcus responded amiably. "Would they not hold the bodies of long-dead pharaohs?"

"But what else?" I pressed. "Art? Treasure?"

The pyramids had been stripped of anything valuable by my time. Since they were essentially giant "FREE GOLD HERE" signs, the looting had probably occurred well before Cleopatra's time, too. Nevertheless, the archaeologist in me felt a burning need to investigate.

"I didn't know you marked tomb robbing among your many talents," Marcus said. "Tempting as your invitation is, I must decline."

"You're not even the least bit curious? We're in a once-in-a-lifetime kind of place! And who said anything about robbing? We're *exploring*. I wouldn't dream of taking anything."

Marcus stopped walking abruptly, then took my shoulders in both hands. "You're serious, aren't you? Need I remind you that I was unable to help you the first time you were imprisoned, and my rank has not changed since then? If the queen throws you in jail, there is very little I can do to free you."

Amenity - A desirable or useful feature
Amiably - In a friendly way
Looting - Theft; robbing

"Jail? For some light archaeology? They wouldn't imprison me for that..."

"Your parents were imprisoned for less."

That silenced me, for a moment at least. "Fine," I eventually remarked. "Fine."

WE SOON FOUND ourselves in the shadow of the pyramids. The slaves made a quick pace despite their heavy load, and a few had trotted ahead to unroll rugs, set up chairs, and unload baskets of food, so Marcus and I didn't get any alone time.

As Cleopatra's monstrous litter approached, I could hear her giggle in response to something Antony said.

"Do you know him well? Antony, I mean?" I asked Marcus.

We were seated on one of the massive rugs, partaking in one of the favorite pastimes of the vacationer — eating.

He shrugged. "Most of the men, including Antony, go back to Caesar's time in Gaul. This is my first posting."

"Is that hard for you?"

"Everyone is new to something, sometime, priestess. The key is to find pleasant company."

I smiled, then lowered my voice. "He seems to be in wonderful spirits, yet I've heard he was furious Caesar named Octavian the heir."

Marcus glanced around, then nodded. "War is brewing. Antony being in Egypt won't stop that. Only one man can rule Rome."

Gaul - A region that roughly corresponds to modern-day France

CHAPTER SEVENTEEN

CLEOPATRA INVITED a different ship to dine with her for each meal. For dinner the third night, ours was selected.

I cleaned up as best I could given the limited facilities, pulling my hair back in a loose updo and letting a few blonde tendrils escape, then crossed the plank connecting the two ships at the appointed hour. Marcus was standing beside it proudly, delivering a lecture to Neby.

"It's called a *corvus*," he said. "Invented by *Romans* to defeat Hannibal Barca. See the hook at the end there? Keeps the ships from separating."

Neby rolled his eyes. "Yes, yes, we all know you lack a functioning navy, so you just decided to board the poor fellow's ships instead. Get a move on, will you?"

Antony was standing on the other side of the plank, dressed in an eclectic mix of Roman and Egyptian fashions.

"*Porco Juno*, Marcus, you're not lecturing this poor man on the Punic Wars, are you?" Antony spread his arms in a gesture of appreciation. "Learn to enjoy where you are, man."

Marcus saluted. "Yes, sir!"

LIKE VIVIANA GETTING READY for a date, dusk took her time in departing. Wrapping herself in pink and purple clouds, she reveled in her own beauty, basking in the glow of the sun.

We were anchored near the pyramids, gently rocking on the shores of the Nile, and I must admit that I was equally enraptured.

So much so, in fact, that I barely noticed the slaves circling, pouring drinks and clearing them, ensuring everyone's needs were met before they arose. I was lounging on a divan, eating Roman-style around one of the tables, but the conversation had faded to a hum.

I glanced at Marcus, who was speaking with a fellow soldier, and Neby, who was telling a raucous story on the other side of the table.

I should've been meeting new people, expanding my circle, but instead turned my gaze to Cleopatra. She was the consummate hostess, laughing at people's jokes and making sure Antony, in particular, was having a good time.

Eclectic - Unusual; chosen from diverse sources
Reveled - Thoroughly enjoyed
Enraptured - Filled with pleasure or joy
Raucous - Loud; wild
Consummate - Showing a high degree of skill; perfect

Then, at once, something snapped me out of my reverie. Mentit was here, and she was refilling Antony's drink.

Good for her, I guess. She's moved up in the world. Better to serve the queen than — what had she called me? A "beggar priestess"? *Her mom must have helped her secure the position,* I thought.

As I weighed the pros and cons of trying to speak with her after dinner, a fly began circling Antony's wine. Waving and *shooing* probably wasn't in keeping with royal etiquette, I decided, and I wouldn't have been able to reach it anyway.

The insect landed on the rim of his golden glass, rubbing its feelers together like a man about to dig into a hearty brunch. The fly drank its fill, then buzzed away in a sugar-filled daze, abruptly falling from the air near my own (not golden) glass.

It took me a moment to process the extraordinary significance of this event.

Antony was raising the glass to his lips when I cried, "Antony! Stop!"

All conversation halted. All eyes turned to me.

"*Priestess?*" Cleopatra said with a forced smile. "I am certain you did not just issue Antony an order, for doing so..."

"I apologize, Your Majesty. But I believe his glass is poisoned."

Dramatic gasps replaced the silence. In the background, a glass shattered as someone dropped a drink.

"You know this how?" Antony growled.

"I am a priestess of Isis. She — she wishes that I warn you." I could hardly say I'd spent dinner watching a fly drink from his glass.

"Hmm," Antony said. "Best get a new drink then."

Iras, Cleopatra's head slave, rushed over in horror. She was personally taking the glass when Cleopatra said, "Stop. Who poured Antony's wine?"

"Mentit," Iras responded. "We believed she was ready..."

"Fetch her."

Guests exchanged meaningful looks, but Cleopatra's gaze was steel. When Mentit emerged, her gaze grew harder still. It wasn't hard to see why. Mentit was terrified, guilt writ large across her face.

Gesturing to the poisoned goblet, Cleopatra said through gritted teeth, "*Drink.*"

Iras passed the glass to Mentit. Mentit gave her a look of pleading terror, but Iras showed as little mercy as her boss.

"Wait," Antony held up a firm hand.

"Thank you, sir! Oh, thank you!" Mentit gasped. "I always—"

"I'm not *pardoning* you," Antony said in disgust. "Who gave you the poison?"

Mentit was hyperventilating now, her breath coming in deep, crying gulps. I clenched my fists until my knuckles turned white. Marcus put a hand over one, shaking his head, silently warning me not to intervene.

"*It must speak,*" Cleopatra said.

When the guards approached, Mentit shied back. "I don't know! He was — he was Roman. He promised I wouldn't have to live in servitude anymore, that I'd get my old life back..."

"Very well," Antony said. "Proceed."

Hyperventilating - Breathing so quickly you almost pass out

Mentit's mother — I assumed it was her mother — came flying up the stairs from the lower deck. She was crying harder than Mentit, and threw herself at the queen's feet.

"Your family received one pardon already," Cleopatra said coldly. "Egypt will not forgive you a second time. *Drink.*"

I looked helplessly at Marcus, but knew there was nothing I could do. I was the one who revealed the poison. To defend Mentit now would only make me look complicit. Most likely, I'd end up sharing the poisoned glass.

I averted my eyes, but couldn't tune out the faint slurp as Mentit took a swig of death. I expected it to sound evil, somehow, but she may as well have taken a sip of juice. She let out a raspy cough, but was clearly still among the living.

"*All of it,*" Cleopatra said.

Mentit was shaking so badly by this point, it was a miracle there was any wine left in the glass. She closed her eyes, tears falling from her long lashes as she gulped.

"Now we watch," Antony said, leaning back.

But I couldn't. I glanced at Neby, who remained uncharacteristically silent throughout the affair, and saw that he too was staring fixedly at the ground.

Mentit begin to wheeze, her breath coming in labored gasps, then she abruptly collapsed. Her mother rushed over, tears mixing with her daughter's as she tried hopelessly to revive her, speaking encouraging words and rubbing her cheeks.

Complicit - Involved in some bad or illegal activity
Revive - Bring back to life

But Mentit's brown eyes, once so filled with life and vanity and jealousy and greed, were empty. Blood trickled from the side of her mouth.

I blinked back tears. A dog didn't deserve to die this way.

Two guards removed Mentit's body, her mother following behind. Conversation remained at a standstill.

"Well!" Cleopatra said. Her voice was steady, but there a terrifying edge to it. "I think we all know who is responsible for this gross act of treason."

"Yet who could imagine he'd act so soon?" After facing death as many times as he had, Antony seemed to regard the situation as more interesting than frightening.

"Poison is in keeping with what you've told me of his character. He'd want it to look like you were weak from the voyage, and died shortly after arriving."

"Clever," Antony admitted. "He always was clever."

"I think it's time we taught our young friend Octavian a lesson. He cannot send poison to *my* dinner table without consequences."

Belatedly realizing that the rest of the ship was shamelessly eavesdropping, Cleopatra addressed us. "Leave us now. Dinner is over."

We filed back to our ship, heading to the upper deck for the drinks and dinner we hadn't finished. Neby, Marcus, and I sat near the railing, some distance from the others, picking at our food.

Eventually, Neby let out a long breath. "Thank the gods for

Belatedly - Later than should be the case

you, priestess! If Antony had died just now...I don't know what she would have done."

"What do you mean?"

"Look at the trouble she's gone to for him. He is her guest of honor. An attack on him is an attack on her. If it should have succeeded...Well, best she not deal with another death so soon."

I decided not to point out that she *had* dealt with a death that evening, even if Mentit's life wasn't worth much in her eyes.

Marcus had been silently nursing his drink. "How did you really know?" he said finally.

I gave him a hard look. "It was as I told the queen."

Sensing some unspoken tension, Neby excused himself. "Perhaps I should give you two some privacy. I think Henuttawy wanted to see me..."

We watched Neby's retreating form, listening to the water lapping at the side of the boat. After a minute, Marcus remarked, "You know I've never bought this priestess of Isis business. It's not that I'm a pagan, but I've *met* priestesses. You're nothing like them."

I bit my lip. I didn't like lying to Marcus; I didn't like lying to anybody. But I couldn't tell him I wasn't really a priestess. What if someone heard me? What if Marcus told someone? I would be out on the street, disgraced, with nowhere to turn and no way to provide for myself.

I had to put my survival over my scruples. I read somewhere that the best defense is a good offense.

Scruples - A moral standard that prevents certain actions

"Just because I'm unlike any priestess you've ever met, doesn't mean I'm not one. I'd like to think I'm unlike anyone you've ever met, period," I said with a suggestive smile, hoping to return to the mood of the day before.

Marcus narrowed his eyes, but said nothing. After a while, I couldn't take it anymore. "I'm going to bed. We've both had quite a night."

"Sleep well…priestess."

HARVEY'S FIELD NOTES

MAY 28:

Nearly gave up hope today. Police conducted raid on an extremist base in the Sinai last night; intelligence indicated they might have Noor. No trace of her.

Father replaced the cup of coffee I'd been staring at for an hour with a fresh one, then sat down across the table from me. I'd started spending weekends with him in Alex. No one left to hang out with in Cairo, and I couldn't handle a dahabeeyah party anyway.

"Harvey, there's something I've been meaning to talk to you about," he said. "It's about Noor."

My head shot up. "What is it? Have they found her? Oh God, is she—"

"No, no, nothing like that," he said quickly. "It's just, I know how hard these past few months have been for you. Between Noor's disappearance and my...*unconventional* intellectual pursuits—"

I snorted.

"Snort all you want, my boy, but I have come to believe the two are related." The professor crossed his legs and calmly took a sip of coffee.

"Right," I said with ineffable sarcasm. "So Noor got sucked back in time, just like Frank and Mary?"

"Precisely."

I rubbed my eyes. "Father, I can't do this with you again. To see you like this…"

Truth be told, he looked better than he had in months. His pants were neatly pressed, his pocket square tidy, and his hair combed.

As though in response to my thoughts, he remarked, "It's the uncertainty of things that drives one mad. I am no longer uncertain as to what happened to Frank, Mary, or Noor."

"How can you say that?"

The professor withdrew a little green notebook from his inner jacket pocket, fingers deftly flipping through months of scribblings until he found the page he wanted.

"It's just as I told Noor all those months ago. Once you have eliminated the impossible, whatever remains, no matter how improbable, must be the truth."

"Mmmhmm. So you're saying it's impossible that Frank and Mary drowned, or that Noor was kidnapped on her way back to

---

Ineffable - Too great to be expressed in words
Deftly - Quickly; with neat skill

Cairo?"

"It is," he said calmly. "I'd bet my life that Frank and Mary never went scuba diving that night, so they could not have drowned."

I shrugged. I'd already begun having suspicions on that score.

"And Noor?"

"I was originally convinced that the inscription fell into the hands of one of my more envious colleagues," the professor said calmly. "Which would mean that we had a break-in on the same night that Noor snuck out. You will forgive me for pointing out that the odds of this are highly unlikely. Far less likely than the possibility that — say — Noor's curiosity got the better of her, and she took the inscription herself."

The word hit me like a punch in the gut. *Curiosity.* If there was one thing that could override Noor's better judgment, it was her curiosity.

The professor slid the notebook over to me, one hand keeping it open to the desired page. Six lines of hieroglyphs were followed by the phonetic version of the text, the English translation below.

I squinted. "Is this the 'incantation' you gave Noor?"

"Close," he said. "Many of the lines are similar — the invocation, the conclusion, but Noor's text only brought her back in time. I believe this is the incantation that reverses it — the text that would bring them home."

"Brilliant. Thanks a heap, Father. So glad you were concentrating your considerable intellectual abilities on ancient spells rather than helping me field Interpol's leads."

Invocation - The act of calling to presence a superior being

He flushed slightly at the insult, but did not retaliate. "Harvey, despite what you may think, I couldn't live with myself if I didn't do everything in my power to bring them home. If that means being the center of ridicule, so be it."

"Father, you know I didn't mean..." I sighed. "What I don't understand is, if you believe in this precious theory so much, why are you still here? You don't have to convince me. Read it yourself."

"If I were a younger man, I would. But the strain of the past few years..." the professor stirred his coffee, the little spoon *clinking* against the cup.

"I've developed a heart condition," he said finally.

"Father! Why—"

"It's manageable with modern medicine," he hastened to assure me, "but I wouldn't last long without it."

"Why didn't you tell me?"

"I didn't want to worry you. As I said, it's manageable."

The professor then pushed the notebook more directly in front of me. "I'm going to leave this with you. It contains all of my research, all of my sources. Look at it. Make of it what you will."

I nodded silently, and he returned to his study.

Retaliate - Fight back; return an attack
Hastened - Be quick to do something

CHAPTER EIGHTEEN

CLEOPATRA'S FIRST ACT upon returning to the palace was to drastically reduce the amount of grain shipped to Rome.

Hearing the news, Antony let out a hoot and a spate of applause. "Egypt is the breadbasket of the world. But if there is no grain in Rome, who will they blame? The man ruling Rome! The mob will have Octavian's head on a platter by week's end."

"My thoughts exactly," Cleopatra replied, serenely rocking Caesarion's cradle.

Antony came to stand next to her. "A fine young lad," he remarked, smiling at the baby in the silly way adults do. "He'll be a fine swordsman, like his father."

Cleopatra hadn't slowed down one whit since the boy's birth, going to great lengths to keep Antony both impressed and enter-

---

Spate - Sudden outpouring
Serenely - Calmly; peacefully

tained. A part of me speculated that feelings beyond basic grati-tude had begun to motivate her, but that wasn't exactly fair. Knowing the future, I knew they would soon fall in love, scandal-izing all of Rome.

One day, she ordered a marvelous fishing expedition in the waters near the palace. Since I'd saved Antony's life in Giza, I ac-companied them everywhere; my powers had never been more highly regarded.

The barge took us out to sea, passing the Lighthouse which remained lit 24 hours a day. I craned my neck to see the top, like a tourist in New York City. Then we hit a sharp wave and my neck jolted forward, like the lid of a box slamming shut.

"*Oy*, alright there?" one of the deckhands asked.

"Perfectly," I responded, taking a seat. I'd grown accustomed to the gentle swells of the Nile, and had to remind myself that we were in Poseidon's waters now, and without an engine.

The Mediterranean was beautiful and reminded me of home, but it also kept Odysseus from his home for ten years. *Best stay seated until we reach calmer waters*, I thought.

Antony and Cleopatra were lying on a mound of pillows under a shaded awning at the back of the boat. Their heads were bent close to one another, and Antony's smoldering gaze was no longer unleashed on anyone but the queen.

The captain eventually dropped anchor further out to sea, where the waves were large but nowhere near as violent. Antony rose to his feet and took one of the fishing lines, joining a handful

---

Speculated - Thought

of other men, including Marcus, at the railing.

"Priestess!" Cleopatra's voice rang out. "Come and join me."

I almost tumbled overboard again, this time from sheer surprise. Though I was almost always in Cleopatra's vicinity, she rarely spoke directly to me. I approached the periphery of her lounge, not wanting to overstep my bounds yet again, and awkwardly hovered just outside.

"Well?" Cleopatra waved a hand over the cushions Antony vacated. "I asked you to join me, priestess. I wish to know more about you."

"More about me?" I cautiously sat. "There is little to tell…"

Her eyes were watching Antony as she spoke. "I cannot believe that. The gods have blessed you with great fortune. Why?"

"I wish I knew, Your Highness."

Antony cast his first line, and almost immediately, a fish bit. Cleopatra smiled.

"Bravo!" she called, then returned her attention to me. "Tell me, then, about this soldier of yours."

I cast a betraying glance at Marcus. "He's not mine," I said. *Not anymore, at least. We haven't spoken since our little tiff on the Nile.* "But he is a good man."

"And not unattractive."

"He is that," I agreed.

Vicinity - The area near a person or place

Periphery - The outer limits or boundaries

Vacated - Left; made empty

I wanted to ask about her own budding romance, but knew it would be monstrously indelicate. I was saved the trouble when she asked, "He speaks highly of Antony?"

"Of course, Your Highness. Everyone does." Not quite the truth, but shattering the romantic fantasies of a queen would be unwise.

"Antony is so unlike Caesar, and yet I find myself..."

"Yes?"

"Drawn to him, somehow."

"I understand."

"How can this be? So soon after Caesar's death? And with Caesarion so young..."

The men were on the other side of the boat, shouting and making jokes at each other's expense as they compared conquests.

I glanced at them before responding. "Sometimes, Your Highness, the gods have unexpected plans for us."

She nodded.

Antony caught another fish. He reeled it to the boat, throwing it with the others. They lay, slimy and dead, on the deck.

"Odd, how they now favor your line!" Marcus called. "They follow you like Helen after Paris!"

"She was always a cheeky little minx," Antony grinned, yanking as yet another fish bit.

"Quite impressive," Cleopatra agreed, scooting to the edge of her lounge so she could look directly down at them. "What is your strategy?"

"It's all in how you throw the line," Antony winked at her. "You must hold it perfectly still. Confuses the creatures, you see."

"Really! And yet I always believed some movement was necessary, to emulate the swimming of a fish."

Antony glanced at his line, and I followed his gaze. A diver from a nearby fishing vessel sank into the water, carrying a single fish in a net. When he re-emerged, the fish was gone.

The man hadn't escaped Cleopatra's notice either. Conversation lulled as Antony reeled in his next fish.

"Not a lot of fight in this one," he remarked. "But no matter. The next one—"

The fish he tossed in the pile was clearly dead. Not just dead; it had been preserved at some point. Salt still clung to the scales.

There were a handful of actual fishermen aboard, brought along to do the dirty work like prepare the bait and take fish off the hooks.

One of them, whose eyepatch and forthcoming speech indicated he was not the most cautious individual, cried, "Oy! That's no' from 'ere! It's river fish. I'd wage my last eye!"

"You doubt my talent, citizen?" Antony purred.

"No, sir. It's only — that's Nile carp, that is. And seeing as we're at sea—"

"What of it?"

"Well, ow'd it get here?"

"Maybe it swam."

Unaware of how many chances Antony had already given him, the fisherman continued to press his luck. "But surely you know that's not possible, sir. And that fishing boat following us. They's not doing any fishing—"

Antony grabbed the man by the back of his shirt and tossed him overboard. The man barely had time to sputter in protest before free-falling into the sea.

Reinvigorated by this act of mild violence, Antony dusted off his hands and smiled broadly. "The wretched fishmonger discovered my ruse, it seems."

Nobody spoke. Cleopatra laughed. "Antony! This entire time, you've had men hooking fish to your line?"

"A veritable army of them," he admitted. "Are you greatly disappointed?"

The question was surprisingly sincere. There was an opening, if Cleopatra wanted it, to mock or belittle him. She didn't take it.

"But why waste your talents on fish? Your sport is the hunting of cities, realms, and empires."

Antony's posture stiffened. "I suppose you're right." He let out a low growl, throwing his fishing pole to the side and bounding upon her in a single leap. I barely had time to get out of the way.

Cleopatra returned Antony's affections, their laughter uninhibited by the thrashes of the drowning fisherman.

"Oh, Antony!" she murmured. "Oh, *Antony.*"

Heedless of our earlier disagreement, I gave Marcus a wide-eyed, "This isn't OK, and if you don't save that man, I will" look.

Reinvigorated - Given new energy or strength

Ruse - Trick

Veritable - Adds emphasis to the noun following it; literally means "able to be proven true."

Uninhibited - Expressed unselfconsciously and without restraint

Marcus grimaced, and was reaching for a rope when the other fishing vessel tossed one into the sea, shouting for the man to grab it.

By the time they heaved him aboard, coughing and retching, Iras had long since closed the curtains to Cleopatra's lounge. She and Antony were so engrossed in each other, they didn't care who lived or died.

* * *

ANTONY AND CLEOPATRA may as well have gone into hiding after that. This suited me, for it gave me time to make discreet inquiries into booking passage to Rome.

Unfortunately, the prospect was nearly impossible for a poor and private citizen. The only ships that regularly crossed the sea belonged to the military and merchants.

With enough money, anything could be accomplished, of course. I could barter passage on a friendly fishing vessel, make friends with a tradesman. But I had no money.

It did occur to me to wonder how my parents had managed it.

After several weeks, however, Antony and Cleopatra were forced to reappear when Octavian's top negotiators arrived in Egypt to plead for more grain.

Neby told me Octavian was so desperate, he'd already offered to double, then triple the price per bushel. Rome's reserves were

---

Engrossed - Having all your attention absorbed by someone or something

dwindling quickly, but Cleopatra refused every offer.

Finally, she agreed to host a small diplomatic dinner where negotiations could take place. Since I made the intimate guest list, however, I suspected she hadn't forgotten the poisoning attempt. The Romans would be lucky if she didn't return the favor.

While waiting for dinner, I decided to explore the servant's quarters, specifically the kitchens. Since the chefs were normally preparing dinner for a hundred, I never wanted to disturb them. But on a night like tonight, when the guest list was the size of a big family, I wouldn't get in anyone's way.

Imagine my surprise, then, when upon arriving to the kitchens I found myself face-to-face with a dozen boars roasting on spits, each one in a different state of preparation.

Some were charred and seasoned, ready for the plate. Others were so raw they could've been asleep, except for the poles through their center.

"Excuse me!" I greeted the lone chef in the center of the room, who was preparing mice for the night's appetizers.

Trying not to watch as he chopped off their little tails, I said, "I didn't realize it was going to be such a large dinner tonight! Do you know how many will be in attendance?"

The chef, an enormous man with biceps the size of tree trunks, smiled at me and set down his knife. "Eight, m'lady."

I looked at the twelve boars in confusion, and the chef continued with pride. "Never been to the kitchens, 'ave ye? Aye, most haven't, but it's no small matter what we do 'ere."

Dwindling - Shrinking; decreasing in size

"I don't understand. I assume some food is for the staff, but you could feed each guest an entire pig and still have plenty left over!"

He chuckled. "We must be ready any time she calls. What if she wants dinner early, or has an extra glass of wine and dinner is late? The food can't be undercooked or dry, so..."

"You prepare the same meal, over and over?"

"Aye," he beamed. "Not one, but many dinners are prepared."

"And you do this every night?"

"Every night."

I stepped out of the way as a middle-aged woman rushed by with bread, fresh from the ovens. Her hair curled in little wisps around her forehead, wet with perspiration.

"Tis going to be an interesting night, priestess," the chef continued. "Antony and Cleopatra 'ave wagered on who can prepare the most expensive meal. And by the gods, does she have a surprise for him!"

CLEOPATRA WAS WATCHING her guests with a catlike grin.

"Well, Antony. After hours of dining on the most exotic and delectable foods available, will you concede that I can prepare a more costly dinner than you?"

"Perhaps. But you *did* say the meal would be worth ten million *sesterce.* What do you think, Lucius? Could we buy a villa in Capri for the price of this meal?"

Lucius was one of the men Octavian sent to negotiate grain

Delectable - Delicious; indulgent

Concede - Admit

Sesterce - A unit of currency in ancient Rome

shipments. He stiffened. "Sir, the people of Rome are starving. Perhaps we could return—"

"And as I've told you," Antony responded, hand to heart, "I care deeply for the people. But if Octavian cannot run Rome, you really must take the matter up with him."

Cleopatra nodded. "So true. Sadly, not everyone is fit to rule. Now if we could return to the subject of my dinner?"

A slave put a goblet of vinegar before the queen. I couldn't see inside, but the smell is quite distinct, even from a distance.

Antony laughed. "Old, fermented wine? I hardly think *that* will tip you over the edge."

"Perhaps not...yet."

Cleopatra lifted nimble fingers to her earrings, pearls the size of cherries. The largest in history, sources had placed their value anywhere from $500,000 to $28.5 million in today's currency.

Unhooking the clasp of the right pearl, she delicately dropped it in the vinegar. It began to fizzle and dissolve immediately, hitting the bottom with a soft *thunk!*

Lucius gasped. His fellow negotiator looked like he was going to be sick. Antony whooped.

"Brava, darling!"

The dissolving pearl was leaving a milky layer on top of the vinegar. Cleopatra gave her glass a little swirl, then took a sip.

"Are we now in agreement that this meal was worth 10 million *sesterce*, or shall I add the other to be sure?" Cleopatra reached for her left ear.

Nimble - Light and quick

"Your Majesty, that won't be necessary!" Lucius interrupted, mopping his forehead with a folded cloth. "I don't believe anyone will ever forget this night."

"No," she agreed. "I should think not."

CHAPTER NINETEEN

"Neby, you should have seen it!"

He was joining me for a postprandial drink in my rooms, and I was regaling him with his cousin's antics.

"The Romans must have been beside themselves, all stoic and stern." He made a forbidding face like a serious grandpa, arms akimbo, hands on his hips.

"They were. I almost felt bad for them! They had no idea how to deal with the queen of Egypt."

Neby didn't stay for long. He departed after one drink, and I crawled into bed by the dying light of the oil lamps.

I began to drift off almost immediately, but a rasping noise soon caught my attention, summoning me back to consciousness. It sounded like someone was dragging a bag across the floor.

Postprandial - Occurring after a meal

Regaling - Entertaining or amusing

Akimbo - Hands on the hips and elbows turned outward

I opened my eyes, wondering if Neby had returned. But moonlight shone through the open window, illuminating shadows the lamps were too lazy to reach.

No one was there.

And yet the sound was coming closer and closer. Then it abruptly stopped.

I threw back the thin blanket, grabbing one of the lamps as I got out of bed. Shaped like Aladdin's, I held the back ring while a flame poked out the front.

I hadn't taken more than a few steps before stopping dead in my tracks, too terrified to move.

An Egyptian asp was coiled just steps from my bare legs. Even in the flickering light, its black, wet skin stood out against the sandy stone. The flared hood reached my knees.

I don't know how long I stood there, paralyzed, trying not to make eye contact with the creature. Occasionally it let out a little hiss, just to remind me of its presence.

The only weapon I had, if you could call it that, was the oil in the candle. If I threw it at the snake, would it retreat, or provoke it to attack? Would oil even come out if I didn't lift the lid first?

Afraid to breathe, I slowly scanned the room, moving only my eyes. There was nothing else that could be used as a weapon, not within arm's length at least.

I risked a glance at the creature. It had begun weaving its head side to side, like a belly dancer, and was looking straight at me.

I couldn't break the connection now. I knew with a sickening certainty that if I wrenched my gaze away from those cold, obsidian eyes, it would strike. I'd be dead within minutes.

Maybe Cleopatra would get the idea to kill herself with an Egyptian asp from me, I thought, trying to cheer myself up. *She'd see my body, decide I looked quite peaceful...*

I took a shaky breath and risked the slowest of steps backwards. The moment my leg moved, the cloth of the nightgown rustling, the monster lunged.

Steel rained from the heavens! Marcus emerged from the shadows, slicing the creature in half as it flew through the air.

I dove out of the trajectory of the beast's fangs. Unfortunately I collided with the wooden frame of my bed, banging my shins and descending into an undignified hop as I clutched my scraped appendages, swearing in a mixture of languages.

My breathing was ragged as I turned to my rescuer.

"Marcus! What are you *doing* here?"

"*Porco Juno*, woman! Do you attract danger everywhere you go?"

He was breathing a little heavily himself.

"The events of the last few months shouldn't be taken as a pattern. Seriously, though. *Why are you here?*"

"Antony and Cleopatra want a portrait of the ceremony in two days' time. They started talking about it after you left, and I volunteered to deliver the message."

"Awfully kind of you."

"Kind, indeed! You'd be dead if I wasn't!"

"I know. I'm sorry, just...jeez."

Obsidian - A dark, glasslike rock

Trajectory - The path followed by a flying object

His eyes softened when he saw how shaken I was. In two long steps, he'd pulled me into his arms.

We stayed like that for some time, until his hand began making exploratory motions along my posterior. I almost laughed. *Seriously? Now?*

I stepped away and said, "So, how do we get the dead snake out of here?"

* * *

I WASN'T IN the right frame of mind to ask Marcus what ceremony he was talking about. I was too busy trying to figure out how a snake had gotten into my rooms — a room on an island, no less.

But soon enough, my addled brain realized the ceremony was the greater of my concerns. There was no way my phone had any battery left.

Maybe I could leverage saving Antony's life against my inability to produce a portrait....But that had been ages ago, and neither Antony nor Cleopatra was the most forgiving of rulers.

It was far more likely that the dead iPhone would be seen as a personal repudiation by the gods. In a culture so steeped in religion and superstition, falling so publicly from Isis' favor would be fatal.

Shortly after sunrise, I rose to see what information I could

---

Addled - Confused
Leverage - Take advantage of
Repudiation - Rejection

gather. Dressing quickly, I crept through the corridors to the kitchens. I suspected they were a hotbed of information, since they had to know how many mouths to feed.

My old friend the chef was already preparing for the day ahead, fetching herbs from the shelves.

Unlike the last time I saw him, when he was only accompanied by one or two others, the kitchens were already as busy as Tahrir Square at midnight.

A small army of women kneaded bread around a low wooden table. Others vigorously polished plates and glasses. Some were sorting less-perishable items, like dates and figs, into large bowls. Boys ran in and out with messages.

"A big event, indeed," the chef rubbed his eyes. "No one knows for sure, of course, but folk say Antony is giving Caesarion his share of Rome when he dies."

"*What?* Then...it's to be a wedding, too."

"Aye. A bit soon after Caesar, maybe, but she does what she wants. Everybody's seen how they are together."

"Is it going to be a big ceremony? Who all is invited?"

The chef looked at me quizzically. "The wedding? 'Twill be private. Before the gods, like. But the ceremony after will be magnificent, too, whether Caesarion is named heir or not. Every noble kitchen in the city is to donate food."

I thanked him for his time, then politely excused myself, pointing to the amount of work ahead of him.

My head was spinning by the time I made it back to my room.

Antony and Cleopatra were to be married, in private, before the gods. Then, to thumb their nose at Octavian, they would announce that Antony's third of Rome would go to Caesarion when he died.

It made sense, really. As Caesar's natural-born son, Caesarion had more of a right to Rome than Octavian, Caesar's nephew.

But Octavian, clever man that he was, would spin the ceremony to his advantage.

Rather than praising Antony for being a wonderful step-father, who was raising his best friend's son and ensuring he was given his birthright, the narrative in Rome would be very different.

Antony has fallen for the charms of the east! The witch Cleopatra has seduced him! He is giving Rome away to Egypt!

War was brewing, indeed. I just hoped I'd live long enough to see it.

* * *

"I CAN'T DO IT, Marcus. My image machine — it's broken."

Seated on one of the divans on my sitting room, Marcus raised a brow as I paced back and forth.

"You cannot fail to produce the portrait for the queen," he said simply. "Your position at court is entirely dependent on moments like this, and what you can do for her."

"I know."

"Well, how did the gift leave you? *Why* did it leave you?" He leaned forward, palms clasped, and studied me intently.

"I — I don't know. It's the device—"

"What about it?"

252

"It's broken."

"Your gift from Isis is broken?"

"It can break like anything else!" I replied. "Like a wheel that gets stuck in a ditch, or —"

"Gifts from the gods do not break."

Marcus intercepted me when I passed him, squeezing my hands tighter than strictly necessary. "You realize you are not entitled to a life of luxury at the palace? If you anger Antony or the queen, you won't retire to a life of quiet anonymity. Prison is the best outcome you can hope for. Or perhaps you'd prefer slavery? Execution?"

"Of course not!" I wrenched my hands free. "But there is nothing I can do to revive it!"

Marcus didn't speak for a moment. Then he said slowly, "I knew you were not who you claimed, and this is merely the final proof I need."

"Marcus—"

"Stop. Let me finish," he said. "You may not be who you claim, I know who you *are*, Noor. Despite your constant flirtation with danger, you are unfailingly, almost stupidly, good. Whatever caused you to lie about your background, I know you have good reason."

I let out a shaky laugh. "I don't think you've ever called me Noor, before."

Marcus ran a hand through my hair, gently stroking my cheek

Anonymity - The state of being anonymous

Revive - Bring back to life

with his thumb. "Even if you aren't one, the term 'priestess' suits you, somehow."

"You're welcome to keep using it."

Some time later, Marcus asked, "If I could get you another device, could you paint the portrait using that?"

"Don't bother. You'll never find another."

"You underestimate my powers of persuasion. I know a certain high priest…"

I decided not to tell Marcus that, not only was I not a priestess, the gift wasn't from Isis. It couldn't hurt to let him think he was helping.

Marcus took his leave, and I remained in my rooms. With the ceremony starting later that afternoon, I racked my brain for any way I could get my blasted phone to work. I laid on the divan and placed my hands under my chin, Sherlock Holmes-style.

What did I know of electricity? Not much. Even if a storm conveniently broke out between now and then, I was skeptical of my ability to harness an iota of energy from it. The best plan I could invent involved climbing onto the roof with a sword. Even then, I'd still need to invent a charger to transfer the energy.

I sighed, doubting even the literary genius could've deduced a way out of my present struggle. Lost in speculation, I gazed out the window at a clear blue sky. Then, to my surprise, I drifted off into a peaceful sleep.

Iota - An extremely small amount
Deduced - Concluded; arrived at the fact based on reasoning

"WAKE UP," Marcus was shaking my arm, his face bent over mine.

"You seem happy," I suppressed a yawn, swinging my feet to the floor.

"You will be too, when you see what I have."

Marcus produced an item from behind his back. It was small, wrapped in a rough cloth tied with string. When I unwrapped it, I nearly dropped its precious contents on the floor.

It was an iPhone.

I must have gone deadly pale when I pressed the "home" button and the device lit up. My own image was reflected back at me, but the background photo wasn't mine. It was of Harvey and me, riding camels in front of the pyramids.

I quickly angled the screen away from Marcus's gaze, knowing the picture would raise questions I wasn't ready to answer.

"Marcus," I said cautiously, struggling to keep my voice even. "Where did you get this?"

"From one of the high priests, of course. I forget his name... You don't look pleased. Surely this helps you?"

"It does! I am! I just need to, um, familiarize myself with the new machine," I said. "Gifts from the goddess aren't always alike. I'll see you at the ceremony?"

The moment Marcus' footsteps faded, I frantically clicked the home button once more. *Thank God.* Trusting soul that he was, Harvey's phone wasn't password protected.

I would never do such a thing under normal circumstances, but this was a life-or-death situation. I opened his text messages and began scrolling through them, trying to glean any information I could about his present whereabouts.

I clicked on his chain with Viviana, dragging my thumb down until I reached the date of my disappearance — more than *six months* ago according to the calendar on the home screen.

"What do you mean she's not in Connecticut??????" Viviana wrote. "*Porca miseria*, what are you doing? Have you called the police?"

"Yes. American, British, Egyptian embassies liaising now," Harvey replied. "Will keep you posted."

I switched over to the messages with Shira.

"Viviana and I arrive in Alex at 16:00," she wrote. "Why didn't you tell us the moment she went missing? First hours in a kidnapping are CRITICAL."

The most recent texts indicated that Viviana and Shira were back in Cairo with Harvey, helping with the search effort.

Guilt gripped my chest. I knew how it felt to look for someone, to hold out hope for months with nothing but false leads to dash them.

I rubbed my eyes, glancing at the top right corner. The phone was already at 50% battery, and draining fast with its frantic search for a signal and WiFi. I put it on airplane mode then powered down, knowing I couldn't turn it back on until the ceremony.

For now, survival had to take priority over my guilty con-

Glean - Gather; collect bit by bit

Liaising - Communicating; cooperating on a matter of mutual concern

science. Without me, Harvey's chance of escape greatly diminished. I clutched the phone to my chest, crossing my arms.

He was here. And if his journey had gone anything like mine, I had a fairly good idea where he was.

Diminished - Became less likely or possible

CHAPTER TWENTY

THE CEREMONY WAS HELD on the mainland, in the city's Gymnasium of all places, but bore only a passing resemblance to a high school pep rally.

Like the candidates for homecoming king and queen back in Connecticut,[8] Antony and Cleopatra sat on thrones high above the crowd.

Unlike back in Connecticut, however, Antony and Cleopatra's thrones were made of pure gold, and Caesarion rocked in a golden cradle between them.

Cleopatra was dressed as Isis, wearing a blue-green sheath so bejeweled she looked like an exotic fish. A crown the size of Caesarion rested atop her head, a disc at the center representing her connection to the divine sun.

Fabric (golden, of course) draped between her torso and arms,

---

[8] *Caitlyn was crowned queen, of course.*
Divine - Godly

so whenever she raised her hands it looked like she had wings.

Antony, seated to Cleopatra's left, was dressed as Bacchus, the Roman god of wine and revelry. A crown of grapes rested atop his dark, tousled hair, with little bunches of fruit interspersed with perfectly aged leaves. His toga was a pristine white, and pinned at the shoulder with an elaborate broach.

Between them, Caesarion's cradle was inlaid with images of Horus, the god of kingship. According to ancient Egyptian mythology, Horus' father was the first pharaoh of Egypt, and he would later go on to rule himself.

The iconography was clear: Caesarion was the young and future king, chosen by Isis and Bacchus, gods of Egypt and Rome.

I snapped a few photos, a mixture of panoramas and zoomed-in versions.

"By the gods, look at them!" Neby wasn't looking at the royal family, but the swirling mass of bodies below.

We'd been given seats up above, the equivalent of a box at an athletic event, and the crowd below was growing increasingly restive, pushing against the guards in an effort to reach their rulers.

"No class. No decency," Neby wrinkled his nose.

As the crowd reached a fever pitch, Antony stood and raised his hands. Within seconds, the people calmed.

Interspersed - Mixed in with something else

Pristine - Spotless; fresh as new

Iconography - The interpretation of images

Restive - Restless; difficult to control

"It is a joyous day!" he called, his resounding voice echoing through the auditorium.

Lacking microphones, the ancients were highly attuned to acoustics, and knew how to build massive theaters where even the listeners in the back could hear every word.

"For today," Antony continued, "we celebrate Prince Ptolemy XV Philopator Philometor Caesar, the son of Julius Caesar, better known to most of us as young Caesarion!"

The crowd exploded in cheers, and Antony allowed them a few moments before speaking again.

"We announce the lands Caesarion will rule when he becomes of age," Antony bellowed as an enormous map unfurled behind him. Sections were designated in color, including modern-day Egypt, Greece, Turkey, Armenia, Syria, and Jordan. "With the full blessing, of course, of the Roman people!"

The roar grew to a deafening pitch, and I had the brilliant idea to switch to video.

Cleopatra stood, joining Antony. "Caesarion will rule as his father did. With justice and reason, restoring order in faraway lands and taking care of our citizens at home."

I clapped with the crowd, which somehow grew even louder when Antony concluded: "And now, we feast!"

I took a few more photos, then quickly turned off the phone. If this didn't earn me some goodwill in the palace, I didn't know what would.

Resounding - Unmistakable; loud enough to reverberate

I POLITELY EXCUSED myself once the feast began, claiming I wasn't feeling well, but I doubted anyone but Neby would notice my absence. Marcus was on the podium below, helping protect the royal family, and the meal wasn't a sit-down affair. Waiters circled with delicacies on trays, and the same was happening among the masses below, only the trays were larger and the food less expensive.

Exiting the Gymnasium, I made my way back to the harbor. If I had any fears about getting lost, they were assuaged immediately. The route was lined with crushed flower petals, since Antony and Cleopatra's procession could never have occurred on a *bare* street.

Even without the petals, though, it wouldn't have been hard to find my way back. Alexander the Great laid out the roads with military precision — nice and straight, with right angles at the intersections. Unlike most major cities, where twisty-turny alleyways confound hapless travelers, all you had to do in Alexandria was pick a direction and start walking.

Upon reaching the harbor, I hailed one of the innumerable little ships that shuttled members of court from Cleopatra's island to mainland Alexandria. When I told the captain I wasn't feeling well, he merely gave a bored "aye" and loosened the sails.

As I inhaled the salty spray of the Mediterranean, I couldn't help but recall the last time I'd made the journey to Cleopatra's island palace. I'd just met Marcus, and had nearly fallen off the

---

Assuaged - Made less intense

Confound - Confuse

Hapless - Unfortunate; helpless

ship in my excitement to see the lighthouse of Alexandria, the coastline, the now-sunken island.

And when I arrived, Cleopatra had sent me straight to the dungeons.

I swallowed the fear rising up in my throat, steeling myself against the task ahead. I was headed back to those dungeons the moment my feet hit *terra firma*.

I DIDN'T PASS A SOUL on my journey to the pits of the palace. Everyone was either at the ceremony or catering to the needs of those in attendance.

Experiencing an unpleasant sense of *deja vu*, I watched once more as the beautiful paintings disappeared from the walls and a familiar dampness began to permeate the air.

Finally, at the end of a long, stony corridor that reeked of dirt and despair, I met two Egyptian guards. Shirtless — as usual — they stood before a petrified wooden door, curved swords at their belts, looking straight ahead.

I tried to gauge who would be more susceptible to my request, but, lacking sleeves, neither was able to wear his personality on one. Both men were in their twenties, with olive skin and dark hair, though one had slightly heavier eyebrows and a prominent five o'clock shadow.

I did my best to project confidence as I said, "Greetings, sol-

---

Terra firma - Dry land; firm land

Permeate - Spread through; pervade

Susceptible - Likely to be influenced or affected

Prominent - Noticeable; standing out

diers. I'm here to inquire about a new prisoner. Orders from the mother goddess Isis and Her Majesty, Queen Cleopatra."

The soldiers looked at me, but didn't move.

"I know you," one said finally. "You were here before."

Sergeant Big Brows' face broke in amused recognition, and he looked me up and down. "Must say, you look much nicer now than you did then."

"Yes, it was all a frightful misunderstanding," I said. "I'm a member of court now, *very* close to the queen. And she'd be happy if you didn't make me wait. So—"

"No can do, miss," the first guard said.

I waited for an explanation, but none was forthcoming. He just continued staring straight ahead, and Sergeant Big Brows winked at me.

Finally I said, "And why is that?"

"We only take orders from certain people. You ain't one of 'em."

"Do you take orders from the queen? Because *that* is who sent me."

Guard number one said nothing.

Guard number two chuckled, "How did I forget this one? So much spirit Lateef had to clip her in the jaw. But I like women with a little spirit..."

He took a step forward, unexpectedly yanking me towards him and squeezing my bottom. I could feel his breath, hot on my face.

"Jesus!" I pushed him away and, thank God, he let me go. I stumbled backwards, then turned on my heel and retreated.

I didn't need eyes on the back of my head to know Sergeant

Big Brows was watching me, and in his own twisted fashion, would interpret any movement of my hips as an invitation to further advances. So I walked rigidly down the long corridor, my back unnaturally straight.

How ridiculous, that I have to walk strangely to protect myself! I could feel my nails digging into my palms, my teeth grinding.

Oh, how I yearned for my confiscated pepper spray — or maybe a Taser? The kind that shoots little probes and makes its victims twitch like dying bugs. Which would hurt more, I wondered?

Mercifully, I eventually turned a corner. When I was sure I was alone, I returned to the task at hand. Obviously, I was still going to free Harvey from prison. Equally obviously, I couldn't get him out on my own — not through the front door at least.

I considered calling in a favor with the queen, but with all that she'd just announced, it could be days before I saw her. Furthermore, without knowing on what charges Harvey was imprisoned, I might endanger myself by coming to his defense. And needless to say, if I was imprisoned, his best hope at rescue went up in smoke.

That left only one option available: breaking in.

I CHANGED OUT OF my palace finery, which had oil stains on it from Sergeant Big Brows' chest, and looked for something more suitable for a prison break. Unfortunately everything I owned

---

Yearned - Wanted; longed (for)
Finery - Fancy clothes

seemed to be of white linen, so I chose a loose knee-length dress, thinking it would offer the most mobility.

Thankfully, a few minutes of army-crawling behind the palace turned my dress into authentic camouflage. For some reason I'd expected a beach, since the front three sides of the palace all faced one, so I was surprised to encounter knee-length, unkempt grass. It looked soft, but left little scrapes on my arms and housed armies of bugs that bit me when I disturbed them.

In retrospect, though, I should've realized that there would be more to the island than just the palace. It was two miles long, after all. The palace may have been large, but it wasn't *that* big.

I held out hope that, like mine, Harvey's cell would have a small window. With all those closed doors, air had to get in somehow, if only for the sake of the guards.

Or if not a window, perhaps a grate? I could pry off the top and climb down through the ancient ventilation system.

One entrance was all I needed. It would have to be expanded, of course, but that's why I'd grabbed a pickaxe from the gardeners' shed. It was currently strapped to my back.

Scanning the terrain, I concluded I must be directly on top of the prison cells.

"Harvey!" I called out softly. "Harvey! Can you hear me?"

I waited in silence for a moment, but there was no response.

I crawled a little further, to just above the outer edge of the prison walls. If any of the cells had a window, I should have been

---

Unkempt - Untidy

Retrospect - Looking back

265

directly in line with them. I looked around and saw nothing but the same windblown landscape, ending in jagged cliffs and the sea before me.

Maybe I hadn't gone far enough? My mental blueprint was far from precise. Incurring another few scrapes on my knees and forearms, I crawled another ten feet. Still nothing.

I stood up and kicked an errant rock. I hadn't the faintest idea what I was going to do once I got Harvey out, but if we were together, we'd think of something.

But if I had to return to the palace, disheveled and alone, with the guards ready to tell Cleopatra a story that would condemn me...

What would she do when she heard I'd tried to issue orders in her name? I shuddered to think.

Swatting away flies, I steeled myself for the task ahead. *I'd done alright for myself so far, hadn't I?*

I turned around, preparing to head back to the palace, but the view from this perspective was completely different.

Little windows were carved into the hills in the landscape. They were hidden from behind, due to the rolling terrain, but clearly visible now that I was looking directly at them. In a fraction of a second, I'd already decided which was the largest and was making a beeline towards my destination.

Cautiously putting my face to the grill, I made sure no guards were near before calling, "Harvey!"

Incurring - Getting; receiving
Errant - Not where it should be
Disheveled - Untidy; disordered

There was no response. The bars weren't wide enough for me to slide through, but if I could enlarge the opening on the right side...

I untied the pickaxe and began hacking away at the earth. Admittedly, the process wasn't exactly silent, despite my best efforts not to grunt.

I shouldn't have been so surprised when, some time later, Sergeant Big Brows grabbed the pickaxe mid-air. I tried to yank it back, but he wrested it away with one hand, leaving splinters in my palms.

"Resourceful little thing, aren't you?"

I ran, but starting from a crouched position and stiff from digging, was at a distinct disadvantage. Sergeant Big Beard had ample time to grab me. "No, no. Don't bother trying to flee. You're coming with me."

He threw me over his shoulder like a sack of potatoes, wisely dropping the pickaxe before I could reach it.

Without thinking, I went absolutely ballistic — kicking, clawing, and gouging any vulnerable place I could find. I pulled his hair and, I think, tried to snap his neck. Sergeant Big Brows threw me to the ground, swearing and clutching his right eye.

I sprang to my feet and began sprinting back to the palace, feeling quite pleased with myself...until I saw his partner. I almost ran into him, the stupid hills made visibility so bad.

I skidded to a halt, my shoes slipping on the grass, then tried to

---

Wrested - Yanked; pulled violently

Ample - Plenty; more than enough

pivot to the right.

"She got the best of you, too, eh?" the partner called, his actions mirroring mine.

Like the games of flag football we played back in P.E., every time I changed directions, he did too — and Sergeant Big Brows was drawing closer with each step.

Eventually — with one guard before me and Sergeant Big Brows behind me — escape became impossible.

"Lateef should have hit you harder," Sergeant Big Brows growled, still clutching his eye.

"Oh, undoubtedly," I said, still catching my breath. "But since he didn't, I demand a *parley*."

"A what?" the partner said.

"*Parley*. Like pirates, you know? I demand to speak with your captain."

"Plenty of time for that, priestess. What did you think we were going to do? Kill ya in this field?"

I glanced warily at Sergeant Big Brows. "Something like that."

"We're taking you to the dungeons. No more funny business, or next time you'll have me to deal with."

AT THE ENTRANCE to the dungeons, Sergeant Big Brows departed with a murderous look, which I returned in kind. Then his partner led me down the earthen hallway to a prison cell.

Look on the bright side, I told myself. *At least you made it in. Not in the way you'd hoped, perhaps...*

Parley - A talk between opposing sides to discuss terms

Taking a row of keys from his belt, the partner swung open a creaky door. I briefly considered going for his sword, but I was standing to his left, and the sword was hooked to his belt at the right.

"See you soon, priestess," he shoved me inside.

It took my eyes a moment to adjust, but some sixth sense immediately told me the cell was larger than the one I'd previously occupied, and that I was not alone. Squinting, I made out three figures — two people leaned against the right wall, one against the left.

The one on the left stood when I entered, and without hesitation I flew into his arms, then did a frantic scan of his anatomy.

No dark patches in his hair indicating a blow to the skull. No significant tears in the clothes indicating a hemorrhaging wound.

Harvey chuckled, then stepped back with his old amused grin. "Thought I might find you here."

"Speak for yourself! It's only dumb luck I found out you were here. I have to keep your phone for a while, by the way."

"My, my, becoming the jealous type already?"

My look must have betrayed some discomfort. Harvey deftly changed the subject. Gesturing to the two other forms in the cell, he remarked with just a hint of criticism, "You remember Shira and Viviana?"

"*What?*" I gasped. "How are you...what are you...?"

Shira and Viviana rose to their feet. Harvey said, "We could

Hemorrhaging - Bleeding profusely
Deftly - Quickly; with neat skill

ask you the same question. You've been gone six months, Noor. You nearly gave me a bloody heart attack!"

"Ah, leave her be, Harvey," Viviana said, pulling me in for a hug. She was wearing a tight red skirt that fell mid-thigh. On top, she wore a fashionable white t-shirt, now tie-dyed with mud. Her glossy locks were held back with ribbon.

I turned to Shira and groaned. Her wardrobe was even worse. *Pants*. I hugged her too, then held her at arm's length. "If you guys came on a rescue expedition, you certainly didn't dress the part. Mini skirts? Cargo pants? Could you stand out any more?"

"We didn't think it would actually *work*," Shira said. "But I can rescue you in this far more easily than..." she eyed my dress critically.

"Thankfully, the rescue is now complete," Harvey dusted off his hands. "We were worried about finding you, but you've found us."

Proudly, as though he'd managed to sneak explosives into the palace, Harvey took off his shoe and removed a folded piece of paper from beneath the sole. "Didn't want to take any risks with it getting lost or stolen. Good thing, too. It's our ticket home."

"What do you mean?"

"The professor found the inscription that reverses the spell. If it's anything like the one that brought us here, all we need to do is read it. We don't even need to leave the dungeons first."

Harvey reached for my hand, and Viviana and Shira came to

Expedition - A journey undertaken for a particular purpose

join. To everyone's surprise, including my own, I recoiled. "Harvey, I...I'm not ready."

"What are you talking about?"

"Harvey, my parents are in *Rome*. Rome! And I haven't a clue how to find them. But if I go back to modern times, I have no chance," I spoke quickly, unloading months of developments in a single paragraph. "And Antony and Cleopatra were married *today*. Octavian will be sending warships to Egypt the second he finds out, and the odds of me safely crossing to Rome after that are *nil*. Octavian's got spies in the palace; he probably knew about the wedding before I did...I thought I had more time — I've been a little distracted — but now with the wedding...we probably only have a few weeks until the Battle of Actium."

His face looked like that of a man watching a tennis match, struggling to process each revelation. Viviana squinted, trying to recall what she could of her country's history, and Shira sat back on the floor and resumed carving a small stick into a spear.

"I'll take your word for it that Frank and Mary are in Rome," Harvey said eventually. "My only concern, Noor, is that the spell is in ancient Egyptian. Who knows if it will work in Rome? I don't know how these magical boundaries work, but..."

"If we go to Rome," I continued his thought, "we have to be prepared to stay."

No one spoke as we pondered the thought of never returning to the present day, the only sound the scraping of Shira's stick.

Recoiled - Sprang back in horror, fear

Revelation - Something (often surprising) that is revealed

Pondered - Thought deeply

I'd survived six-plus months in ancient times, but that was like studying abroad. Could I really decide never to see Mitzi again? To forgo modern medicine and a proper toothbrush?

The alternative, though, was to never see my parents again. Parents or Mitzi?

"The risk should be mine," I said eventually. "I would've had no idea how to get home without you; I'll never be able to repay you. But you should all go back. Just leave me a copy of the inscription before you go."

Harvey looked hurt. Shira said, "Eh, this is not how a rescue works, Noor. One does not find the person and then leave them."

Only Viviana looked torn, but before she could say anything, Harvey interjected, "I'll pretend you didn't just say that. Obviously I'm staying with you, whatever you choose to do."

"Obviously," Shira added, still whittling her stick.

"Of course," Viviana nodded. "But if I could have a copy of the text, just in case..."

I laughed, tears dripping down my cheeks. "I insist we all have one, in case we get separated. And everyone has the right to do what is best for them, at any time."

I eyed Viviana pointedly, giving her a reassuring nod, and she relaxed.

"In that case, how are we going to get out of here?" Harvey said.

"There's a larger window in one of the other cells," I said. "I was trying to climb in when I was pinched."

Forgo - Go without

"Interesting, but I'm not sure how that will help. Any other useful information I should know?"

I brought them up to date on everything that had happened since I arrived — how I accidentally burned down the Library of Alexandria (Harvey paled, but refrained from comment); how I'd also been tossed in jail on my first day; how I was now a respected priestess at court.

I didn't tell them about Marcus.

"A fascinating tale," Harvey admitted. "A brute force exit does seem to be out of the question. Unless — Shira?"

She grimaced. "The guards are well-armed, and we're not exactly a crack fighting force."

I nodded. "We'll keep strategizing. In the meantime, is there anything I should know on your end?"

Harvey leaned back, cracking his knuckles. He and I were leaning against the left wall, Shira and Viviana the right, when he began, "We shouldn't have been arrested, honestly! We didn't vandalize anything or — heaven forbid — burn down the Library of Alexandria. We just look funny, I suppose."

He gestured to his tan slacks and white button-down, his shoes with machine-perfect stitching and the watch at his wrist.

"We *have* been trying to rescue you, all of us, for months," he said. "About a week ago, Father told me he found the 'spell' that reverses the one he showed you. I couldn't take it anymore. Shira and Viviana were in Cairo to help with the search party, and I shared my...concerns...about his well-being with them."

Refrained - Held back

"We were sitting on the couch, reading the text," Viviana added impatiently. "*E presto.* We are here."

"More or less," Harvey admitted. "We woke up near a bunch of rubble. Presumably it's what remains of the library. I was checking to see if my mobile had any signal when a horde of blokes wearing eyeliner jumped me. I was too startled to fight back."

Shira grunted, the emerging bruise on her cheek making it clear that she was the only one who had done anything of the sort. "Yes, well," Harvey continued. "They took my phone, then turned us over to the Romans."

"Phones are a bit of a sore spot with the high priests," I explained. "They must have been thrilled to find another!"

"There's not much else to tell," Harvey spread his hands before him. "The Roman tribune ordered us thrown in here, and we've been languishing in prison since mid-morning."

My head snapped in his direction. "Tribune, you said? Did you catch his name?"

"Marcus something-or-other. Why?"

No reason. Only that my erstwhile love interest had you imprisoned, and because of him, we might perish in these dungeons and lose my parents forever.

WE ROTTED IN PRISON for three days. The only contact from the outside world came in the form of meals, slid across the floor through a little flap in the door. We never encountered a human we could attack.

Presumably - Something that is likely, but not certain (think: "probably")

All of this left me with plenty of time to kick myself for being such a trusting fool.

Could Marcus be behind all of this? If he was secretly working for Octavian, he would need an "in" with Cleopatra's court. I provided that.

When he saw my friends, he must've noticed the similarities between us. He would've had no choice but to imprison them — if there were an abundance of magicians, my power would be diluted and his connection would become less valuable.

When we started to fight in Giza, he needed a way to get back in my good graces. He probably planted the snake in my room himself, so he could save me from it. The bastard could've killed me!

I looked at Harvey, quietly doing his own mental calculations against the back wall, and thanked God I was here with him and not Marcus. We'd camped together in the Black and White Desert often enough to know when to give each other space. If I had to guess, he was analyzing ancient accents, just as I'd done during my first stay in prison.

His clothes were wrinkled, shirtsleeves rolled to the elbow, with stains below the underarms. I knew I looked just as bad, if not worse, having crawled through the rugged terrain before being captured. But thankfully, being a larger cell, this one was slightly better appointed.

A side room contained its own makeshift toilet (a hole in the floor that opened up to the outside, the contents of which were

---

Diluted - Made weaker

swept out to sea), so we weren't sleeping in a glorified urinal. The train to Luxor was far more repulsive, but Viviana was perfectly happy to complain about both.

When the rattle of chains alerted us to a visitor on the morning of the fourth day, Harvey, Shira, and I leapt to our feet. Viviana remained seated, perfectly content to watch the proceedings from a distance.

I wasn't surprised to see Marcus' perfect form, broad shoulders and pristine battle armor silhouetted against the light behind him. Viviana scrambled to a standing position, adjusting her skirt and smoothing her hair, but Marcus wasn't looking at her.

In three long strides he'd taken me in his arms, heedless of the bug bites and wild-woman-of-the-forest appearance. I thought he was going to do something romantic, but instead he gave me a shake. "Why are you down here? *Again?*"

I remained stiff as a statue. "You should know," I said. "Wasn't this all part of your plan?"

"What are you talking about, woman?"

"You're working for him. Octavian. You've been keeping me in Alex to reinforce your own position at court. I could've been on my way to Rome! You threw my best friend in jail—"

Marcus took a step back. "Working for Octavian? Why would I do that? I've sworn an oath to Antony! And in case you forgot, *I'm* the one who told you your parents were *in* Rome! I would've taken you there months ago, if you'd let me."

He gave me a meaningful look, reminding me of his proposal,

Pristine - Spotless; fresh as new

and I flushed.

"Then why," I scrambled, "why did you cheer for the crocodile? And why did you have Harvey's phone?"

Marcus looked at me with pity, clearly believing I was losing my wits after three days in prison. Then he noticed Harvey, Shira, and Viviana. They'd stood motionless throughout the exchange, except for Viviana, who was still simpering.

"I know you," Marcus said.

It was the longest Harvey had ever been silent amid a conversation. He responded for the group: "That you do. You threw us in this pit."

"His name is Harvey," I added, doing my best to sound sane. "He's been my closest friend since we were children. And this is Shira and Viviana, my..." I couldn't think of the ancient word for "roommates," so I settled for, "other close friends."

"Nice to meet you," Viviana said in adorable Latin. She'd probably studied the language since childhood, the way many Americans take Spanish.

"I'll need subtitles, please!" Shira waved her spear. "Good or bad things happening? Do I attack?"

"No!" Viviana and I cried in unison.

Viviana began translating for Shira, and I returned to Marcus. "When I found out they were here, I had no choice but to try to free them. You understand, don't you?"

"But why didn't you tell me?" Marcus demanded. "By the gods, I could've spoken a word and had them released! Don't you know by now that I'd do anything for you?"

I could practically see the big red hearts over Viviana's eyes.

"I...it all happened so fast," I stammered.

Eventually Harvey cut in. "I hate to interrupt what is clearly a very tender moment, but perhaps it would be better conducted outside these walls? I'd give my right arm for a bath."

Marcus wrinkled his nose. "Perhaps you're right. Follow me."

We passed Sergeant Big Brows and his partner on the way out. I didn't say a word before Marcus began berating them in the strongest invective I've ever heard, in any language.

They did not have the authority to arbitrarily imprison people. That dubious authority rested with Antony, Cleopatra, and a small cadre of men far more important than they would ever be.

Sergeant Big Brows caught my eye and foolishly decided to mount a defense. "But, sir, she—"

"You will be *silent* when I speak, soldier. And next time you forget your place, I'll have you defenestrated."

"How oddly specific," Harvey said in tones of mild amusement.

Marcus shot him a look, then finished upbraiding the guards. When he was done, and the guards were out of earshot, he reassured me, "They won't bother you again. That is, assuming we can invent a credible story to explain your absence to the queen. She's been asking for you."

"Since when?"

"Yesterday. She wanted to see the images from the ceremony."

Invective - Highly critical language

Cadre - Small group of people

Defenestrated - Thrown out a window

Upbraiding - Scolding

Credible - Believable

"*Merde.* Can I say I went for a walk and was thrown in the dungeons? That *is* basically what happened."

"You can try. What about them?"

Marcus gestured at my companions, walking behind us. When I turned around, Harvey was looking at me in the oddest way.

"We'll have to explain their presence, too," I said. "I'll think of something."

"You always do," Harvey muttered.

* * *

HARVEY WAS A wealthy merchant from faraway America, which explained why we shared an accent, how I knew him, and why his clothes were so unique. He'd been foully robbed on his journey to Alexandria, then mistaken for a criminal upon his arrival.

I explained this to Cleopatra in the most dramatic of terms, then told her flat-out that I'd been falsely imprisoned while trying to rescue him. What he deserved, I said, was our sympathy, not our fear.

"I can hardly blame you for coming to the aid of a friend," she said disinterestedly. "But next time, don't disappear for so long. It is terribly inconvenient."

"Of course, Your Majesty." I bowed, repressing a grin. It was as close as I'd get to an official pardon.

No one asked about Shira and Viviana. Since they arrived with

---

Repressing - Suppressing; holding back

Harvey, everyone assumed they were his wives, and would therefore receive the same pardon he did. Their clothes were the product of bizarre — and slightly barbaric — American fashions.

Antony was sprawled in a second golden throne, now installed beside Cleopatra's. His sandaled feet draped over one of the arms, he waved an impatient hand. "*Bene, bene.* Now let us see these *renderings* of yours."

Iras approached me, palm outstretched. I gave her Harvey's phone and she stared at it intently, whispered something at it in ancient Egyptian, then tapped on the screen. Needless to say, it did not turn on.

"*Bona dea...*" Antony rubbed his eyes. "Priestess, *come!*"

Like a little dog, I fetched the phone from Iras, trotting past the guards to the royal podium. I stood between the royals, moving the phone closer to each one as I showed them the images.

"But why are they so *small?*" Cleopatra said, the novelty of the item already wearing off. "Make them larger. I should see my likeness on the side of a temple."

"Unfortunately, Your Majesty, the gift does not extend—"

"What she means to say," Harvey interrupted in the politest of tones, "is that she *has* received a new gift from the goddess, just not that one. Yet."

I shot him a *"what are you talking about now is really not the time!"* look.

"*The video,*" he coughed in English. "Play the video!"

Just as I was kicking myself for not remembering I'd taken one, and thanking myself for remembering to tell Harvey, Antony said. "You see? What is it you see, boy? Speak up!"

Pesky roots. The word "video" is Latin for "I see." Harvey was basically repeating, "I see! *Gibberish gibberish* I see!"

"He sees," I said smoothly, "how blessed you are to receive such a gift.

I flipped to the video, bringing the phone near Cleopatra, and pressed play.

Her brows raised and she leaned forward to get a better look. "Extraordinary," she said. "Quite extraordinary."

Antony leaned towards us, lurching over the arm of his throne. He nodded and frowned, in an impressed sort of way.

Cleopatra ordered me to play the video four more times. I adopted my serene priestess voice. "The goddess sees all, and now, so can you."

But she wasn't listening. A smile curved the queen's painted lips, but eventually Antony waved me away. "Leave us now."

Though Harvey was absolved of any wrongdoing in the eyes of the queen, the relationship did not extend so far as to provide a suite of rooms.

She probably assumed he would leave Antirhodos (which made me wonder, why had Marcus brought him here in the first place? Surely not every prisoner ends up on the royal island? Unless it was because, due to their similarities with me, they were seen as somehow important?)

But since Cleopatra hadn't explicitly ordered him to leave, I

Absolved - Released from guilt, blame, or wrongdoing
Explicitly - Clearly; directly

brought the three of them back to my quarters. Viviana cooed in Italian, running her hands over the furniture before standing appreciatively at the balcony. Shira joined her, and once the two of them were lost in animated conversation, I pulled Harvey aside.

"Antony wasn't at all himself back there," I said. "He's always been a character, but he was...distracted, somehow. He'd rather be planning for war."

"In that case, whether the war has actually begun may be irrelevant," Harvey said slowly. "Once they are on the war*path*, Antony and Cleopatra may wish to keep your wise counsel."

I nodded. "I'd say we have days to leave for Rome. Not weeks."

CHAPTER TWENTY-ONE

SOMETIMES THE SIMPLEST THINGS in life are the most difficult.

Technically, all we needed to do was board an Italy-bound ship. Now that Marcus and I were back on speaking terms, he could find a nice one and secure safe passage.

But to do this meant, essentially, that I was accepting his hand in marriage. How could I possibly explain wanting to bring Harvey, Viviana, and Shira along? Maybe the last two would back out, but to bring only Harvey would be even stranger.

And sorry, but *married*? At 18? To an ancient Roman soldier? Infatuated I may have been, but I was nowhere near ready for that level of commitment.

I groaned. If the voyage had been costly before, it was four times as expensive now, and I was equally impecunious. Not knowing the ramifications of reading the text, Harvey and co.

Impecunious - Having little or no money
Ramifications - Consequences

hadn't brought any money.

My situation was decidedly unique to the time. Unlike in modern days, not having any money didn't mean I was destitute or in debt. No one asked me to pick up the check at the end of a meal or pay rent at the end of the month. I simply had no income. No one paid me a salary to hang around and act like a priestess.

Naturally, I only explained the financial component of my rationale to Harvey. We hadn't spoken about Marcus, and I was in no rush to bring it up.

"Larceny it is, then," Harvey concluded.

The four of us were on the divans in my sitting room, the balcony open to the sea and sky. The curtains billowed gently, as enraptured by the sea breeze as we were.

"To steal something, in these times..." Shira grimaced. "It may not be wise. Was it ancient Egypt where they cut the hands off thieves?"

Viviana grew pale, then leaped from her seat to go stand by the balcony. She wiped sweat from her upper lip. "Just catching some air!" she trilled.

"Shira's right," I said. "And not just because of the potential punishment. Most people here are like me. Their families might have money, but it's not accessible in the day-to-day."

"But, *someone* must have money," Harvey insisted. "I mean, look at the amount of *stuff* in this place. Someone's paying for it."

"You know as well as I do that most of this was inherited." I

Destitute - Extremely poor; going without basic necessities

Component - Part of a larger whole

Larceny - Theft; stealing

inhaled sharply as an idea struck me. "And yet, there is something we buy copious quantities of every day."

"And that is?"

"*Food.* Even if Cleopatra does commission expensive sculptures from time to time, a craftsman might get paid once, at the beginning or end of a project. But butchers and bakers need regular payment. The kitchens might actually be our best bet."

"Do you know where they are?"

"Better. I'm friends with the chef."

As we considered ways to rob the man who'd always welcomed me, I reminded myself that the money we'd steal wouldn't actually be his. He wasn't financing palace dinners out of his own pocket. We were taking *Cleopatra's* money, which he just happened to handle. The chef would be fine.

ntain eye contact with the chef as Harvey snuck in through the side entrance.

"They were all talking about it!" I gushed. "Sounds like it's going to be masterful."

Harvey was behind the chef now, quietly opening cabinets and rifling through jars.

"But...cakes take time. Loads of time. And we haven't the people today..."

The chef wiped his forehead with his forearm. In doing so, he turned his head and saw Harvey.

Copious - A lot of; an abundant supply

Commission - Order the production of

"You, there!" he shouted, brandishing his knife.

Harvey dropped the jar he was holding and ran. It made a satisfying crash, and I added to the chaos by bumping into a rack of jars, all of which shattered to the floor.

"Oh my goodness!" I said. "Look at this mess. Here, let me help you..."

The chef surveyed his orderly kitchen with horror. Shards of glass, pottery, and dried herbs covered the table, the floor, and everything in between.

I really did feel awful about it, and started helping him pick up.

"Ye'll cut yourself if you're not careful, priestess," he said with a deep breath. "Best you leave now."

I WAS CONVINCED the chef was going to lose his job because of us, that he'd end up begging on the street with a brood of starving children.

"We're keeping an eye on him," I insisted. "And if anyone gets upset, I'm covering for him."

"Obviously," Harvey said. "But until then, we need to come up with another plan. I couldn't find so much as a *piastre* on those shelves."

Harvey stretched. Viviana eyed his admirable musculature, now on full display in ancient Egyptian garb. We'd all adopted the local wardrobe, but none represented such a marked change as Harvey. He was wearing a white skirt that fell above the knee, and

---

Brandishing - Waving or flourishing in anger or excitement

Piastre - A unit of currency worth a small amount

a thick pectoral necklace instead of a shirt.

Apparently chest waxes were routine down at the bathhouse. I nearly died laughing when he described the horror that gripped him upon seeing the ominous bowl of wax, and how when he refused, the aestheticians attacked him with little clams.

"Clams?" I asked.

"Some kind of ancient tweezers," he said, jovially pinching my midsection. "*Snap, snap, snap!*"

He'd escaped with most of his chest hair intact, and looked like a gorilla compared to the smooth Egyptian men at court.

A smile quirked the edge of my lips as I returned to the subject at hand. "Bartering is still common. Think we could trade your old clothes for safe passage?"

"I don't know what the going rate is, but it's worth a try."

"Maybe your soldier boyfriend can help," Shira piped in. She and Viviana were playing *senet*, the ancient Egyptian form of chess. "Seems like a powerful figure around here."

The air went still. Of course Shira didn't know what happened between Harvey and me before I left. There was no reason she shouldn't mention my new "boyfriend." (Though the word seemed far too pedestrian to describe a figure like Marcus.)

Harvey and I spoke at the same time.

"I need to—"

"Maybe we can—"

By then Harvey was halfway to the door, patting his skirt. "I

Aestheticians - People knowledgeable about beauty
Pedestrian - Lacking excitement; dull; common

forgot something in the — ah — throne room? Back in a mo'."

"Harvey, wait—"

But he was already gone.

THE NEXT DAY, without telling Harvey, I sent a message to Marcus.

"Can we meet?"

I penned the note in Latin with my own hand, then gave it to a member of Antony's personal guard, asking if he could see it delivered. The man looked annoyed, but gave a curt nod.

Truthfully, I didn't know how else to reach him. He always just seemed to appear every few days on some business or another; I'd never had to seek him out before.

The day progressed with no response, but that wasn't altogether unexpected. The soldier on duty had to return to camp before passing my message along.

But as dusk rolled in, I started to wonder how Marcus would reply. A messenger at midnight? Throwing rocks at my window a la *Romeo and Juliet*? No, that wouldn't do. The window was sea-facing...

In any case, I'd have some explaining to do with my houseguests. With the four of us in a suite designed for one, Harvey and I were sleeping on the divans while Shira and Viviana shared the bedroom. No one was sneaking in or out unobserved.

I was spared from an awkward explanation by the simple fact that Marcus didn't respond. Not that night, or the next day. Nor the day after that, nor the night after.

I finally ran into him at Cleopatra's levee some days later.

"Priestess," he said, as was his custom, on the way out.

"Marcus," I returned his salutation. "You didn't get my message, then?"

"Message?"

"It doesn't matter. Do you have a minute?"

We made our way back to the hypostyle hall, where he'd first proposed, and I squared my shoulders.

"I haven't forgotten your offer, and I *am* thinking about it. But before I can make any decisions, I have to get to Rome to find my parents. And I need to leave soon, before the fighting begins. If I could just *borrow* some money—"

Marcus took me by the arms and looked down at me fondly. I could feel the warmth of his hands on my skin. "It's not about the money, priestess."

"I know, I know. You want—"

"No, it's not that. Well, yes I do. But about you getting to Rome—"

"Yes?"

"The fighting may not have begun, but you'll never find a ship."

"What are you talking about?"

"The royal navy commandeered anything sturdy enough to make such a voyage. Unless you're willing to trek around the sea, through a thousand miles of desert, travel will have to wait until after the war."

Hypostyle - A building with a roof supported by large pillars

Commandeered - Seized for military use

"Of course I'm willing."

Marcus chuckled and rubbed his eyes. "I know. But alone and on foot? You'd be dead by the first oasis."

I clenched my jaw, even though I knew he was right. When Hannibal made a similar journey, albeit on a different route, he'd lost tens of thousands of men.

"What are we going to do then?" I asked.

"*We*? Priestess, there is no 'we' in this situation, thank the gods. I'll go to battle. You'll stay at the palace. You can read an incantation, or do whatever priestesses of Isis do, and pray for my safe return."

"Battle?" I went rigid.

"That is, conventionally, what opposing armies do."

"But, you don't have to go, do you?"

"Can't get much field experience staying here at the palace."

"But you won't be on the ships, right? You'll be strategizing behind the scenes, like the last battle?"

"Unfortunately, no. We won't have the same level of infrastructure in Actium." Sensing my alarm, he added, "But don't worry! With our share of the Roman navy, plus Cleopatra's fleet, we vastly outnumber Octavian's forces. The battle will be quickly won."

I felt sick. In the echo of the hall, the phrase had the ominous ring of "famous last words" from the walking dead, a man charging into a losing battle.

Albeit - Although

Ominous - Suggests something bad is going to happen

CHAPTER TWENTY-TWO

THE PALACE DESCENDED into an eerie calm after Antony and Cleopatra departed. The lavish dinners halted. Meetings of the "The Inimitable Livers Club" stopped wreaking havoc on the sleep of innocent farmers (Antony and Cleopatra dressed in costumes and ding-dong-ditched people — don't even ask).

The air felt thick with anticipation, our movements syrupy. I spent day after day on the balcony, staring out to sea.

If I just knew one more fact — just one — about the ancient world, I thought, head in my hands. *Will Marcus survive the battle?*

I imagined the fighting through his eyes — chaos and blood and sharks circling the fallen bodies. Ships on fire, men screaming...

Eerie - Strange and troubling

Inimitable - So good or unique it cannot be copied

Wreaking - Causing (damage or harm)

Several weeks into my malaise, Harvey approached me.

"Noor," he said. Why don't you sit down?"

"I'm fine. Sit down for what?"

Harvey gently steered me to one of the divans. Sitting down next to me, he began, "I haven't said anything, since I haven't minded staying on longer than we thought."

"You've had unfettered access to Cleopatra's palace," I snorted. "You're living every historian's fantasy."

"I am," he agreed. "But Shira and Viviana aren't historians. They didn't even know they'd be coming here. People will be worried."

"Send them back, then."

Harvey's brow furrowed. "I'm worried about you, Noor."

Why do people say that? I ground my teeth. *It's the stupidest phrase. It solves absolutely nothing, and just makes you feel worse.*

I breathed deeply through my nose, resisting an overwhelming urge to snap at him, then went back to the balcony. Waves crashed on the rocks below. Birds swooped to snatch their prey between crests. Neither of us spoke.

Finally, hands gripping the railing, I whispered, "I lost them, Harvey. *Again.* And now I might lose..."

Thick, hot tears fell down my cheeks. Harvey, forgetting he was dressed as an ancient Egyptian, came over and pulled me in for a big hug.

I loved him for that, loved that there was no jealousy over

Malaise - General feeling of discomfort or uneasiness

Unfettered - Unlimited; unrestrained

Marcus in my moment of need, just the knowledge that I needed comforting. He felt warm and safe, except for the pectoral necklace digging into my cheek.

"It'll be OK, Noor," he cooed, rocking me slightly. "It'll be OK."

His chest was damp by the time my tears stopped falling, but I didn't pull away. He smelled like home and sandalwood oil, his skin soft against mine.

The door creaked. "We are interrupting something, eh?" Viviana asked, her tone unmistakably laced with innuendo.

I jumped back in alarm. "No! No, it's just—"

Shira *tsked*. "Can't you see she is grieving?"

Viviana covered her hand with her mouth. "*Scusa*, I did not mean to joke about... that is, I am sorry."

"It's fine," I sniffled. "And it's I who should be apologizing. Thank you — all of you — for being so patient with me."

"I cannot imagine," Viviana murmured. "Take all the time you need."

"Within reason," Shira added.

I let out a choked laugh, joining them in the sitting room. "It's time we talk about next steps. I think the two of you should go back. How can you explain even being gone this long?"

Shira shrugged, plopping down on one of the divans. "We'll think of something, but you are right. We say our goodbyes tonight — disappearing without explanation may lead to questions. It's unlikely they'd lead to the truth, but we don't need to take the risk. Then we read the spell first thing tomorrow."

Innuendo - A suggestive reference

I nodded. Trust Shira to cut right to the heart of the matter. "Who do you need to say goodbye to?" I asked curiously. I hadn't realized they'd made so many friends.

As Shira and Viviana rattled off the names of people I'd barely spoken to, I realized how isolated I'd become since learning I couldn't get to Rome — and that Marcus was sailing into a losing battle.

WITHOUT WARNING, Cleopatra's gilded barge sailed into the harbor early that evening. Oars made of silver dipped into the water. Perfumed sails lent a pleasant smell to the wind. Flowers and other symbols of victory graced the rails.

My first thought was to wonder how anyone aboard could breathe through all that perfume, if I could smell it from here.

Harvey and I were back on the balcony. Viviana was saying goodbye to a certain soldier, and Shira was with her, playing the silent chaperone.

"But...what?" Harvey sputtered. "Antony and Cleopatra lose. They *lose*. What's happening?"

I frowned at the horizon and started to speak, but Harvey pressed on. "This is bad, Noor. If Antony and Cleopatra win, our world looks radically different — borders redrawn, languages reconfigured, governments reimagined...The American Constitution was based on Greece and Rome. If Rome never becomes an empire, who's to say America will even be founded?"

"Do *not* discuss American history with me right now."

Reconfigured - Put together differently

"The Battle of Actium is a cornerstone moment in history, Noor. If Antony and Cleopatra win, nothing is safe. That includes us."

Cleopatra was waving at the crowds from the deck of her boat. Throngs of people had run to the harbor to see her, waving back and crying tears of relief that the war was won so quickly.

"Where's Antony?" I said. "Shouldn't he be on deck with her?"

"Injured, maybe, or on a different ship with his men?"

"Hmmm."

CLEOPATRA ORDERED an enormous feast in honor of Egypt's victory. Antony would be returning shortly, she announced, and he of all people wouldn't mind if the celebrations began a bit early.

Since there wasn't time to prepare a victory dinner, drinks were passed around freely instead. Nobody minded the lack of a proper meal.

To Egypt! people said. *May Neptune wipe his butt with Roman ships!* one rather inebriated fellow added, raising his drink in a toast.

I hid my laugh with a sip of wine and decided not to point out that, technically, Antony was also Roman. Antony and Cleopatra may be ruling as equals now, but Egypt hadn't exactly kicked Rome to the curb.

The voices faded into the background as Harvey considered

Inebriated - Drunk

the positive implications of Egypt's burgeoning hegemony.

"There's no guarantee it will last, of course. Based on this fellow's remarks, the Egyptians may be every bit as imperialistic as the Romans or Brits," he tilted his head. "But the implications for East-West relations—"

With a sudden *crack*, the double doors to the Great Hall flew open. Antony stood in the center, bloody and disheveled, one arm on each door. His eyes went immediately to his queen.

"Ah! The conquering hero has returned!" Cleopatra called. "Won't you have a drink, my love?"

"I believe I will." Antony grabbed the entire tray from a nearby slave, spilling generously before slamming it on a table in front of the royal thrones.

Cleopatra laughed nervously. "Not that I don't appreciate how ruggedly handsome you look, but perhaps a bath is in order. Iras, summon Antony's..."

"I'm fine," Antony snarled, downing the first glass. "Enjoy each day while you have it, nay?"

More soldiers were starting to file in, looking in confusion at their surroundings. I stared anxiously until I could take it no more. I jumped from my seat, leaving Harvey to fend for himself, and ran directly into the melee.

*Too tall, too short, too young, too old...*I grabbed many a surprised soldier, trying to see his face. They shook me off and carried on.

Burgeoning - Beginning to grow

Hegemony - Dominance

Imperialistic - Extending a country's power through diplomacy or military force

Melee - A confused mass of people

Goosebumps erupted on my forearms. I felt sick. *Where was he?*

An arm stole around my waist; a face nuzzled my hair. Instinctively I elbowed the miscreant, then doubled over in pain. My funny bone had collided with the man's breastplate.

I turned, but by then, had already realized who the presumptuous individual must be.

"Marcus," I nearly fainted with relief. His arm was bandaged, his face smeared with smoke and sweat, but he was intact.

He pulled me in with his uninjured arm, giving me a kiss, then asked, "What is the meaning of this?"

"The meaning of what?"

"This...*celebration!*"

Oh, no. He hit his head. He has amnesia. But he remembers me, at least!

"It's in honor of Egypt winning the war!" I said encouragingly. "You fought bravely, I'm sure!"

"Priestess, I...we...the war isn't won. Octavian is in pursuit. He'll be here by morning."

"What?"

"*She,*" Marcus spat in Cleopatra's direction, "turned and fled when the fight got thick. Took all her ships. We were surrounded."

Harvey approached in time to hear the last sentence. He was about to clap Marcus on the back in an awkward "welcome home" gesture, and it grew even more awkward when Harvey's hand stopped mid-air.

Miscreant - A person who behaves badly

Presumptuous - Going beyond what is permitted or appropriate

"You lost?"

"Retreat was the only option," Marcus said, eyeing Harvey's frozen appendage. "The Egyptian flank was gone. It was retreat or suicide."

"I'm not blaming you," I said. "No one is! We're just happy you're alive."

"Alive," Marcus repeated hollowly. "For now, yes."

Harvey and I made somber eye contact. History was back on course.

BRAVELY AS CLEOPATRA attempted to continue the charade, news that Octavian's armada would surround the harbor by morning quickly spread throughout the palace.

And yet, somehow, the party continued. The chefs had started cooking by then, and the queen ordered a never-ending supply of food and wine.

She sat clear-headed on her throne, watching the court enjoy themselves as though it were any other Tuesday — if a slightly celebratory one.

Antony, on the other hand, was a wreck. He'd ripped off his armor, letting it crash to the palace floor, before settling bleary-eyed on his throne.

Now he slouched in a filthy red tunic, holding drinks in both hands, grumbling to himself as he stared out the window. I was dying to know what he said, but all I could hear were his ex-

---

Appendage - Something attached to something larger or more important

Somber - Grave or solemn in mood

Armada - Fleet of warships

traordinary hiccups.

Cleopatra put a hand over his. "Easy, my love. We must be good hosts."

Harvey, Marcus, and I were seated on floor pillows before a low table, some forty feet from the royal couple. The mood of the room was festive, but Marcus scowled at the queen. "I'm half-tempted to believe the lies they tell about her in Rome, that she is a sorceress who has bewitched and unmanned him."

Harvey rolled his eyes and took a sip of his drink. "She has no reason to, er, 'unman' him. She suffers the consequence of his loss worse than anyone."

"Explain," Marcus reached for a piece of bread, roughly tearing off a chunk with even white teeth.

"If Antony loses, *so does she*," Harvey said, his tone insufferably condescending. "Octavian becomes the sole ruler of Rome. Cleopatra and her son by Caesar get nothing."

Marcus scowled. "None of this would've happened if she hadn't fled."

"Wouldn't it? No chance she saw the tide of battle turning and didn't want her ships falling into Octavian's hands? Or would you have preferred she burned the ships, like Caesar when he destroyed the library?"

"Harvey!" I said. "A little tact, please?"

Then, in an attempt to redirect Marcus' attention, I asked him, "What do you think will happen next? Will there be another battle?"

Condescending - Talking down (to someone)

Marcus glowered. "Antony isn't planning for one. He's announced no meeting. He doesn't appear to be planning any strategy. I fear..."

"Yes?"

"If I were Octavian, I would lay siege to the palace. An island is laughably easy to surround. Before long, we'll be cut off from food and water."

I looked around. Half-eaten food littered the tables; spilled wine stained the pillows. I gestured dramatically, "There must be weeks of provisions here. Months, maybe. Surely Antony and Cleopatra will come to their senses by then!"

"Octavian may not give them the time," Marcus swallowed. "He's far more ruthless than I. It'd be simpler, I think...for him to trap us inside, then set the palace on fire."

"*What?* He couldn't! He's a slave to public opinion. What would the people say?"

"If not for them, we'd already be kindling." Marcus reached over and took my hands. "Priestess, I don't know what Octavian will do, but there's a chance I can negotiate a pardon. Octavian would rather have my family's gratitude than vengeance, I think. Even so, I'll be stripped of everything I own. I'll be exiled, forced to live in the provinces with no rank...But you—"

"Marcus—"

"I will do everything I can. *Everything,*" he said fiercely, "to protect you. But if Antony and Cleopatra will not fight, they must surrender. If they do, Octavian will have no reason to burn the palace. You will be safe."

To my surprise, tears were streaming down my cheeks when

Harvey rudely interrupted.

"Noor?" he said politely. "Might I speak to you for a moment? *Alone?*"

He stood up, not waiting for me to respond before dragging me into the shadow of a nearby column. I looked back at Marcus, who was clearing his throat, then at Viviana and her new soldier, giggling in the shade of another column.

Shira was watching them from a distance, expression surly and arms folded, like an FBI agent on the spring break shift in Miami.

"Harvey, who is this soldier of Viviana's?" I asked. "Shira's no killjoy, even if she doesn't speak the language. She's watching them like she's worried—"

"Have you lost your bloody mind?" Harvey demanded, shaking me by the shoulders. "It was one thing to go after your parents, but you're acting like you're going to stay here! To be burned alive with a soldier, or follow him to Gaul and be a farmer's wife! I swear to God, Noor!"

"I never—"

"There is *nothing* we can do to help Antony and Cleopatra," Harvey continued. "Antony is lucky he hasn't already drowned in a vat of wine, and Cleopatra doesn't have a chance without his army. And I will *drag* you out of here kicking and screaming if you say you're staying with Marcus."

"Alright," I shook off his arm. "Alright! You want to know what I'm thinking? I haven't decided yet!"

"*Decided?* Decided *what?*"

It was a good question. What did I need to decide? Whether to stay or to go, certainly, but whether or not I could save my parents was no longer the only factor motivating my decision.

I'll admit it — I wanted more time with Marcus. I needed to figure out how it was possible to love two people at once, but in entirely different ways. Why couldn't I love them both, but not wed myself to either one just yet? I was only 18, for goodness' sake!

I needed to buy myself more time. I'm not proud of how I did it, but the words I spoke *were* true, even if they weren't really what I'd been thinking.

"Here's what I do know," I waved a hand at the throngs of people surrounding us. "I'm not ready to let all of these people be burned alive. Are *you*?"

Harvey grimaced. "They'll be fine. If we don't interfere..."

"Our very existence here is an interference, Harvey! We've already seen that things can change. We can't assume that every detail will play out like it does in the textbooks. I — I need to think. Marcus! Come here."

Once again the stoic soldier, Marcus joined us, cheeks slightly shinier than they'd been a minute ago.

I sat down, my back against the wall, and pulled the two men down with me. Here, we were more or less secluded from the crowds.

"We are three intelligent people," I said. "There must be some scenario we're overlooking — something that enables us to avoid further loss of life, save Marcus' future, and get to Rome to find

---

Throngs - Densely-packed crowds
Secluded - Shut off from; isolated from

my parents. We just need to find it."

Neither of them spoke.

"Ok, I'll start," I said. "Marcus, you are correct that our fates depend on the actions of Antony and Cleopatra. We could never sneak everyone out of the palace before Octavian burns it; the only means of egress is by sea. Is there *any* chance of another battle? Or could we dig in and fight them off from here? I could pour scalding oil on their heads..."

Harvey looked at me with a sour mixture of amusement and exasperation. "Do try to control your rampageous imagination. We're trying to avoid death and deformity here, remember?"

Marcus rubbed the back of his sunburned neck. "Your friend is right. We've barely enough loyal men left to form a legion, much less repel the entirety of Octavian's forces. Antony...we left many men at sea."

"But there must be some way to keep us all alive!" I said, belligerently adding, "Octavian, Antony, *and* Cleopatra."

As far as Harvey was concerned, the latter two were already dead. That's how it happened in the history books.

Marcus's shoulders, normally so broad and capable, slumped inward. "Where there's a war, there's a winner. The loser rarely survives."

"Especially not in this case," Harvey added.

Egress - Exit

Scalding - Burning; very hot

Exasperation - Extreme annoyance

Rampageous - Violently uncontrollable (like a rampage)

Belligerently - Aggressively; war-like

I shot him a look. "Is there a palace architect? Someone with a layout of the grounds? There must have been *some* pharaoh who wasn't stupid enough to let himself get surrounded like this. An underwater tunnel, a secret exit..."

Marcus just looked at me like I'd lost my mind, and Harvey gently reached for my arm.

"Harvey, I won't ask you to stay with me until the end. But please — don't go yet."

He looked at me for a moment, then nodded.

WE REMAINED in the Great Hall until the wee hours of the morning. Early on, I grabbed Shira and looped her into our conversation.

"Why are you standing sentry over Viviana like that?" I asked. "Do you know something I don't?"

"Just a feeling," she shrugged. "Certain people don't handle losing well. Then you add alcohol..."

"She'll be fine. And we're just a stone's throw away if not. Join us."

We returned to our table, sitting on embroidered floor cushions. Shira and I sat cross-legged, and the men laid on their sides, propped up on their elbows.

Sometimes we spoke in Latin, translating for Shira; other times in English, translating for Marcus. Somehow, the conversation turned to stories of our childhood.

Harvey's curiosity momentarily overpowered his impatience as

Sentry - Guard

Marcus described his patrician upbringing.

"My family is not famous, not like Brutus'," Marcus said, gaze hardening at the mention of Caesar's murderer. "His family founded the republic, but now I suspect they'll be famous for something else."

Sitting up and refilling his drink, Marcus continued, "In any case, we are an old and noble family, if a weakening one. Once we were consuls; now we are senators. Father is keen that we not drop any lower."

"What did your education look like?" Harvey asked. "Were you tutored at home?"

Marcus gave him an odd look. "How else would I learn? Oh yes, we had all the finest *magistri*. Swordsmen, orators, mathematicians, all came to teach me the art of serving the republic."

Setting his drink down, Marcus flopped on his back in a moment of dramatic self-indulgence. Long legs stretched out, bare and hairy from the waist down, he sighed. "Not anymore. It's death or exile for me."

"I lost my family, too," I said, reaching for him. "The reason I came here—"

Harvey shook his head slightly.

"Why shouldnn-I tell him?" the drink beginning to affect my enunciation. "We're all in now."

Harvey shrugged in a, *"He'll think you're crazy, but I warned you"* kind of way.

Patrician - Aristocratic; of noble rank

Magistri - Latin for "teachers"

Enunciation - The act of pronouncing something clearly

"Marcus," I said. "What I'm about to say may surprise you, but I swear it's the honest truth." I kneeled before him, one hand on my heart, one hand raised like I was about to be sworn in as president.

He draped an arm across my legs, mouth curving in a sardonic smile. "You're not a priestess of Isis."

"That is true, but you already knew that." Looking down at him, I said, "I was born more than 2,000 years from now."

Then I had a moment of intense *deja vu*. There was a crash. Something falling — not an explosion. But there were shouts! Angry shouts, in a mixture of languages.

My head swiveled in the direction of the chaos. Shira was already halfway there, worry lending wings to her frame. Her concerns had been well-founded. Viviana was being strangled by the soldier.

Viviana swatted at his hands, violently shaking her head in an attempt to escape. Hair kept getting in her mouth. "*Basta!*" she gasped, tears squeezing out of her eyes. "*Basta! Basta!*"

Harvey, Marcus and I immediately scrabbled to our feet. Unfortunately I tripped on my stupid dress in my haste to sprint over; Marcus wasn't the most agile in his armor, coming from a lying down position; and Harvey was the last to see it, his back facing the scene.

Still running, Shira was flailing her arms like a psychotic windmill. At first I thought it was some Israeli fighting maneuver.

Sardonic - Mocking or cynical
Basta - Italian for "stop"
Scrabble - Scramble or crawl quickly

Maybe she's winding up for an aggressive smack, I hoped. *Or she's intimidating him by making herself seem larger, like when you see a bear.*

Unlike me, Viviana understood immediately. Remembering that night in our dorm so long ago, Viviana raised her right hand, twisted, and crashed her weight on the soldier's forearm with the remainder of her strength. His grip broke immediately, and she proceeded to elbow him in the armor before doubling over in pain, coughing and clutching her elbow.

The soldier was reaching out to grab her again when Shira snatched Viviana from the jaws of defeat.

"This is why you run away!" Shira cried, thrusting Viviana behind her. "When you are done, you run away!"

The soldier snarled. "Out of my way, or you'll get it, too."

Shira couldn't understand him, of course. Light on her feet and hands raised near her face, she never broke eye contact, but I could see her identifying his vulnerabilities. *20 points for the head, 50 for the crotch...*

The soldier lunged. Shira smashed her palm into his nose, then used his own momentum to hurl him into a column. By then, Harvey, Marcus and I were on the scene.

Harvey went immediately to Viviana. "My God," he said, gently moving Viviana's hair. "Your neck. And Shira, holy—"

I turned my attention to the centurion who tried to kill my ex-roommate. Marcus already had the man's arms pinned behind him, so I contributed in the only way I could.

Voice thick with tension, I said, "You have made a grave mis-

---

Centurion - A relatively senior position in the Roman army; commander of about 100 men

take, centurion. This girl was under *my* protection. May your bones wither and your liver rot! May Pluto feast on your innards; may—"

He spat at me, and I was forced to nimbly hop out of the way. Marcus yanked the man's arm behind him, nearly dislocating his shoulder. Two other soldiers had arrived by then.

"Put him in arms until he sobers up," Marcus said. "We'll deal with him in the morning."

The soldiers saluted, grabbing the centurion and dragging him to the exit.

"Well!" I said. "Well, well, well."

WE PUT COOL rags on Viviana's neck to help with the swelling, Advil and ice not being an option, then put her straight to bed.

Shira was standing beside her, making sure she stayed in a slightly elevated position. Without looking up, she said, "Noor, it's time we go."

"I know."

"As soon as she wakes up..."

"I understand."

Neither of us spoke for a minute. Then, to my surprise, I started crying. *Again.* Shira pulled me in for an enormous hug.

"You've been through a lot, Noor..."

"It's not that," I sniffled. "It's just — thank you. You and Viviana, you're..."

"I get it."

"No," I stepped back. "I mean it. There are only a few people I really trust, and most of them I've known my whole life. But you and Viviana, I *love* you guys."

Shira laughed. "A sentimental drinker, eh? Better than a violent one." Then, seeing the look on my face, she said, "I love you too, Noor."

I gave Shira another hug, lightly kissed Viviana on the top of the head, and quietly left.

HARVEY AND MARCUS waited in the sitting room, like visitors at a hospital.

"How is she?" Harvey leapt up.

"Fine," I said. "Sleeping."

Harvey nodded, and I turned to Marcus. "Let me show you out."

I took Marcus out into the corridor, pulling the door shut behind me. There was no handle, merely a little lever that raised and lowered over a latch, like a barn door.

Marcus spoke first. "Of all the ways I envisioned this evening ending, this wasn't one of them."

He gave me the Antony smolder and leaned over me, leaving no doubt in my mind as to how he envisioned the night ending.

I smiled back, but just before our lips met, I fell. Not "head over heels," fell. I *literally* fell, stumbling backwards in a clumsy attempt to catch my balance before landing on the hard, cold stone.

"What the—?"

Harvey stood over me, the door in his hand. "Did I do that? Apologies."

"You know you did," I grumbled.

Harvey hoisted me to my feet, giving me a far more perfunctory examination than he'd given Viviana, and said, "Tribune, we will see you in the morning."

Then he closed the door. I didn't bother objecting. Marcus could take a hint. Apparently Harvey couldn't.

I woke up several times that night. Harvey was always awake, pacing back and forth in front of the door.

Perfunctory - Carried out with minimum effort or reflection

CHAPTER TWENTY-THREE

"Noor, wake up." Harvey's voice. My skin felt sticky, my eyes puffy.

"Not now..." I groaned into the pillow.

"Noor, you need to get up," Harvey gave me another shake. "Antony's gone missing."

I twisted bolt upright. "Missing? How?"

"I don't know. But I'm inclined to believe history will play itself out the way we know it."

Head still spinning, I stumbled to the armoire in a daze, careful not to wake Shira or Viviana. Changing behind its open door, I ran my fingers through my hair and rubbed my eyes, struggling to make myself as presentable as possible.

"All the books and TV shows play with the timeline to suit their own purposes. But we know..." I struggled to even say it.

Inclined (toward something) - Feel favorably about; lean towards a certain opinion

"We know Antony is going to kill himself. How long do we have?"

"I'm struggling to recall a primary source," Harvey admitted.

I grabbed his arm. Sandals slapping against the stone floor, I strode briskly past columns I would've sold my soul to study the year before, powering in the direction of the Great Hall.

"Have you been able to locate Cleopatra?" I asked.

"No. Marcus has been looking for them both all morning. We decided it was time to fetch you."

"All morning? What time is it?"

"11:00 or so."

I let out a frustrated sigh. "We won't have long now."

Marcus intercepted us just outside the throne room, but a sickening feeling in my gut had already taken hold.

Somewhere in the distance, I could hear Cleopatra crying.

"Antony's body was just discovered," Marcus said gruffly. "He died by his own hand."

"But — why?"

People had been asking the same question for 2,000 years. No one knew the answer, but the prevailing theory did Cleopatra little credit.

Most historians think she tricked Antony into believing she was already dead — in effect, forcing him to kill himself.

Devastated at losing the love of his life, and fully aware that he'd be taken to Rome for a public trial and execution without her (and her gold) backing him up, Antony would be left with little

---

Prevailing - Having most influence; existing at a particular time

choice.

But why would she do this? Those same historians — heartless creatures they are — say Cleopatra would try to use Antony's death to barter for her own freedom with Octavian.

She'd be less of a threat with him gone, since the Roman people wouldn't follow her, and she had a fairly good track record when it came to winning over Roman rulers. First Caesar, then Antony — who's to say she couldn't seduce Octavian, too?

But that all-important question was fated to remain unanswered, for now at least.

"Why did he do it?" Marcus repeated. "Cursed if I know. But I don't think it would be wise for you to go in there."

I ignored him and approached the great aperture. Remnants of the previous night's debauchery lingered — spilled drinks, rumpled cushions, the odor of too many people who have never heard of deodorant.

There were three bodies in the room. Only two of them still drew breath.

Antony was seated on his throne, his lifeless limbs stretched out on the arms. Cleopatra was curled on his lap, crying and begging him to come back. Iras stood to Cleopatra's side, as she always did, but said nothing.

I silently retreated, re-joining Marcus and Harvey.

"Noor, it's time to go," Harvey said. "I'm sorry you have to leave her like this, but if Antony is dead—"

Aperture - Opening

Debauchery - Excessive indulgence

"*If* Antony is dead?" I snapped. "He *is* dead, Harvey. We failed. We failed to save my parents. We failed to save the Library. And now we've failed to save Antony and Cleopatra."

Neither man spoke for a moment, then Marcus gently remarked: "Your friend is right. Gods, the questions I have for the two of you! He was telling me this morning — but there isn't time. If there is any possibility of you getting off this island, going to a place where you'll be fed and protected, I insist that you take it."

"*Et tu,* Marcus? It was bad enough having Harvey on my back! How my future plays out will be *my* choice. Not yours," I spun to Harvey, "and not yours."

Marcus didn't retreat. "It is the right choice. And I will die well knowing you are safe, escorted by a man who I've come to realize is as honorable as any I have fought beside..."

Harvey's lips twitched at the saccharine speech, but he nodded respectfully and clasped his rival's forearm as they prepared to say goodbye.

I, however, stood still as a statue, not giving Marcus' moving speech nearly as much attention as it deserved. A germ of an idea was growing in my brain, and I was afraid the slightest movement might shake it loose.

"Ready?" Harvey asked.

Abruptly, I turned back towards the throne room. "A lovely speech, Marcus," I called behind me, "but no one else is going to die! Not you, not Cleopatra, not Harvey, and not I!"

Saccharine - Excessively sweet or sentimental

***

"IMPUDENT WENCH!" Cleopatra gulped through her sobs. "You dare — interrupt — my mourning? Guards!"

"Please, Your Highness!" I knelt before her, leaving Harvey and Marcus awkwardly shuffling their feet by the entrance. "I share in your grief. But I bear a message from the goddess — a message I believe you will wish to hear."

Cleopatra blinked, her eyelashes sticking together as the tears mixed with her makeup. "The goddess? I believed she had forsaken me...Tell me, priestess!"

She clambered off of Antony's lap and stumbled over to me. She clasped my hands in what may have been a sign of devotion, but felt more like a prison grip.

"The goddess shares in her daughter's pain," I stood up and winced, trying to free my fingers. "Isis too lost her husband, but was reunited with him in the afterlife. You shall be as well."

Cleopatra nodded vigorously, "What else does she say?"

"She urges you to live on, to continue fighting."

At that moment, I had a sickening realization. What if Cleopatra didn't want to live on without Antony? Could I in good conscience manipulate her into doing so, speaking as the voice of her god? I shifted uncomfortably.

"How do I continue to fight?" she wailed. "My armies are defeated. Octavian's dogs surround my palace. His messenger says I must surrender myself, or my people will dream of fire!"

Impudent - Disrespectful; impertinent

"Do you wish to live on, Your Majesty?" I asked quietly. "Do you wish to see the sun rise again? Do you wish to see your son, Caesarion, grow old?"

The mention of Caesarion caused Cleopatra to shake violently.

"Whomever else Octavian may spare, Caesarion will surely face the sword. 'There can only be one son of Caesar,'" she quoted, as though she'd heard the line a thousand times. "Tell me, what must I do?"

"If we succeed, you can live long, happy lives. Caesarion can grow old and marry, and you can live to see his children."

"I live *only* to see him avenge his father's name!"

"I'm afraid not, Your Highness."

Cleopatra shot me a look that could've shattered glass. "We *will* make Octavian suffer for what he has done. No son of mine will live in peace after such a loss."

I didn't say anything for a moment. Then I remarked: "The only way I can save you, Your Highness, gives you life without victory."

"Life without victory?" she snorted, as though I had proposed life without water. "You'll sneak us out of the palace dressed as peasants, is that it? We'll live the rest of our lives in hiding? *Brava*, clever girl! But I'd rather follow Antony into the afterlife."

Obviously finished with our conversation, she began blindly walking back to Antony. I averted my eyes.

"Sneak you out of the palace, yes. Dressed as peasants, no. You'll go as yourselves. You will hide from no one. You will live in luxury you cannot imagine...but you will never again be queen of Egypt."

She turned back to me, then hiccuped. "My crown for my life? I've yet to devise a strategy that leaves me with both. You speak truthfully, priestess? You can take me — and my son — to a place where we can live safely? *Comfortably?*"

"I can try," I promised. "But since this is so risky, you should have all the facts...You'll find out soon enough anyway. You should know that I'm not actually a priestess of Isis."

Her face hardened as the truth of my betrayal sank in. I fell back a step, remembering the night she unflinchingly forced Mentit to drink a glass of poison.

"You interrupt me in my most vulnerable hour, *claiming* to have a message from my holy mother, and now you tell me you are not who you say?"

I tried to reply, but she shrieked. "Guards! Take this woman! Imprison her! Execute her! Get her out of my sight!"

"Not everything I said was a lie, Your Highness!" I cried, shying back from the guards. "I *will* help you and Caesarion escape, if you just let me! I just thought you wouldn't listen unless—"

Marcus subtly positioned himself between me and the guards. "*Noor.*"

I called out to Cleopatra one last time. "Remember my offer, Your Highness!"

Marcus nodded at the guards in tacit acknowledgement that he would escort me out. I had officially done everything I could to save the last queen of Egypt.

Devise - Come up with; plan; invent

Tacit - Silent; understood without speaking

* * *

"SHE'S ALREADY CALLED in the sorcerers and snake charmers," Marcus said after we returned to my quarters. "She intends to follow in Antony's footsteps."

"Poisonous snake bite?"

"Indeed. She got the idea from your snake ring, I hear."

I looked down at the ring in surprise. I'd almost forgotten I was wearing it, not having taken it off since my run-in with Mentit.

Harvey and I looked at one another. I knew he was also remembering our trip to the Khan el-Khalili on my first day back in Egypt. His jaw clenched and he looked away.

Viviana chose that moment to emerge from the bedroom. She looked like a gorgon, hair askew, makeup running, and skin bruising.

We all turned to stare, but not before she'd done the same to us. Raking a cool gaze over me, Harvey, and Marcus, she said in Latin, "Noor, you will speak to me in the bedroom, yes?"

The moment the door closed, I faced a verbal hail of bullets.

"You are hiding something," Viviana said, switching to English. "What is it? Oh, I have known for many months that you are Harvey's *inamorata*. All this time, he has done nothing — *nothing* — but look for you. But you? You and this soldier are together now. This much is clear. But there is guilt with you. A feeling to

---

Gorgon - A fierce or frightening woman; Medusa-esque
Inamorata - Beloved (from Italian, but now also an English word)

Harvey that was not there before."

Shira was changing back into her modern clothes. She stopped with her tank halfway over her head. "Well *this* is getting interesting."

"You're right," I admitted. "We kissed."

Viviana squealed and brought her hands together. "When?"

"The night I came back here."

Shira raised her eyebrows and finished getting dressed. "No wonder he's been so obsessed with finding you."

"A lover's passion, interrupted!" Viviana cried, before I could note that he would've looked for me either way. "He has gone mad with grief. And now you treat him like this?"

I flushed. "It was one kiss, Viviana, and it was almost a year ago. We hardly exchanged vows. You're saying he hasn't been interested in *anyone* all this time? That *you* haven't made a pass at him?"

"My actions are of no consequence. He is never interested."

"She's not lying, Noor," Shira said. "Harvey's been waging a one-man international manhunt since you disappeared. I don't think anyone at the embassy's gotten more than two hours' sleep since he found out you were missing."

I looked out the window. The breeze rustled the curtains, as it did every morning. The sun shone upon each and every wave, undistracted — as I was — by the dozens of ships in the harbor.

A flurry of activity surrounded the most majestic ship. I cursed as it began unloading passengers onto a dinghy.

"As much as I'd love to stay here and discuss my love life, we have more pressing matters to attend to."

I exited the bedroom and strode to the balcony in the sitting room, craning to catch a better view of the harbor.

"Looking to join the star-crossed lovers, are you?" Harvey called.

"I wasn't in the slightest danger of falling," I replied. "And now is not the time to quote Shakespeare. Octavian is *en route.*"

"To the palace?" Harvey shot out of his seat like someone pinched his bottom.

"Entourage in tow, by the looks of it. I bet that's Agrippa next to him."

In two long strides, Harvey was standing beside me. He grabbed me by the wrist with one hand and fished a folded note card from his pocket with the other. It looked like one your grandmother might write a recipe on, except that it contained a magical time-travel formula instead of a recipe for turkey chili.

"Thank God I kept the hard copy," he muttered, shooting a mutinous look at Marcus. "Any chance of getting my phone back?"

"Your what?"

"Hang it. It's time. Shira! Viviana! Get out here *now.*"

Harvey cleared his throat and spun in a circle, unsure which direction to face in order to address the unknown forces of the universe. Eventually he settled on the window and took a deep breath.

Amid the flurry of activity, my gaze locked with Marcus'. "Do

Entourage - A group of people surrounding an important person
Mutinous - Willful or disobedient

you...do you want to join us?"

Harvey didn't wait for an answer. Instructing Shira, Viviana and me to hold hands, he began to invoke the ancient Egyptian spell that would bring us home. His tone was faltering, uncertain. If he'd been speaking in English, it would've sounded like: "My mouth has been given to me that I may — er — what does this bloody thing say? Oh, that I may *speak—*"

Marcus and I still hadn't broken eye contact. He began to reach for me when everyone, including Harvey, froze. Surely that was the sound of footsteps barreling down the hallway?

Cleopatra burst through the door, Caesarion in her arms. She dashed past the furniture in the sitting room until she reached us. Iras was by her side, skirts hitched at the knee to enable her to follow the queen's rapid pace.

Her personal guard, on the other hand, was having a difficult time maintaining their phalanx. They kept trying to march in sync, arms and legs extending at once, but had to break into a trot every few steps to keep up.

When the furniture in my sitting room became an extra obstacle, they began bumping into one another, and only some quick maneuvering prevented unintentional amputations.

Eventually they sorted themselves out, standing in rows on either side of their queen.

Harvey had stopped talking entirely, his mouth ajar.

Faltering - Hesitant; unsteady

Phalanx - A body of troops moving in formation

Amputations - Cutting off limbs

Ajar - Open

"I've had a message from the goddess," Cleopatra's eyes were alight. "A real message. A dream. A vision. We are to go with you, Caesarion and I!"

"That's — that's wonderful!" I said, feeling a bit whiplashed. "We were just about to leave."

Cleopatra scanned my chambers in confusion. "You have a rope, a ladder sequestered away? Very well. Fetch it! Octavian is approaching the gates!"

"We, ah," I forced myself to stop stuttering. "We're going to the future. We don't need a ladder."

I must say, she and Marcus took the news better than Harvey and I did, the night the professor first told us.

I suppose if you lived *before* the discovery of the scientific method — before absolute declarations of what is possible and what is not — it would be easier to believe in the improbable.

"Very well," she said. "Get on with it!"

Harvey's jaw was clenched. I could see him doing mental calculations. With obvious effort, he drew his eyes from the notecard and said, "There's just one thing, Highness."

She gave him a look that said, "Hurry up and tell me, worm."

"What about your people? When Octavian realizes you've gone missing, he'll assume you've escaped. He'll burn Egypt to the ground in his search for you. And he'll probably still set fire to the palace, just in case you're in hiding."

Cleopatra wheeled on me, "You said it was my crown for my freedom! You said nothing about my people paying the price!"

Sequestered - Hidden

Her nerves were in tatters. Mine were little better.

"There is a way," Iras said quietly.

"Speak," Cleopatra replied.

"I — I resemble Your Majesty. Octavian only knows you from a distance, in bejeweled wigs and heavy paint. None of his men have had the opportunity to study your face."

"You propose standing in for me?"

Iras nodded. "It would be my greatest honor."

"Would it be blasphemy?" Cleopatra turned on me, forgetting that I wasn't actually a priestess. "I am the goddess incarnate, her representative on earth. What would she think if another, a slave, paraded around in my place?"

"*More* to the point," Harvey interjected through gritted teeth. "Could you live with yourself, knowing what this girl has done for you? You know what Octavian will do when he captures you."

Harvey turned to Iras. "You would take imprisonment, torture, and a public execution for your queen?"

"I do not know you," Iras responded, "and I appreciate your kindness. I would gladly do what you've said for my queen, but I do not believe I will have to."

"How do you figure? Last I checked, we're a little short on manpower."

"I will not be tortured by Octavian," she said, "because I will not be alive when he finds me. In this way, everyone can live — Her Highness, the young heir, the people of Egypt."

"Out of the question."

Blasphemy - The act of offending God or religious doctrine

"Where you come from, death is sad, no?"

"I'd say that."

"It is for us as well," Iras said slowly. "We mourn, we beat our chests, we pull out our hair..."

Harvey made a face and muttered, "I thought that was just an exaggeration for the tomb paintings..."

"But when I die, and my heart is weighed on the scale against the feather of Ma'at, I will not fear. I've spent my life serving the living incarnation of Isis! Ammit will get no supper from me."

"Ammit's the monster that eats the bad people's hearts," I muttered to Marcus, who, as a Roman, was struggling to follow Iras' speech.

"I insist, Your Majesty," Iras repeated.

"Very well," Cleopatra said. "I cannot imagine that Isis would want me to survive, but my people to perish. So, Iras...thank you."

I looked at Iras, feeling the same as Harvey, but he spoke before I could.

"Nope," he said. "No cigar. It was one thing to step back and watch history unfold, but I can't send an innocent soul to her death."

He said the English word for cigar, but the spirit of the phrase seemed to translate.

"Is that so?" Cleopatra's temper rose as she spoke. "And who are you, exactly? Last I saw you, you'd just slithered out of my dungeons. You live now *only* because you help me!"

"You're a real piece of work, you know that?" Harvey glared at her. "What a ball of fun you'd be at Disneyland. Noor, I'm not even sure we should be bringing her—"

Cleopatra's guard, which had been staring blankly ahead until this point, leveled their gaze on Harvey.

"Ha, ha, ha!" I interrupted with a forced, high-pitched laugh. "What a joker you are, Harvey!"

A smile plastered on my face, I grabbed his arm and nodded at the queen in apology, then dragged him into the bedroom.

My smile fell the moment Cleopatra was out of sight. "For Pete's sake, Harvey!" I hissed. "Can you display a little more tact? She's royalty! She's a brat! We know this!"

Harvey started to protest, but I cut him off. "I'm not saying we should let Iras go poison herself. Obviously! But there's no harm in letting her play the hero while we finish concocting a better plan. It doesn't scare her! Ancient Egyptians prepare for death their entire lives!"

"Yeah, and what if she's wrong? I'm not convinced that her heart is going to be weighed against a feather and Osiris will shepherd her into heaven. What if we're actually consigning her to eternity in the bad place?"

"Again, I am *not* saying we let her go through with this! I'm just saying you need to be careful when you speak to Cleopatra. Getting home becomes a lot more complicated if we have to break you out of the dungeons again. If they take the notecard from you —"

We bickered for a few more minutes until Marcus appeared in the doorway.

"What is it?" I asked.

Concocting - Coming up with

"Iras is gone."

HARVEY AND I dashed back into the sitting room, calling Iras' name as we scanned our surroundings.

"Iras?" Harvey bellowed.

"Iras!!!" I added a bit more frantically, scrutinizing shadowed corners before throwing open the door and scanning the hallway.

"Calm yourselves," Cleopatra snapped. "We'll find her."

"How did she get out?" Harvey demanded.

"Slinking from room to room unnoticed is her life's work," Cleopatra shrugged. "She's a slave."

Harvey snorted. "Fine way to talk about a girl who just offered to sacrifice her life for you."

Cleopatra sniffed, but Harvey was already out the door. His shoes slapped against the cool stone with each step, and the rest of us soon caught up with him.

"She's going to take the matter out of our hands," Harvey predicted. "Give us no choice. Where are the snake charmers, the sorcerers Cleopatra summoned?"

"The throne room," Marcus responded, leading the way.

And so we returned to the room where I'd seen so much transpire — where Cleopatra had decided to imprison me, where we'd all gathered in revelry, and where I found out Antony had ended his own life.

A hideous foreboding passed through me as I had that final

Scrutinizing - Closely examining; inspecting

Transpire - Happen; occur

Foreboding - A feeling that something bad will happen

thought.

When we burst through the doors, Iras was seated on Cleopatra's throne. She was wearing the queen's garments, and an Egyptian asp coiled around her arm. The snake charmer was still present, as were a number of sorcerers.

Iras' death would be in vain if any of them saw the real Cleopatra, who was hot on our heels.

"Out," I pointed to the side door that led to the servants' quarters. My tone brooked no room for argument, and Iras' nod confirmed the command.

They shuffled out just in time. Cleopatra stepped through the front door a moment later. Harvey was making calming noises to Iras, saying things like, "You don't have to do this...We'll find another way. There's always another way..."

Iras raised her chin. "I am not afraid. And there is no other way. None in which my queen can live and my people survive."

I longed to help Harvey, but feared any additional movement would prompt the snake to strike. A tear slipped from Iras' eye. "Goodbye, my queen. Live well."

"No!" Harvey, Shira, and I lunged forward. We'd been speaking in ancient Egyptian, but you didn't need to know the language to comprehend that Iras was in grave danger. She was crying and holding one of the most poisonous snakes in the world.

The soldiers stood still. Viviana turned away in horror, hand over her mouth. Caesarion started crying.

At first, the noise was the worst part. I could hear the vile creature hiss as it lunged, hear Iras's low whimper as its fangs pierced her innocent flesh. But of course that wasn't the worst part. The worst part came after, watching Iras grow pale, her breath turn to gasps.

At least Cleopatra had the decency to join Iras in her final moments. She passed Caesarion to a startled Viviana, then took Iras' hand and whispered something in her ear.

Iras smiled at the queen, shutting her eyes for the final time.

CLEOPATRA SAID a brief prayer, then stood and smoothed her gown.

"We, in this room," she began, "are the only people who truly know what has happened here."

She turned to address her personal guard directly. "You won't be coming with me. But as I have done since I became your queen, I do in my final moments. I trust you with my life and my kingdom."

The soldiers — who normally looked like automatons, remaining blank-faced at every outlandish scene — were looking directly at Cleopatra. She walked past each one of them in turn, and each one pounded his chest in salute.

"When Octavian finds Iras," she continued, "he *must* believe it is I he sees. If any of you gives him reason to believe otherwise, it would not only be grossly dishonorable, but you, your family, your people will be the ones to suffer. Octavian will not stop hunting me until Egypt is devastated, our women and children sold into slavery, our fields burned and sown with salt.

Automatons - Robots
Outlandish - Bizarre; strange

"But, if Octavian believes he has won, he will leave. Egypt will become a protectorate of Rome. It is a future I never wished to see, but better a protectorate — our people alive and our temples preserved —than the carnage we can expect if he believes I plan to fight another day. We would become Carthage — a mighty civilization reduced to rubble and poisoned soil, never able to support another life."

A suppressed shudder ran through the men.

"When Octavian arrives, you must let him believe he has won," Cleopatra concluded. "He can take my gold. He can take my kingdom. The war is over."

CLEOPATRA'S MEN stood guard near the door, and we burst into a frenzy of activity to ensure the ruse would work. Iras' death would be for naught if we failed to sell the deception.

We examined her clothes, her shoes, her wig, triple checking that no detail would betray her rank. Adding a layer of verisimilitude, Cleopatra removed her own rings, placing them on Iras' fingers.

If Octavian wasn't already ashore, he would be momentarily. Pausing for a moment, Cleopatra took Iras' jeweled hand and placed it over Antony's.

"It's how I would have gone," she said quietly.

As though summoned by my fears, I saw Octavian through the windows of the throne room.

Carnage - Death and destruction
Verisimilitude - The appearance of being true or real

Cleopatra cursed. "If I am not there to give the order, how will my men know to open the palace gates? How will they know not to fight?"

"I'll go, Your Majesty," her chief in command bowed in her direction. "It has been an honor."

Cleopatra nodded, then turned to us. We had only moments to make our escape.

* * *

HARVEY HADN'T SAID a word since Iras' death. He cleared his throat and told Cleopatra, "We all must be touching for this to work — if it works at all. It's never been tested this way round."

He reached for her hand. She narrowed her eyes, but took it, holding Caesarion in the other arm. Harvey reached for the note-card and I looped my arm through his.

"Marcus," I asked crisply, "are you coming?"

He pressed his lips together. "If Octavian wins, which we've just guaranteed, I'm dead anyway, exiled at best. I'll never see my family again. I'll be penniless—"

"Yes, yes," Harvey said. "In or out?"

Marcus grasped my hand, and we smiled at each other as Harvey finished issuing the instructions.

"Marcus, loop your other arm through Cleopatra's, or put your hand on Caesarion's back," he ordered. "We don't know what kind of energy is at work here. If you're the furthest removed from the source — me — you may as well get it from two sides. Complete the circle, so to speak."

Cleopatra's captain shouted something from the gates. The mammoth doors began rumbling open.

Retrieving the notecard, Harvey began to speak, boldly this time, though the sound of approaching footsteps almost drowned him out.

The bloody Romans hadn't even waited until the gates were fully open to storm it! They were entering as soon as the space was large enough to admit them. Sweat beaded my brow, but I didn't dare release my arm to wipe it away.

Suddenly the wind grew louder, the waves crashing against Octavian's ships. That wouldn't slow them down now, though. They were already in the palace.

"Oh you who guard them, I know you and I know your names," Harvey called. *"Let the gates be opened!"*

* * *

I THRASHED AND WRITHED, fighting some immutable force. I couldn't breathe. I was being crushed, and feared we'd stretched the limits of time travel too far until I realized Cleopatra was passed out on top of me.

Caesarion was crying. *Where was he?* I turned my head and found him curled up, frog-legged, on Marcus' chest. Cleopatra's arm was still draped over them.

"Harvey!" I called, afraid to move the queen in case Caesarion also fell. "Harvey, where are you?"

Immutable - Unable to be changed

I heard grunts and groans, the sounds of people inspecting themselves for damage.

Then Viviana — thank God she made it too! — gently moved Cleopatra's arm and took Caesarion. The baby secured, Harvey mercilessly rolled Cleopatra off me. She landed on the concrete with a *thud*, then started muttering.

Tenderly, I sat up and hugged Harvey, then reached for Marcus. He was breathing and starting to stir. Shira was in the same condition. Both were safe, just waking up.

Everyone accounted for, I sat down and pressed my palms to my eyes, trying to scatter the little stars. The rush of my pulse melded with the roaring of the sea below. The air felt hot and sticky, and it smelled like...*pollution.*

My head shot up. Unable to contain my curiosity any longer, I stumbled to my feet and scanned my surroundings.

We were on a rooftop. It wasn't particularly distinctive. Concrete below, a table and chairs by the ledge, the Mediterranean in the distance. But immediately, I knew exactly where we'd landed.

"Harvey," I croaked. "We're home."

I smiled and gazed at the horizon. A world of problems still awaited me. I hadn't found my parents, I hadn't solved anything regarding Harvey and Marcus, and now I had to figure out what to do with Cleopatra in the 21st century.

She'd have to get a job, of course. The very thought sent a chill down my spine.

Melded - Mixed; combined

Yet for all my failures, my optimistic spirit refused to be extinguished. I'd seen firsthand how much one person could influence the tide of history. Whatever my future held, at least it would be a future of my own making.

AFTERWORD

It amuses me to no end that, after reading a story such as mine, the publishing world was less interested in *time travel* than how they could possibly market a book with so many "big words."

Apparently they've decided it's going to be an SAT prep book? It's part of some collection at vocabbett.com.

Hey, whatever works. If all these scary "big words" help you in any way, I'm happy to be of service.

Cheers,

Noor

P.S. This story isn't over, obviously. Keep reading for a peek at Cleopatra's (mal)adjustment to modern living. I haven't finished the whole story yet, but you can sign up at vocabbett.com/sequel to be notified when it's done. Until then!

A SNEAK PEEK AT
CLEOPATRA'S PANTSUIT

CLEOPATRA STARED AT the sleek new Macbook in consternation.

"This machine is deliberately trying to enrage me," she snapped. "Take it away."

The last pharaoh of Egypt was sitting at my Grandma Mitzi's desk in Connecticut. It was my Macbook before her, however. Mitzi would never own such a device.

The office resembled the rest of Mitzi's sprawling mansion. Every ounce was lavishly decorated, and this particular room looked like Lawrence of Arabia served as the interior designer. It was all dark wood, dusty paintings of 19th century explorers, and red-tinged lamps.

"Your Highness, you've mastered every modern device but the computer," I lied. "The lights, the refrigerator, the fireplace…"

Consternation - A feeling of anxiety or dismay
Lavishly - Luxuriously; elaborately

"I do enjoy the perpetual illumination," she admitted. "But what do I care for fire and food? Never before have I had to *prepare* what I eat!"

"Yes, I know how difficult it can be to make a sandwich."

"The indignity," she muttered. "Like a slave!"

"But you are the queen of Upper and Lower Egypt," I rallied, trying to steer the conversation in a more productive direction. "There is nothing you cannot do! And in this time, in this place, it is nearly impossible for a young person to survive without knowing how to use a computer."

"I am not so young."

"Trust me, Your Highness — where we are now, 29 is still young."

Cleopatra turned a wary eye in the direction of the Macbook. "Tell me again what this machine does."

I paused. "Consider this. How long does it take a scribe to write a court document? To carve inscriptions in tombs?"

"That is two different questions. To prepare a tomb takes years, but court documents can be completed with immense efficiency." She waved a golden hand. "A day, no more."

I gently re-opened the computer, pulled up a word processor, and began typing. "Imagine if the same work only took minutes."

She sniffed, unimpressed.

"That's not all," I continued. "This device contains all of the information in the entire world."

She sat up straighter. "*This* device? And why do *you* possess it?"

Perpetual - Never-ending

I ignored the veiled insult.

"The information isn't *only* on this device, but this device allows me to *access* all of the world's information. It's like—like a little machine that allows me to view all of the Library of Alexandria, without actually traveling to Alexandria."

She blinked more quickly than normal.

"If it contains all of the information in the world, as you say... Does it know history? Can it tell me what happened after we fled?"

"It can."

I directed her to the Wikipedia page on the Battle of Actium, detailing how Cleopatra and her lover Marc Antony suffered a devastating defeat at the hands of Octavian, the first emperor of Rome.

It also detailed how Antony had killed himself, believing Cleopatra had done the same.

To Cleopatra, it had been a mere summer since the devastating loss of a man she saw as her husband, not her lover. Yet the page read with the clinical coldness of time passed.

"It is believed that Cleopatra purposefully misled Antony," her voice cracked when pronouncing his name. "With Ant—him gone, Cleopatra could forge an alliance with Octavian. She had successfully seduced two other Roman rulers. Why should she not have success with a third?"

Cleopatra turned to me. "This is how the world remembers

Mere - Something small or slight

337

me? As a harlot?"

"Your Highness, your name lives on. If anything, people respect the lengths to which you went in order to save your kingdom."

Her eyes narrowed. "Show me what happened to the worm, Octavian. I assume he was assassinated? Brutally?"

I pulled up his Wikipedia page, and Cleopatra clenched her jaw.

"41 years?" she repeated. "He ruled for *41 years?* And lived to be *77?*"

An intense discussion of time had been necessary when we first arrived, for Cleopatra to understand what jumping 2,000 years into the future entailed. Once I explained that Americans measured time like the Romans, the minor adjustments were easily comprehended.

"I'm afraid so. He presided over one of the most stable, prosperous eras of Rome. The '*Pax Romana*,' he called it."

"The Roman peace," she spat. "Peace at what cost?"

"Yes...I'll leave you to this," I indicated how she could switch between tabs, if she wanted to read more about the battle.

Then I gently closed the door to Mitzi's office, leaving Cleopatra reading her story through the eyes of history.

Harlot - A woman with loose morals

Entailed - Involved

Comprehended - Understood

ACKNOWLEDGEMENTS

I could never have written *Ahead of Her Time* without the support of the incredible people below:

1. My auntie Tootsie, who has made writing fun since our childhood days at the lake
2. My mom, who enabled me to take the adventures I needed to tell Noor's story
3. My husband, who brought me treats and kept me on track when my inclination towards procrastination overtook me
4. My son, who's the best little writing buddy a mama could ask for
5. My students, who made history more fun than I ever thought possible
6. My editors, auntie Wendy (I have great aunts) and Thalia Suzuma, who both provided invaluable feedback
7. Noor herself, who wouldn't leave me alone until I told her story. I hope she's happy with the result.

ALSO BY ERICA ABBETT

Death at the Villa Tarconti (A novelette)

Hera and the Headmaster (A short story)

Casting Call: Author Seeking New Villain (A short story)

And much more at www.vocabbett.com!

GLOSSARY OF TERMS

When there are multiple definitions of a word, the definition provided matches the context of the sentence.

1. (To no) avail - With little or no success
2. Abject - Total; to the maximum degree
3. Absolved - Released from guilt, blame, or wrongdoing
4. Abstemious - Restrained; disciplined; not indulgent
5. Abyss - A deep or seemingly bottomless pit
6. Acquire - Get; obtain
7. Acutely - Intensely; sharply
8. Adamant - Determined; unwilling to change his/her mind
9. Addled - Confused
10. Admonishing - Scolding
11. Adonis - An extremely handsome person
12. Aestheticians - People knowledgeable about beauty
13. Aforementioned - Previously mentioned
14. Ailment - Illness
15. Ajar - Open
16. Akimbo - Hands on the hips and elbows turned outward
17. Albeit - Although
18. Alibi - A reason given to avoid blame
19. Allayed - Diminished; put to rest
20. Allegations - Accusations
21. Altruistic - Selfless; looking out for others
22. Amassing - Gathering; accumulating

23. Ambiance - Mood; atmosphere
24. Amenable - Agreeable; responsive
25. Amenity - A desirable or useful feature
26. Amiably - In a friendly way
27. Amiss - Wrong
28. Ample - Plenty; more than enough
29. Amputations - Cutting off limbs
30. Anachronistic - Belonging to a different time period
31. Anatomy - Body
32. Anguish - Pain; suffering
33. Annual - Yearly
34. Anonymity - The state of being anonymous
35. Anthropomorphic - Assigning human characteristics to something not human
36. Apathy - Lack of interest; not caring
37. Aperture - Opening
38. Apparently - As far as one can tell; capable of being seen
39. Apparition - Ghostlike image; an unexpected appearance
40. Appendage - Something attached to something larger or more important
41. Apprehended - Caught; arrested
42. Apprehensive - Nervous
43. Apt - Appropriate under the circumstances
44. Arbitrarily - Randomly
45. Arbitrated - Settled; judged
46. Archaic - Old; outdated
47. Armada - Fleet of warships
48. Ascent - The act of going up

49. Ascertain - Figure out; make certain of something

50. Assailant - Attacker

51. Assuaged - Made less intense

52. Auspicious - Favorable; good

53. Automatons - Robots

54. Auxiliary - Helping; giving supplemental assistance

55. Avert - Prevent; turn away

56. Banter - A playful and friendly exchange of teasing remarks

57. Barge (n.) - A large ornamental boat used for pleasure or ceremony

58. Bartering - Trading

59. Bask - Bathe in; revel in

60. Beckoned - Encouraged someone to come nearer

61. Begrudge - Hand over unwillingly or resentfully

62. Beheld - Saw something remarkable

63. Belatedly - Later than should be the case

64. Belied - Contradicted; failed to give a true impression of something

65. Belligerently - Aggressively; war-like

66. Bewilderment - Confusion

67. Blasphemy - The act of offending God or religious doctrine

68. Blithely - Showing casual and cheerful indifference

69. Bowel movements - Number two's

70. Brandishing - Waving or flourishing in anger or excitement

71. Bristle - React angrily or defensively

72. Brusque - Abrupt; perfunctory
73. Bulbous - Round or bulging
74. Burgeoning - Beginning to grow
75. Burrowed - Dug
76. Cacophony - A harsh, unpleasant mixture of sounds
77. Cadre - Small group of people
78. Callous - Insensitive; showing a cruel disregard for others
79. Canon - Model; something that is generally accepted or recognized
80. Carnage - Death and destruction
81. Ceased - Stopped
82. Celestial - Relating to the sky or heavens
83. Centurion - A relatively senior position in the Roman army; commander of about 100 men
84. Chagrined - Distressed
85. Chronicled - Recorded, especially in a detailed way, organized by time
86. Circumstantial - Suggesting something without actually proving it
87. Circumventing - Finding a way around
88. Clambered - Climbed
89. Clamor - Loud, chaotic noise
90. Cliches - An unoriginal phrase or idea
91. Coherent - Logical, rational
92. Cohorts - Companions
93. Commandeered - Seized for military use
94. Commence - Begin
95. Commission - Order the production of

96. Commune - Communicate, especially on a spiritual level

97. Comparative - Involving a comparison

98. Complicit - Involved in some bad or illegal activity

99. Component - Part of a larger whole

100. Compound - Make something bad even worse

101. Comprehensible - Understandable

102. Conceded - Admitted

103. Concocting - Coming up with; devising

104. Condescending - Talking down to someone; showing a feeling of patronizing superiority

105. Confidant - A person you confide in, share secrets with

106. Confound - Confuse

107. Consigned - Committed decisively or permanently

108. Consternation - A feeling of anxiety or dismay

109. Consummate - Showing a high degree of skill; perfect

110. Contemplating - Thinking about

111. Contemporaneously - With/for the time period (related to "contemporaries", below)

112. Contemporaries - Living at the same time

113. Contented - Happy and at ease

114. Contingent - A group of people united by a common feature

115. Contorted - Twist or bent out of normal shape

116. Contours - An outline representing the shape or form of something

117. Contrived - Made-up; invented

118. Conveyed - Communicated; carried from one place to another

119. Convoluted - Complex and difficult to follow

120. Copious - A lot of; an abundant supply

121. Cosmopolitan - Containing people from many different cultures

122. Credence - Belief

123. Credible - Believable

124. Crepuscular - Relating to twilight

125. Cretin - An offensive term for a stupid person

126. Curt - Rudely brief

127. Dahabeeyah - A type of sailboat popular among early 20th-century travelers

128. Dank - Unpleasantly damp and musty

129. De Facto - In effect, whether intentional or not

130. *De rigueur*- Required by current trends (from French)

131. Decrepit - Old, worn out

132. Deduced - Concluded; arrived at the fact based on reasoning

133. Deem - Decide; consider something a certain way

134. Defenestrated - Thrown out a window

135. Defiance - Open resistance; stubbornness; disobedience

136. Deftly - Quickly; with neat skill

137. Delectable - Delicious; indulgent

138. Delineated - Outlined; portrayed precisely

139. Demeanor - Behavior; personality

140. Demise - Death

141. Denizens - Residents

142. Derisive - Judgmental; expressing contempt or ridicule

143. Destitute - Extremely poor; going without basic ne-

cessities

144. Detainees - People being held somewhere, especially for political reasons

145. Deteriorating - Becoming worse

146. Detritus - Waste; debris

147. Devise - Come up with; plan; invent

148. Diaphanous - Light; delicate; sometimes a little see-through

149. Diligence - Determination; persistence

150. Diluted - Made weaker

151. Diminished - Became less likely or possible

152. Discern - Determine; figure out; distinguish

153. Discernible - Understandable; recognizable

154. Discreetly - In a not-obvious way; unobtrusively

155. Disembark - To leave or get off a ship, aircraft, or other vehicle

156. Disentangle - Free (from something)

157. Disfigured - Spoiled the attractiveness of

158. Disheveled - Untidy; disordered

159. Disparaging - Derogatory; critical

160. Disperse - Go out in different directions

161. Distorting - Disfiguring; pulled or twisted out of shape

162. Distraught - Devastated; deeply upset

163. Diversify - Make more diverse or varied

164. Divine - Godly

165. Docile - Submissive

166. Domineering - Dominating; asserting one's will over others in an arrogant way

167. Donning - Putting on

168. Dubious - Suspicious; unable to be relied upon

169. Dwell - Live

170. Dwindling - Shrinking; decreasing in size

171. Eccentric - Unconventional; slightly strange

172. Eclectic - Unusual; chosen from diverse sources

173. Eerie - Strange and troubling

174. Effused - Spoke excitedly

175. Egress - Exit

176. Elder - A person of greater age

177. Elusive - Difficult to find, catch, or achieve

178. Embarrass des richesses - An overabundance of riches; literally translates to "an embarrassment of riches"

179. Emissions - The production and discharge of something

180. Emulated - Copied

181. Encasing - Enclosing; holding

182. Endeavored - Tried

183. Engrossed - Having all your attention absorbed by someone or something

184. Engulfed - Covered completely; swallowed whole

185. Enraptured - Filled with pleasure or joy

186. Entailed - Involved

187. Entourage - A group of people surrounding an important person

188. Enunciation - The act of pronouncing something clearly

189. Enveloping - Covering; surrounding completely

190. Ergo - Therefore

191. Errant - Not where it should be

192. Erudite - Scholarly

193. Exasperation - Extreme annoyance

194. Excursion - A short journey or trip

195. Explicitly - Clearly; directly

196. Extricated - Freed; removed

197. Facade - The face of a building

198. Faltering - Hesitant; unsteady

199. Fastidious - Attentive to detail/cleanliness

200. Fatal - Deadly

201. Faux - Fake

202. Feat - Great achievement

203. Fending (off) - Defending oneself

204. Fertile - Lush; green; growing abundant crops

205. Fervor - Passion; emotion

206. Finery - Fancy clothes

207. Flotilla - A fleet of ships

208. Flourish - A bold or extravagant gesture

209. Foreboding - A feeling that something bad will happen

210. Foremost - Best

211. Foreshadowing - Hinting at a future event

212. Forestall - Prevent

213. Forgo - Go without

214. Fray - A place of intense activity

215. Furtive - Secretive, usually because of guilt

216. Futile - Pointless

217. Gaggle - A flock of geese; a derogatory term for a group of people

218. Galabeya - Unlikely to be an SAT word, but it's a

traditional Egyptian garment that looks like a big, long-sleeved dress

219. Garishly - Excessively bright and showy

220. Gauge - Measure

221. Gaul - A region that roughly corresponds to modern-day France

222. Genealogical - Relating to one's ancestry

223. *Geneh* - A unit of Egyptian currency

224. Genuflecting - Kneeling

225. Giddy - Excited to the point of being dizzy or unsteady

226. Gilded - Covered with a thin layer of gold

227. Gingerly - Carefully; cautiously

228. Glean - Gather; collect bit by bit

229. Gorgon - A fierce or frightening woman; Medusa-esque

230. Gossamer - Very light, thin, delicate

231. Gratified - Pleased; satisfied

232. Gravitating - Moving towards or being attracted to something

233. Grimace - A twisted or pained face

234. Grin - Smile

235. Guileless - Sincere; honest; without deception

236. Halal - Having meat prepared in accordance with Islamic law

237. Hapless - Unfortunate; helpless

238. Harebrained - Rash; not thought through

239. Harlot - A woman with loose morals

240. Hastened - Be quick to do something

241. Hastily - Quickly

242. Haven - Safe place

243. Heedless - Not caring

244. Hegemony - Dominance

245. Hemorrhaging - Bleeding profusely

246. Hereditary - In the genes; passed from parents to children

247. Hijab - Headscarf; a garment to cover the hair

248. Hindquarters - Back legs

249. Hordes - A large group of people (often used in the context of an invasion)

250. Hue - A color or shade

251. Hyperventilating - Breathing so quickly you almost pass out

252. Hypostyle - A building with a roof supported by large pillars

253. Iconography - The interpretation of images

254. Ides - The 15th of the month

255. Illiterate - Unable to read or write

256. Illuminated - Lit up

257. Imminent - Happening very soon

258. Immutable - Unable to be changed

259. Impeccably - Perfectly; faultlessly

260. Impecunious - Having little or no money (I told Noor *we* would end up "impecunious" if she insisted on using all these big words)

261. Imperative - Crucial

262. Imperialistic - Extending a country's power through diplomacy or military force

263. Impetuous - Impulsive; prone to acting quickly without thought or care

264. Implications - Consequences; something that happens as a result of something else

265. Imply - Indicate or suggest without being explicitly stated

266. Imposing - Grand and impressive

267. Impudent - Disrespectful; impertinent

268. Inadequate - Insufficient; not enough

269. Inadvertently - Accidentally

270. Inamorata - Beloved (from Italian, but now also an English word)

271. Inane - Silly or stupid to the point of annoyance

272. Incapacitate - Prevent from functioning normally

273. Incarnate - In human form

274. Incinerated - Destroyed by burning

275. Inclined (toward something) - Feel favorably about; lean towards a certain opinion

276. Incoherently - Spoken in a confusing or unclear way

277. Incompetent - Unskilled; unqualified

278. Inconceivable - Unbelievable; not able to be understood

279. Incurring - Getting; receiving

280. Inebriated - Drunk

281. Ineffable - Too great to be expressed in words

282. Inevitable - Unavoidable

283. Inexorable - Unable to stop or escape

284. Inexplicably - Impossible to explain

285. Infernal - Fiendish; diabolical

286. Inflection - The intonation or pitch of the voice

287. Infrastructure - The basic structures and facilities needed for the operation of a society

288. Inherently - Permanently; in an essential way

289. Inimitable - So good or unique it cannot be copied

290. Inlet - A small part of a body of water

291. Innuendo - A suggestive reference

292. Innumerable - Too many to count

293. Inquiring - Seeking information

294. Instantaneous - Happening instantly

295. Insurrection - Uprising

296. Intently - Intensely

297. Interjected - Said abruptly, usually interrupting a conversation

298. Interlude - Period of time

299. Intermittent - Occurring at irregular intervals; not continuous

300. Interspersed - Mixed in with something else

301. Interval - A space between two things

302. Intervened - Interrupted; came between people to change something

303. Intoned - Said melodically, with a rise and fall of the voice

304. Intricately - In a complicated or detailed manner

305. Invective - Highly critical language

306. Inverse - Opposite

307. Invocation - The act of calling to presence a superior being

308. Invoking - Calling on; summoning

309. Iota - An extremely small amount

310. Irony - When the full significance of someone's words are not known to them

311. Irrelevant - Not related; not important in connection to something

312. Irrevocable - Unable to be taken away or reversed

313. *Joie de Vivre* - Liveliness; "joy of life" (from French)

314. Jostling - Push or shove, especially in a crowd

315. Jovial - Cheerful; friendly

316. Labyrinth - A maze

317. Labyrinthine - Twisty and confusing, like a maze

318. Laden - Weighed down

319. Languish - Suffer from being forced to remain somewhere unpleasant

320. Larceny - Theft; stealing

321. Laterally - Sideways

322. Latter - Closer to the end than the beginning

323. Lavish - Luxurious; rich; elaborate

324. Levee - A formal reception of visitors or guests

325. Leverage - Take advantage of

326. Lewd - Crude; rude

327. Liaising - Communicating; cooperating on a matter of mutual concern

328. *Lingua Franca* - Common language

329. Litter - A bed or seat that is enclosed by curtains and carried by people

330. Longevity - Having a long existence or life

331. Looting - Theft; robbing

332. *Magstri* - Latin for "teachers"

333. Malaise - General feeling of discomfort or uneasiness

334. Malicious - Mean; bad; intending to do harm

335. Maritime - Relating to the sea

336. Medieval - Relating to the Middle Ages, a time period that lasted from around the 5th to the 15th century

337. Meek - Quiet; gentle; submissive

338. Megalomaniacal - Being obsessed with your own power

339. Melancholia - Gloom; sadness

340. Melded - Mixed; combined

341. Melee - A confused mass of people

342. Mendicant - Poor; relying on charity

343. Mere - Something small or slight

344. Meticulous - Careful; precise; showing great attention to detail

345. Miasma - An unpleasant or oppressive atmosphere

346. Milled - Moved around in a confused mass

347. Millennia - Thousands of years (the plural of millennium)

348. Minaret - A tall, slender tower rising up from a mosque

349. Miscreant - A person who behaves badly

350. Misinterpreting - Understanding something the wrong way

351. Missive - Message

352. Modicum - A small amount

353. Monarch - King, queen, or emperor

354. Monosyllabic - Having one syllable

355. Monotonous - Having one tone or pitch

356. Mortuary - Having to do with death (in this case, a temple honoring her after her death)

357. Mottled - Blotchy

358. Muse (n.) - Someone who serves as the inspiration for an artist

359. Mused (v.) - Wondered

360. Mutinous - Willful or disobedient

361. Naiveté - Lack of experience, wisdom, or judgement

362. Nasal - Coming from the nose

363. Necromancy - Communicating with the dead

364. Neoclassical - In the style of ancient art (literally "new" classical)

365. Nimble - Light and quick

366. Notoriously - Well known, usually in a bad way

367. Obdurately - Stubbornly refusing to change one's mind

368. Obliged - Did as someone asked or ordered

369. Oblivion - Unaware; unconscious

370. Obsequious - Excessively obedient or attentive

371. Obsidian - A dark, glasslike rock

372. Ogling - Stare at admiringly or covetously (usually used to describe a man eyeing a woman)

373. Omen - A sign of good or bad things to come (related to "ominously," above)

374. Ominously - Suggests something bad is going to happen

375. Omnipresent - Always there

376. Onerous - An extremely burdensome amount of effort

377. Opting - Choosing; taking the option of

378. Opulent - Ostentatiously rich or lavish

379. Origins - Roots; the place where something begins

380. Ousted - Driven out; removed

381. Outlandish - Bizarre; strange

382. Overzealous - Too eager or enthusiastic

383. Padding - Walking quietly

384. Palpable - Intense; touchable

385. Panoramic - Wide-ranging; including all aspects of a subject

386. Papyri - The plural of "papyrus," the ancient Egyptian form of paper

387. Parley - A talk between opposing sides to discuss terms

388. Partake - Take part in

389. Patrician - Aristocratic; of noble rank

390. Pedestrian - Lacking excitement; dull; common

391. Penchant - Fondness (for); liking (something)

392. Perceptible - Able to be seen or noticed

393. Perennials - Remaining active all year

394. Perfunctory - Carried out with minimum effort or reflection

395. Perilous - Dangerous

396. Periphery - The outer limits or boundaries

397. Permeate - Spread through; pervade

398. Perpetual - Never-ending

399. Perplexing - Confusing; baffling

400. Petrified - Changed into a stony substance

401. Phalanx - A body of troops moving in formation

402. Phenomena (*Plural of phenomenon*) - Something or

someone remarkable

403.   Phonetic - How something sounds; the correspondence between symbols and sounds

404.   *Piastre* - Unlikely to be an SAT word, but it's a unit of currency worth a small amount

405.   Pilferage - The act of stealing something small

406.   Pique - Awaken; make greater

407.   Plausible - Probable; reasonable

408.   Plenipotentiary - Diplomat; someone who has the full power of their government

409.   Poignantly - Evoking a keen sense of sadness or regret

410.   Pompous - Self-important; conceited

411.   Pondered - Thought deeply

412.   Postprandial - Occurring after a meal

413.   Potent - Powerful

414.   Precarious - Uncertain; dependent on chance

415.   Predicament - Problem

416.   Premise - Point; a statement that forms the basis of a theory

417.   Prestigious - Having high status; respected

418.   Presumably - Something that is likely, but not certain (think: "probably")

419.   Presume - Assume

420.   Presumptuous - Going beyond what is permitted or appropriate

421.   Prevailing - Having most influence; existing at a particular time

422.   Prevalent - Widespread

423. Prevaricate - Speak or act in an evasive manner; try to get out of something

424. Pristine - Spotless; fresh as new

425. Probed - Questioned; tried to uncover information

426. Profane - Obscene; blasphemous; not respectable

427. Prominent - Noticeable; standing out

428. Protruded - Stuck out

429. Provoke - Make something happen

430. Proximity - Closeness (to)

431. Pulchritudinous - Beautiful

432. Pungent - A sharp smell

433. Purgatory - A place of suffering where sinners wait before entering heaven, in Roman Catholic theology

434. Quibble - Object to something small or trivial

435. Quirking - A sudden twist, turn, or curve

436. Quizzical - Indicating mild or amused puzzlement

437. Quorum - A group of people; the minimum number of people to make certain proceedings valid

438. Ramblings - Speaking in a lengthy and confused way

439. Ramifications - Consequences

440. Rampageous - Violently uncontrollable (like a rampage)

441. Rankled - Bothered

442. Rapt - Fascinated

443. Raucous - Loud; wild

444. Rebut - Refute; make a comeback against

445. Recoiled - Sprang back in horror, fear, disgust

446. Reconcile - To make different things compatible

447. Reconfigured - Put together differently

448. Reconvene - Get back together

449. Recurring - Happening repeatedly

450. Redolent - Smelling of

451. Redouble - Double down on; make greater or more intense

452. Re-emerged - Came back into view

453. Refrain (n.) - A comment that is often repeated

454. Refrained (v.) - Held back

455. Regalia - The emblems, insignia, or wardrobe of royalty

456. Regaling - Entertaining or amusing

457. Regally - Fit for a king or queen; magnificent and dignified

458. Reimburse - Pay back

459. Reincarnation - A new version of something from the past; rebirth in a new body

460. Reinvigorated - Given new energy or strength

461. Relapsing - Falling back into

462. Reluctant - Unwilling

463. Reminisce - Talk about the past in an enjoyable way

464. Remorse - Regret; shame

465. Repressed - Suppressed; held back

466. Repudiation - Rejection

467. Requisite - Required; necessary

468. Resonate - Evoke emotions

469. Resounding - Unmistakable; loud enough to reverberate

470. Respective - Belonging to separate people

471. Resplendent - Shining brilliantly

472. Restive - Restless; difficult to control

473. Restorative - Restoring strength and well-being

474. Retained - Hung on to

475. Retorted - Said sharply/wittily in response

476. Retrospect - Looking back

477. Revelations - Something (often surprising) that is revealed

478. Reveled - Thoroughly enjoyed

479. Reverence - Deep respect

480. Revitalized - Brought back to life; given new life

481. Revive - Bring back to life

482. *Riad* - Unlikely to be an SAT word, but it's a traditional Moroccan house or palace

483. Rudimentary - Basic

484. Ruminated - Thought deeply

485. Ruse - Trick

486. Saccharine - Excessively sweet or sentimental

487. Sadist - Person who takes pleasure in hurting others

488. Salutations - Greetings

489. Sardonic - Mocking or cynical

490. Scalding - Burning; very hot

491. Scaled - Climbed

492. Scarcely - Hardly; barely

493. Scintillating - Sparkling; clever

494. Scoffed - Made a scornful noise

495. Scrabble - Scramble or crawl quickly

496. (Bowing and) Scraping - Make deep bows; backing out of the room in reverse

497. Scruples - A moral standard that prevents certain

actions

498. Scrutinized - Closely examined; inspected

499. Secluded - Shut off from; isolated from

500. Sediment - Particles that settle at the bottom of a liquid

501. Semblance - Something that resembles something else

502. Senility - The state of losing one's mental faculties (especially the memory) as a result of old age

503. Sentry - Guard

504. Sequestered - Hidden away

505. Serenely - Calmly; peacefully

506. *Sesterce* - Unlikely to be an SAT word, but it's a unit of currency in ancient Rome

507. Sheepish - Embarrassed

508. Shrapnel - Fragments of a bomb or other item thrown by an explosion

509. Shrewd - Clever; resourceful; astute

510. Sidelong - Sideways; from the side

511. Simultaneously - At the same time

512. Singed - Slightly burned

513. Slink - Move quietly, unobtrusively

514. Slothful - Lazy

515. Smattering - Small amount

516. Solemnity - The state of being intensely serious or dignified

517. Somber - Grave or solemn in mood

518. Spar - A fast-paced argument

519. Spate - Sudden outpouring

520. Spectacle - A show; a visually striking performance

521. Speculated - Thought

522. Stifled - Restrained

523. Stints - Periods of time

524. Stoic - Restrained; controlled

525. Subtle - Delicately complex or understated

526. Suburbia - The suburbs

527. Succumbed - Yielded to an overpowering force or desire

528. Suffice (it to say) - Saying enough to make one's meaning clear, without going on about it

529. Superseding - Taking over; replacing

530. Supine - Lying face-up

531. Suppressed - Repressed; prevented

532. Surreptitiously - Secretly; trying to avoid attention

533. Susceptible - Likely to be influenced or affected

534. Syntax - A branch of linguistics dealing with the arrangement of words and phrases

535. Tacit - Understood without speaking

536. Tactician - A person who carefully plans a strategy to reach a specific end

537. Tamper - Mess with; interfere with

538. Tangible - Touchable

539. Teemed - Swarmed with; was filled with

540. Telepathy - The ability to communicate through psychic means

541. Tentatively - Hesitantly

542. Tenuous - Weak or slight

543. Terminology - The terms used in a specific field

544. *Terra firma* - Dry land; firm land

545. Territorialize - Expand into more territory

546. Thoroughbred - Pure; complete; embodying the essence fully

547. Threshold - The bottom of a doorway; a point that must be exceeded for something to happen ("I've hit my threshold for...")

548. Thriving - Flourishing; doing very well

549. Throngs - Densely-packed crowds

550. Tinny - Having a thin, metallic sound

551. Tomes - Books

552. Trajectory - The path followed by a flying object

553. Transatlantic - Across the Atlantic

554. Transpire - Happen; occur

555. Traverse - Travel through or across

556. Tresses - Long locks of hair

557. Unabashedly - Not embarrassed or ashamed

558. Unanimous - Agreed on by everyone involved

559. Unassailable - Unable to be attacked, questioned, or defeated

560. Unceremoniously - Abruptly; with a lack of courtesy

561. Undulating - Moving in a wave-like motion

562. Unerringly - Accurately; without hesitation

563. Unfathomable - Unable to be explored or understood

564. Unfettered - Unlimited; unrestrained

565. Uninhibited - Expressed unselfconsciously and without restraint

566. Unintelligible - Not capable of being understood

567. Unkempt - Untidy

568. Unperturbed - Undisturbed

569. Untoward - Unexpected; inappropriate; inconvenient

570. Upbraiding - Scolding

571. Upended - Turned upside down

572. Utmost - The most extreme; the greatest

573. Vacated - Left; made empty

574. (In) Vain - Useless; producing no result

575. Vanquished - Thoroughly defeated

576. Vassal - A person or country in a subordinate position to another

577. Veered - Changed directions

578. (In this/that) Vein - In a certain way

579. Veneer - A thin layer of something

580. Vengeance - Revenge

581. Venture - Undertake a risky journey

582. Verdant - Green; rich with vegetation

583. Verify - Make sure something is true

584. Verisimilitude - The appearance of being true or real

585. Veritable - Adds emphasis to the noun following it; literally means "able to be proven true."

586. Vicinity - The area near a person or place

587. Vile - Wicked; morally bad; terrible

588. Visage - Face; sight

589. Vivid - Lively

590. Viziers - Advisors

591. Voluptuous - Curvy and attractive

592. Vulgars - Vulgars - A rude way to describe average

people; the masses

593. Wade - Walk through; get involved in

594. Wreaking - Causing (damage or harm)

595. Wrested - Yanked; pulled violently

596. Writhed - Squirmed; twisted and turned

597. Yearned - Wanted; longed (for)

Made in the USA
Monee, IL
01 October 2021

79182878R00215